King's Road

art camino
fiction

Third edition 2025. First Published December 2012
by Art Camino Fiction.

This book is a work of fiction any resemblance to events or
people past or present is absolutely amazing, but is wholly
a product of the author's imagination.

A CIP record for this book is available
from National Library of Australia

ISBN 978-0-9806049-4-8

COPY SALES
Kings Road is available on **amazon.com**
Purchase direct from **artcamino.com/fiction**

Distribution enquiries:
Art Camino Fiction

sales@artcamino.com

ISBN 978-0-9806049-4-8

9 780980 604948

art camino
fiction

King's Road

Set in London during the cultural turmoil of the '70s and early '80s, King's Road is a funny and revealing story of divisions in society and a young man's search for love.

By

Sean De Siun

Dedicated to my friends and
Londoners of all ages, races, creeds,
philosophies, orientations and genders.

For
Patricia Laffan

Although readers would be correct to assume that this book is largely drawn from my own personal life and experiences, the characters and events depicted here are certainly not autobiography. The characters are not in any sense true portraits of real people. The main protagonist is written in the first person, however, the 'I', is not the author but an invention of convenience created to carry the narrative.

Other characters that were of no less importance may have been omitted from the text, but not the spirit of the novel.

SDS November 2012

1

In July 1969, just as my family and I were digging into a big tub of ice cream and home made apple pie, the big moment arrived.

'...the Eagle has landed,' beeped and crackled the voice attached to the ghosted image on the TV. Neil Armstrong and Buzz Aldrin had arrived on the moon. We had been watching and waiting for hours, but it was too late - the ice cream and apple pie were a far greater attraction.

We were used to major TV events. A few weeks earlier, Charles was invested as the Prince of Wales at Caernarfon Castle. 'I Charles, Prince of Wales, do become your liege man of life and limb ...'

As the Queen placed the coronet on Charles' head my father walked through the door. 'What do you have under your coat, Daddy?' squealed my little sisters. He pulled out a puppy that we instantly named Charlie, of course.

We lived in a house on Sloane Avenue, one block from the King's Road in the Royal Borough of Kensington and Chelsea. Originally built as a private route for King Charles, it crosses Chelsea from Sloane Square in the east, to the border of Fulham opposite Stamford Bridge.

In 1969, the King's Road was the grooviest stretch of pavement on the planet. It was lined with clothes shops, some very upmarket, others selling hippie gear. People came from all over London, to buy, gawp and be seen. All we had to do was wait on the corner of Sloane Avenue and the King's Road, and watch the spectacle pass by.

Rich old men strode along in double breasted suits, smelling of expensive of cigars followed by soldiers with stiffened moustaches and pushed out chins as if still on a mission to 'fight the Gerry, what'. Super-fashionable women in pink boots, mini skirts and fussy-but-casual hairdos were followed by elegant men in flounced white shirts, groomed beards and pony tails and more girls in see-through blouses with no bras. Long haired freaks wafting musky odors with broad smiles walked slowly by with girls in Afghan coats and large pink-rimmed sunglasses.

This was 'swinging London', and even at the tender age of ten, I appreciated the generosity of the girls in their flimsy blouses and tiny skirts.

We had only recently arrived in London. I had been brought up in Australia, but for some time before coming to London my mother, father, three younger sisters and me lived on Juhu beach India. My eldest sister and two brothers had remained in Australia.

Juhu, is seven miles long stretching down the coast from the city of Bombay, and our house was just behind a row of coconut trees that separated the sand from a small village. In the evenings Mother and I, Memsahib and Bubasaheb, appeared from our siesta out onto the first floor balcony.

The mixed smells of incense, curries, wood fires and tropical flowers wafted like waves through the air. The servants and their bidi smoking friends from the village rose and stood to attention as we imperiously strode down the steps and out the front gate, dragging my little sisters behind us to the beach.

I jumped in the surf and crashed around in the warm foamy waves. My blond hair was bleached white by the sun and, my pale, freckled skin forced to a bronzed tan color, and my blue eyes shone through pure white eyelashes.

As dusk fell the beach filled with fruit sellers, snake charmers, mongoose dancers, elephant and camel rides, jewellery sellers, sitar players, fortune tellers and sadhus who lay on beds of nails or buried themselves in the sand with just a hand poking up. It was a carnival as the shimmering orange sun dropped precipitously into the Indian Ocean leaving ripples of purple, pink and orange on the water.

We didn't go to school. Instead a private tutor gave my sisters and me lessons for one hour a day. Mrs. Patel taught me about the Indian struggle for independence and how to stand on my head, which I did from then on for the duration of the class. She sat cross legged on the veranda while I stood on my head in the corner and my sisters ran around screeching.

One day Dad came in and said, 'We're moving to London. Isn't it exciting?'

'Where's London Daddy?'

The weather in London was a shock to our systems. We arrived in spring, but it was considerably colder than winter in Sydney, and frigid compared to Juhu. Mum marched my sisters and me up to Peter Jones, the department store on leafy Sloane Square and bought us anoraks and Aran sweaters.

We walked back down the length of King's Road, and Mum stopped to gaze in all the shop windows. We paused on a bench in the square outside the Duke of York's barracks. I pointed at a shop called The Chelsea Drugstore, 'Lets buy some drugs Mum.'

'Don't be cheeky Eamon. Anyway, it seems to be a clothes shop.'

As we walked past the entrance I strained my neck to peer in and could see girls wearing multicoloured tights and plastic mini skirts.

Continuing further west we came to Chelsea Town Hall and the Chelsea Register office. Mum pointed at the impressive front door and said, 'Judy Garland was married here just a few weeks ago. I recognise the door from the photos in the newspaper.'

We turned left into Flood Street and walked down to Cheyne Walk and the Thames. Standing on the embankment we watched barges pass under the elegant light-festooned Albert Bridge. Going back up to the King's Road, we arrived at World's End, the heart of London's hippie counterculture, and Granny Takes a Trip, the hippest of the hippie boutiques.

Eventually we crossed Edith Grove and Lots Road, where King's Road crosses into Fulham and changes name to New King's Road. Mum stopped and said, 'Okay, this is far enough.'

We walked back up to our new home bundled up for winter on a bright, sunny day while everyone else was in shirt sleeves. Our white heads poked out of our thick coats, and our tanned faces made us look as though we were of a different race from everyone else.

Like Juhu, the King's Road had a carnival atmosphere and exotic looking people, but that was where the similarities ended. Instead of the far away sounds of Indian music drifting on the warm, fragrant breeze, the cough of red double-decker buses and the beep of taxi horns rattled my ears. Fresh spring flowers, fish and chips, and acrid car exhaust fumes confused my sense of smell. My skin, used to warm air and foamy water, felt trapped by the weight of several layers of clothing.

I wondered how long would it be before Daddy came home one night and said, 'Pack up we're all going home to Sydney.' But I soon realized that our lives had changed and that this was not a vacation.

I didn't know it then, but the next twelve years of my life would be spent walking up and down the King's Road, perhaps more than a thousand times.

'One small step for [a] man,' beep, crackle pop.

2

My brother Vincent, flew from Sydney, to join us and was enrolled in the London Oratory, an expensive private Catholic school.

Back in Australia Vinnie played cricket and rugby, he was an outdoor, sporty person, but he now became more serious and was always doing his homework. He stopped playing sport, and instead joined the Oratory's brigade of the Army Cadet Force.

The Cadets met each week at a school hall in Cale St, around the corner from our house. I was only ten years old - officially too young, but they let me join anyway. Our branch was attached to the Coldstream Guards whose role it is to protect the Royal personages. We assembled in the school hall in the early evening and spent most of the two-hour sessions learning how to march.

Sergeant 'Fatgut' taught us how to salute, 'Longest way up, shortest way down,' and bellowed at us as we stomped around the parade hall, 'Left right, left right.'

Sometimes we went to the Duke of York's for special training sessions or to march around their parade ground. There were weekend trips and up to two week long training camps further a field. We had to make our beds so tight that the inspecting Non Commissioned Officer could bounce a half crown on the blanket.

We marched around the quadrangle for hours, and ran through obstacle courses carrying big bags of stuff. Vinnie was four years older than me and seemed so talented and naturally athletic. He was my big brother, my protector.

After a few months, we moved from Sloane Avenue to a house in Harrow, a suburb on the northwest outskirts of London and nowhere near the cosmopolitan heart of the city. I was used to moving house and expected it. We never seemed to stay anywhere for long. Vinnie continued going to the Oratory in Fulham, but I had to change to a school close to our new house. I felt out of place once again trying to get used to a new school and kids. However, on Tuesday evenings the two of us took the train to South Kensington Station to go to cadets. It was strangely comforting and familiar to hear the sergeant bellow at me.

Vinnie was so self assured, tough, smart and worldly. Everything a big brother is supposed to be, but when we moved to Harrow he began to change. Mum and he went to buy furniture for the new house and returned with an enormous Russian radiogram. It had a radio and a turntable and two large stand alone speakers. Vinnie bought *Everybody Knows This Is Nowhere* by Neil Young, sewed patches on his jeans even though he didn't need them and grew his hair longer.

My eldest brother Brian was at university when we left Sydney, and he soon came to London but didn't move in with us. Instead, he shared a house with friends in Edith Grove just off the King's Road at World's End.

Brian was the liveliest of all of us always carrying on wildly, moving, wrestling and dancing. When we were kids in Sydney, he liked to try out the karate chops and commando fighting moves that he learned from his cadet troop on me and Vinnie. If I bumped into him in the kitchen, he would shout, 'Ah-ha stand and fight coward,' put me in a half nelson and make me say uncle before he would let me go.

In India, we received a letter from him with a cutting from the *Sydney Morning Herald.* We were surprised to see a picture of his smiling face with long hair and a moustache at an anti-Vietnam war demonstration. When we left Sydney he was clean shaven with a side parting in his neatly trimmed hair. He wrote, 'We aren't hippies, we're happy.' I was disgusted. Outrageous, I thought. After all, *I* was the Bubasaheb.

Brian's birthday was just a few weeks after he arrived in London, and Mum took Vinnie and me into town to visit him. I wondered what he would be like as I hadn't seen him since we were in Sydney.

We walked up Edith Grove, an elegant but dilapidated street, to his house, knocked on the front door and it creaked open. We tiptoed into a dingy hallway and strange music echoed down the corridor, 'Brian, Brian!' we shouted.

Brian stumbled out into the hallway and hugged us all. I was amazed how short he seemed. I must have grown several inches since we had last met. He had long brown hair and a moustache and was wearing round rimless glasses like John Lennon.

'Brian, I hardly recognize you,' I said looking down at his red leather boots and bell bottom leather trousers.

'Come in, my friends are throwing a birthday party for me.'

Strange smelling incense blew in our faces as we followed him into a dark room. Mysterious looking girls with long blonde hair and flowing robes lounged on mattresses and sofas with guys sprouting moustaches and beards. Nobody spoke much - they just lay around grinning and listening to the music.

'Hey Eamon, how's school?'

'Er, alright I guess. It feels weird being around all the kids in my class. I didn't go to school in India.'

I felt strange sense of detachment having not seen him for so long. I wanted to know him, to understand him, but he seemed to have changed so much. Seeing him made me feel even more out of place in London.

What are you doing now, Brian?'

'I'm trying to find my soul and discover inner peace.'

'I thought you were going to university?'

'I was, but when I finished they were going to draft me into the army and make me go kill Vietnamese people.'

'I thought you liked being in the cadets and all that?'

'That was just kids stuff, playing cowboys and Indians.'

'So, what are you going to do here in London?'

'I don't know Eamon. I'll see what comes up. I'm serious about finding my soul. I've been learning to play the guitar, let me play this song for you.'

He picked up an acoustic guitar and began to pick out a ragtime tune,

'You can get anything you want at Alice's restaurant ...'

The song went on for about twenty minutes. It was actually a monologue with guitar backing. It recounted the story of a young American guy who had managed to avoid being drafted to fight in Vietnam because he was a litter bug. When he finished we clapped, but his hippie friends just grinned more intently.

'Right, right, I get it,' said a guy sitting next to me, sage-like with a knowing smile.

Brian gave my mother a piece of birthday cake, and I wanted to eat it, but she said 'NO! Don't touch it,' and stuffed it her handbag.

Brian didn't have the same accent as me. He sounded more American because his early school years were in the USA and Canada. My family moved to Australia from Canada, but actually, they were Irish. I say they were Irish. My three eldest siblings were born in Dublin, but my father always insisted that my little sisters and I were Irish, as well.

'Daddy, where am I from?' my sister Mary asked.

'Sure, you're from Cork, aren't you darling?'

'But Daddy, I was born-ed in 'Stralia.'

'If you were born in a stable would you be a horse?'

'Course not, don't be silly Daddy!'

'Well then there you are Mary. Never forget you're Irish. The Irish are the greatest poets, musicians, orators, writers, singers and dancers in the world. Even more important than being Irish we're Catholic Christians, and we're all going to go to heaven. So, always say you're prayers and be a good girl.'

My parents told me that I was Irish. My tutor in India tried to convince me that I was a Bubbasaheb, my brothers talked like Americans, yet, here I was in London.

Before we arrived, I knew next to nothing about England. At school, in Australia I had seen a picture in a book showing English school boys wearing short pants ankle deep in snow throwing snow balls at each other. I had no idea that snow was cold until I ran out into it that first winter. 'Errragh! This stuff is freezing and wet. I wanna go home!'

Soon afterwards I asked, 'Mum, what are we doing here?'

'How do you mean Eamon? We live here you go to school, and Dad goes to work.'

'But what are we doing here? I thought we lived in Sydney.'

'We used to live in Sydney. Now we live in London.'

'Forever, can't we go home?'

'We are home Eamon. Home is where the heart is. We love each other, and we're a family. This is our home now.'

When we went to India, I thought it would only be temporary, and that we would soon return to Australia. When we moved to London, I figured that we were just taking the long way back. But, this it seemed, was it - the outer suburbs of London. Instead of running around in the sunshine I was always staring through glass windows to the cold world outside.

In India Mum seemed so elegant and enjoyed living in a warm, humid climate. Dad was often away on business and as my brothers had stayed in Australia, I was the man of the house.

Most of the time only Mum, me and my little sisters were at home - plus the servants. We were the only non Indian people in the area so, I was the only person that she could have a conversation with, and the two of us grew close.

We didn't have a TV or radio, but we were surrounded by high pitched Indian music ringing from the radios in the village. A large reel-to-reel tape player was installed in the voluminous open living room, however the only tape we had was *The Desert Song,* a 1920s operetta. We listened to it incessantly and Mum taught me how to waltz swirling around with electric ceiling fans whumping above us.

It went to my head - being able to boss the servants around. However, Mum would bring be back down to earth. 'Remember Eamon, your just a human being like everyone else. You must treat people with respect.'

Not long after we visited Brian for his birthday, he moved away and left his entire record collection with us. Vinnie and I suddenly had lots of new records to listen to by bands such as, The Velvet Underground, Led Zeppelin, Jefferson Airplane, The Mothers of Invention, Janis Joplin, the Rolling Stones, Jimi Hendrix, Arlo Guthrie. Of course, there were also Bob Dylan records. *The Freewheelin' Bob Dylan*, *Highway 61 Revisited, Blond on Blonde.*

Vinnie had a transistor radio and listened to Radio Luxemburg. He stayed up late at night watching *Disco 2* on TV which played all the latest music. I hung onto Vinnie's shirt tails and he became my window into the counter-culture.

The radiogram was in the dining room, but we usually had our meals in the kitchen, and it soon became the de facto music room. Vinnie and I took it in turns to play records. I was his stupid little kid brother, and he didn't want me to be hanging around bothering him. So I listened outside the door to hear what records he put on and I played them for myself when he had finished. 'I'm going to read in my room. Don't play the music too loud,' he barked at me as he brushed past.

Just before we moved back to Chelsea, the new record by The Rolling Stones, *Exile on Main Street* came out. We listened to it and all our records constantly, with Vinnie singing along to every word.

Vinnie read voraciously. He had *The Electric Kool-Aid Acid Test* by Tom Wolfe and *Hell's Angels: The Strange and Terrible Saga of the Outlaw Motorcycle Gangs* by Hunter S. Thompson. He even had a copy of the banned School Kids edition of *OZ* magazine and numerous copes of *Playboy* which he assured me, '…have terrific articles, you should read them.'

When he wasn't there I did read them, especially the pages with staples in the middle. He collected *Rolling Stone* magazine, which told us everything about American music, politics and popular culture. *New Musical Express* told us about the British music scene, but the best music was American anyway, or so we thought. Vinnie read *Rolling Stone* from cover to cover plus any other magazines, newspapers or books he could get hold of that mentioned music, culture or politics.

When we moved to Harrow, Vinnie was a short haired army cadet of the Coldstream Guards. Two Years later when we moved back to Chelsea, he was more widely read and knew more about popular music and the hippie counter-culture than any journalist. In fact, he should have been one. But he had to go to school.

Our three little sisters, eight, five and three years old ran around screaming all the time. Our eldest sister Mairead finished her degree in Sydney and moved to London. She became a Meditation teacher and spent most of her time away on courses in Switzerland. When she was at home, she took over the kitchen and cooked us nut loaf.

'Maharishi says that if you meditate twice a day you'll attain cosmic consciousness and eventually bliss consciousness,' she told us. Mum nodded but didn't like the nut loaf. Brian was around even less. He also wanted to achieve higher states of consciousness - assisted by herbs and modern chemicals.

Dad went to work, came home late and fell asleep in front of the TV. On Sundays, he took us to Mass and for drives, 'around the world for sport' or 'as far as turn back'. He clapped his hands together and said, 'What are the chances of something E-X-O-T-I-C like cake?' Before dinner he sang, 'Wash your face and hands and comb your hair, oh wash your face and hands and comb your ha-a-air,' and urged us to, 'tell the truth and shame the devil'.

Our house was large and rambling with a deep back garden. Charlie the dog frequently escaped into the neighborhood and I had to chase him for miles. We had what we thought was a tom cat until one day, he had a litter of kittens in my wardrobe. We had guinea pigs, a mynah bird, and I kept racing pigeons.

Our mother, Mother Machree, held us all together. She was our heart and soul. She seemed to understand all our foibles and never judged us. A friend of Vinnie's bemoaned, 'You're lucky, you have a hippie mother.'

Meanwhile, living in Harrow away from the groovy centre of London a new menace appeared. Gangs of violent, racist, teenage boys with cropped hair roamed the streets. They wore steel toe-capped footwear called 'bovver boots', jeans held up by braces, short sleeved button down shirts and black Crombie coats. Paki bashing - attacking immigrants who they presumed to be from Pakistan - was their favored pastime. Menacing and frightening, they called themselves, skinheads. I was too young and too white for them to bother with, but when I started secondary school things became more serious.

First, however, I had to take the Eleven Plus, which was an exam, since abandoned, that all school kids in England had to sit at the age of eleven. If you failed, you were branded a dunce and were sent to herding pens called secondary modern schools. There, you were prepared to join the police force, army or some other lowly job. If you passed the Eleven Plus, you could go to a real school.

On the day of the exam, I thought it was just an end of term test. I didn't realize it was important as I had only been in the English school system for a short while. No questions were asked about Indira Ghandi or head-standing, and I failed.

My first secondary school, St Thomas', was a comprehensive where kids attended the same school, but in separate streams depending whether they passed the Eleven Plus or not. I was sent to the dunce's stream to play with pencils and flick elastic bands around.

We lived a few miles from St Thomas' and I took the bus there each day. As we drew closer to the school more and more kids crowded on the bus, until it was filled with scruffy uniformed boys and girls.

The school was Catholic and mixed sex - well, nearly mixed sex. The boys and girls were segregated into different classes with the girls in one building and the boys in an adjacent one. We shared the same playground, but a white line had been painted down the middle. Girls had to stay on one side and boys on the other. In order to meet a girl, you had to mosey around by the white line and pretend to be talking to a boy while whispering over your shoulder. When I started at the school I didn't want to meet girls anyway, but by the time I left at age thirteen, I most certainly did.

The boys in my class aspired to be skinheads, they talked about being 'hard' a 'tough nut' and 'proud'. 'Oy let's go paki bashing tonight. You gonna come Eamon? Nah, course not, you're a bleedin' hippie int ya.'

They didn't actually go bashing anyone. It was their version of cowboys and Indians - make-believe. However, the older boys in the school genuinely were 'skins' and they were terrifying.

At the end of the school day, I was relieved to go home to my family and our animals. I retreated to the shed where I kept my pigeons. I was scared at school but felt safe in my coop.

Soon, a new offshoot of the skinhead fashion evolved - suedeheads. They wore more formal clothes such as Brogue shoes or Tassel Loafers, and two-tone tonic suits made from shiny, iridescent blue-green material, and wore their hair slightly longer. They liked reggae which seemed strange because reggae was West Indian music and they didn't like 'wogs' or 'jungle bunnies'.

Each morning a boy the same age as me jumped on the bus when it was about a half way to school. Unlike most of the kids he always had his nose in a science or mathematics text book as the bus bumped along. One day he sat beside me and answered my question, 'I'm a suedehead, course I am. Bleedin' obvious i'n' it?'

I was apprehensive talking to him at first but soon got the feeling that he wasn't violent or racist. He just liked the fashion and had a passion for music - reggae in particular. From the first day I met Chris I waited for him at the bus stop after school, and we traveled home together.

'Eamon, come around to my place and listen to some music.'

He had an extensive record collection. 'Wow Chris, where did you get all these records, do you have a big brother?'

'No, I'm the only child. I just collect them. I'm always down at the record shop.'

'We don't have any of these records at my house.'

Chris had all the skinhead reggae hits. Many of them were banned in England as the lyrics were pornographic. Songs like Prince Buster's *Big Five* and *Wet Dream* by Max Romeo. He had *Skinhead Moonstomp*, *Skinhead Jamboree* and *Skinhead Girl* by Symarip, and Laurel Aitkin's *Skinhead Train*.

'Crikey Chris, how did you get into this music? My brother and I listen to Bob Dylan.'

'I heard Derrick Morgan's *Tougher than Tough* one day, I just loved it and I've been into reggae ever since.'

He had reggae from Jamaica and white reggae from England but preferred the authentic West Indian music. He also liked American soul music such as the Chi-lites and the Stylistics and had many Tamla Motown records including The Four Tops and the Temptations.

'Why are you a suedehead Chris? You're not a tough nut.'

'I like the look, the fashion. I don't like all that hairy hippie stuff. Peace and love and all that crap - do me a favor! No, I like to look smart.' By smart, he meant, sophisticated, sharp.

After listening to music, we played football in his back garden. Chris changed into his Levi jeans turned up neatly at the bottom, Dr Martin boots, braces and Ben Sherman Shirt. When I was at home, I wore tie-died shirts with laces up the front that my sister made for me and flared jeans. By the time I was thirteen, my hair had grown down to my shoulders. The skinheads shouted after me, 'Oy, look, it's a poofter - bleedin' hippie!'

By now Vinnie and I were old enough to look after ourselves, but we always came home for dinner - the evening screaming and shouting match - the food was always so delicious and plentiful.

Mum made friends with a lady who lived across the road and visited her for coffee most afternoons. Sometimes she came home looking alarmed as if something terrible had happened. 'Mum, what's the matter?'

'Oh, it's just Janet across the road. She seems to have so many problems and wants to share them all with me. Sometimes I just can't get away from her. She gets very depressed and her doctor prescribed Valium for her.'

'What's Valium?'

'It's a terrible drug that makes you talk in a drawl as if you're half asleep, 'mother's little helpers' she calls them. I think if I spend much longer out here in the sticks I'm going to end up like her, a Valium addict.'

I soon realized that the suburban scene freaked our hippie mother out. She wanted to move back to the centre of the city and immerse the family in the life and culture of the great capital.

A year and more passed by and I began to feel at home and less of an alien at school. In fact, I almost began to feel English, at least I thought I did. I slowly figured out the sensibilities and humour of the country. Chris also had records of the Goon Show and we listened to them intently and rolled around in laughter.

'Oh, God that was funny weren't it Eamon?'

'Yeah Chris, cor, absolutely hilarious, ha ha.' I pulled a fake smile, as in fact, I couldn't understand a word Harry Secombe or Spike Milligan said through their thick accents.

'Eamon, they aren't English anyway.'

'Oh well, what about the guys in Monty Python's, are they English?'

'Yeah, I think so, they must be,' Chris said scratching his chin.

Gradually, as the months went by I unravelled the lingo, and even started to sound like a local. Eventually I was reluctantly accepted by my classmates. 'You're still a bleedin hippie Eamon, but you're alright I suppose,' the biggest kid in my class said to me one day.

Yes, I was feeling more comfortable and at ease being in England, until one Sunday evening I came home for dinner. Dad was away on business and Vinnie who was now sixteen years old was out with friends. We usually had a formal Sunday meal but as only me and the girls at home we ate in the kitchen.

'What's for dinner Mum?'

'Just chicken Eamon as Dad's not home tonight.'

We sat around the table and watched the evening news on the TV in the corner. I was expecting the Vietnam war, as always, and Prime Minister Ted Heath to be warbling on about the European Economic Community which Britain wanted to join. Mum was dishing up when she stopped and stared, open-jawed.

Earlier that day here had been a demonstration in Derry, Northern Ireland. The BBC announcer spoke while images of soldiers flickered on the small black and white screen.

> 'British troops have opened fire on a crowd of demonstrators in the Bogside district of Londonderry, killing 13 civilians. Seventeen more people were injured by gunfire ...
>
> ... It was by far the worst day of violence in this largely Roman Catholic city since the present crisis began in 1969.
>
> Bogsiders said the troops opened fire on unarmed men - including one who had his arms up in surrender ...'

We watched in horror at images of soldiers running through streets guns firing with people fleeing in all directions. A priest waving a white handkerchief passed through a cordon of crouching soldiers followed by several people carrying a dying boy draped in a white sheet.

A crowd stood in a circle looking at a dead man lying on the street covered by a blanket, blood pouring from his head, and scattered in fear as more shots rang out.

The interviewer asked a British officer what had happened. He said that the army had fired three rounds and that the dead, '... may well not have been killed by our soldiers.'

The dead …

My sisters paid no attention and carried on shouting. 'Pass the 'taties, I want butter …'

I looked over my shoulder. Mum was standing with her arms clenched tightly around her waist and back against the wall. She was crying, her head bowed.

'Mum,' I called.

She looked up at me. Her eyes were red and face was dripping, 'They just want us dead. All they do is kill us, just murder us.'

Until that moment, the nightly news was entertainment to me. Something I watched after *Star Trek*. I knew it was serious for the people involved, but it was always abstract, far away, in Vietnam or somewhere else. The only other time that I could remember seeing my mother cry was when John Kennedy was assassinated. I spent the rest of the evening watching TV - the seven o'clock news, the nine o'clock news, News Night. All that they talked about was the 'Irish problem'.

On Wednesday morning, I read in *The Times* that several of the dead were to be buried that afternoon in Derry. A demonstration was planned to take place at the Houses of Parliament in London to protest at what had already been dubbed, 'Bloody Sunday'.

'Mum, do you think we should go to the demonstration this afternoon?'

'I don't know Eamon. I feel we should do something to show how we feel.'

The two of us took the train to St James's Park and walked up to the Houses of Parliament. A small crowd of people had gathered in Parliament Square, and several people spoke on megaphones in Irish accents.

'These outrageous murders must not go unpunished. The British army must be brought to account, and they must leave Ireland immediately!'

It was a dark, winter's evening, and a cold mist enveloped us. STim faced policemen wearing tall Bobby's helmets surrounded us. The leaders of the demonstration said we should march to Downing Street, so we left the square and crossed Bridge Street into Whitehall. The people around us were mostly middle aged men and women. No one spoke much, but looked grim and sad, huddled up in overcoats and woolly hats, their breath pouring out as steam.

Mum and I were in the middle of the crowd and banners waved on poles ahead of us. Thirteen symbolic black coffins were carried on men's shoulders at the front. We shuffled along up the middle of grand Whitehall with the imposing buildings of Her Majesty's Treasury and the Foreign Office flanking us.

Without warning, about fifty yards in front of us, several scruffy young men barged into the crowd from the left and right hand sides of the street. They punched and pulled people dragging them to the ground. Two men ran towards us from the left carrying empty metal garbage cans over their heads. They hurled them into the middle of the crowd, and the throng of people fell around us in panic.

Mum looked at me and said, 'agent provocateurs'. I had never heard the term before, but I understood what she meant. We tried to back away from the violence, but the people behind were unable to retreat fast enough, and we were stuck, unable to move in any direction.

'Get 'em,' cried a man ahead of us, and the men who had thrown the garbage cans were chased to the right and into a line of policemen blocking a side street, Derby Gate. The police opened their ranks and let the provocateurs through, closing the line behind them. Could I believe my eyes? They were clearly thugs sent to cause a riot.

Policemen on enormous horses appeared at the front wielding truncheons and tore into the column of people. The crowd rushed in a falling heap back towards us. I grabbed Mum's arm, and we turned and fled in fear of being crushed or beaten.

We reached the corner of Westminster Bridge, and I looked back up Whitehall. People were running in all directions, and the street was already nearly cleared. A column of policemen walked down the road truncheons in hand. The metallic crunch of their boots falling in unison echoed around the canyon-like street. Police horses clip-clopped past us snorting, steam rising, their riders with tight reigns in hand. Off key sirens of police vans eee-awwed, their blue lights circled past.

Terrified, I gazed up at the Houses of Parliament, the home of British democracy and the symbol of civil rule. Big Ben its solid square structure promising stability towered above us and across Parliament Square was Westminster Abbey, the church of God where the monarchs of England are crowned. We were in the political, historical and cultural epicenter of the country. My pulse pounded in my temples and palms sweated. Why were they doing this to us? What were we doing here, us foreigners?

We cowered and edged our way around the square back to the tube station. Eventually, unharmed, we stood in silence in a packed train carriage filled with sullen, depressed demonstrators.

My fear subsided and was replaced by a deep sense of injustice. Now I knew what it was like to be one of the countless victims that filled the TV news each night.

No one in the carriage said a word. Like Mum and I, they stared downwards, gently shaking their heads. The tube train squealed and hissed through the tunnel, chug-a-dah-chug-dah- chug-a-dah-chug. The troubling odor of stale London-underground air and damp overcoats filled my nostrils. I closed my eyes and imagined I was a bird soaring towards the sun, my beating wings forcing me higher and higher.

We had been living in England for three years, nearly a quarter of my life. By this time, I felt as if we were part of the country and had a place here - but what now? Who were my people that they should be feared so? I told myself, try to fit in. You've got to fit in. I had nowhere else to go. I had to make my way somehow in this cold, harsh country.

Mum's eyes had the same cold look that my heart felt. It was as if a chill wind had blown through us - not like the wintry cold outside, but a howling wind that brought goose bumps up on my skin. A wind filled with sleet and screeching banshees warning us to flee and hide lest wolf in the night should catch us.

3

Not long after Bloody Sunday, I woke up in the middle of the night and heard murmurs coming from my parents bedroom. They talked through the night and in the morning seemed resolute, as if a decision had been made. A few days later real estate agents came around with measuring tapes and clip boards. Our house was put on the market, and a sign put up in the front garden.

Everyday Mum and Mairead scoured the classified section of *The Times* and wrote numbers and addresses in a note pad. They took the train into the city and came back in the evenings exhausted. One day they returned home early and said they had found the perfect apartment for us on the border of South Kensington and Chelsea. In August, we moved back to the Royal Borough.

We arrived at the new apartment just as the moving company had finished unloading the last of our possessions and dumped them in the front hallway. My little sisters ran from the front to the back of the flat and back again screeching with every discovery, 'What's in here? Mummy it's a big cupboard eeeeee...'

Charlie the dog barked and the cats slinked off to hide among the unpacked boxes. On the second floor of a mansion block, the apartment was larger than our house in Harrow with five bedrooms, a large kitchen, an enormous living room, and a dining room. Previously, it had been occupied by American Navy officers who were obviously bachelors. One of the bedrooms had a sauna built into it and another had been painted in Day-Glo with psychedelic scenes.

The Yellow Submarine from the animated Beatles movie was painted on one wall surrounded by sunbursts, stars, and flowers. Multicolored psychedelic images filled the other walls and ceiling. Vincent (now he was older we had to stop calling him Vinnie) said, 'Those navy guys must have had a lot of fun here. Imagine the parties they had.'

He grabbed the psychedelic room as his own. I couldn't argue. He deserved it, not just because he was bigger than me - it was clearly his room.

The flooring in the hallway and vestibule was black and white tessellated tiles which looked particularly elegant. But, the enormous living room was carpeted in thick green shag pile carpet. 'It looks like a golf course in here,' I said.

Mum and I walked across the room to the windows that opened out the front of the apartment onto elm-tree lined Royston Gardens. A narrow balcony overlooked a glass-covered walkway leading up to the front door of the building. We looked down as an elegant man in a double breasted, pin-striped suit emerged, he threw his head back haughtily and sauntered up the street with one hand in his pocket. 'Oh this is much more like it Eamon. Elegant people, culture, art, style. Thank God we're out of the boondocks at last.'

Royston Gardens is in South Kensington crossing the Old Brompton Road, Fulham Road, the King's Road continuing down do Cheyne Walk and the Thames. Going west from the corner of Royston Gardens and Fulham Road was the ABC cinema, the Penguin bookshop, Finch's pub, Saint Stephen's Hospital, and the Marist Convent where my sisters went to primary school. Further along is Hortensia Road then Stamford Bridge, Chelsea Football Club, and the London Oratory where Vincent went to school. This was our new neighborhood.

The back of the apartment looked out onto single story mews houses and further across to the backs of the buildings in the next street. We soon discovered that Blakes Hotel, where rock stars stayed when they were on tour, was opposite us. Vincent said, 'Led Zeppelin are staying there at the moment. I read it in New Musical Express.'

I soon began to miss the reggae music Chris used to play. I imagined him in his Levi's and boots stomping to the staccato beat. Chris was just about the only friend I had ever had. Yet, the family had moved again, and I didn't know when I would see him next. But it was a relief to have left my school and all the skinheads behind. I didn't have to do anything - not even run away. I just moved house, again, and left my troubles behind.

Vincent acquired an electric guitar, a 100 watt Hiwatt Amp and a Marshall speaker. So, as well as singing, he played guitar along to his records. My bedroom was next door to his at the back near the kitchen.

Now in his final year of school Vincent was taking his A-Levels. He had been to expensive schools and taught by priests in Australia and London for his entire primary and secondary education. His education was the Catholic equivalent of going to an English public school. The academic schooling he received was top grade, but more importantly an attitude, a self belief was imbued in the students and Vincent exuded confidence and self assuredness.

For Vincent the move simply meant that he had a short bus ride to school instead of a tedious train journey, but once again, I had to be found a new school. Mum enquired with the Inner London Education Authority. Due to my abysmal failure of the Eleven Plus there was only one local school that I would be able to get into. It sounded okay, Chelsea School. 'That'll look good on your résumé,' said Vincent.

On the first day of the new academic year in September, Mum and I walked down Fulham Road to the school and knocked on the office door. The headmaster came out and seemed amazed to see us. He was not about to refuse a new volunteer. After filling in some forms, I was sent to my allocated class, 3B.

As I entered I could see no teacher in the class room, and a bunch of kids crowded around to see who the new boy was. 'Oy, shit-face, where did you get expelled from then?'

'I didn't get expelled - we moved house.'

The class burst into uproarious laughter. 'Eh-ha-ha-ah, you poor bastard!'

They thought it was hilarious that I wasn't forced to go to Chelsea School but sent there by a simple twist of fate. 'Where did you rank in the fighting?'

'Er, I tried to avoid fights.'

''Ere, listen to this posh git will ya. Are you a bleedin' Yank or wot?'

'No, I'm Australian, kind of …'

'No, eeze not a Yank, eeze a fuckin' kangaroo'

Chelsea was probably the worst school in London. It was small with only three hundred or so students. I use the term, students, loosely. Inmates would be a better description. It was boys only, and nearly a third of the kids were West Indian. The rest were a rag-tag bunch of thugs and bullies from Fulham and Hammersmith. I was one of less than a handful of boys that lived in Kensington and Chelsea. Most of the inmates had indeed been expelled from other schools. Chelsea was the bottom rung, with nowhere else they could be sent.

The West Indians were tough. However, they stuck together, and if you weren't in their circle they left you alone. So I was considered new blood for the white bullies to torture. One boy gave me some advice. He said, 'When you go to a new school you have to pick a couple of fights, win and act tough. Then everyone will be scared of you and leave you alone.'

I didn't pick a fight, but I soon had the opportunity test his theory. A bully stopped me in the school yard. He stooped over me grimacing down into my face.

'Oy, mush, gimme a quid. Come on hand it over you tosser!'

I felt like a bamboo pole being pushed over by a hurricane wind.

'I'm not giving you any money.'

'Look you little turd, gimme all your money or I'll smack your 'ead in!'

I was afraid of him, but the way he looked at me, as if I were worthless, enraged me. I discovered something about myself that day - I had a powerful, left hook. I already knew about my bad temper. As soon as he stopped yelling I sprang back upright

THWACK

One punch and he was on the floor. After that, I was left alone.

'Eeze mad 'e is,' they said. Even the West Indians were impressed. 'Yar a'right man, ya biff 'im good!'

A boy called Albert and I gravitated together, and he became my best mate. Albert looked like a potato with a round face and squashed bulbous nose. His mother was Scottish, and his father wasn't at home anymore.

He lived on the corner of Whetherby Street and Fulham Palace Road in Hammersmith, opposite Charring Cross Hospital. His mother ran a corner grocery, and the family lived in the rooms above the shop with a store room out the back. I often went over in the evening to help him unload the boxes of tins and restock the shelves. Albert had difficulty reading and writing, and as we sat among the boxes in the store room, he moaned, 'Every day of my life I am told 'ow ig'orant an' stupid I am.'

His mother was friendly enough, although she was 'as rough as the Old Kent Road'. In the evenings, she chain-smoked and watched 'tellie' with his uncle who was a taxi driver. When we finished re-stocking the shop, we walked around Hammersmith looking for mischief. Albert was quite, but no pushover. He noticed details about people and would point out things out to me.

'He works on the railways,' he said.

'How do you know?'

'Look at his donkey jacket. That bloke's a carpenter, you can tell by the pencil sticking out of his back pocket.'

The shop was around the corner from the Hammersmith Odeon. The band, The Who, had recently released *Quadrophenia.* The album included a booklet with lots of photographs from the area including one of the band members outside the 'Hammie Odeon' and others of West Pier in Brighton. 'Ve Oo', as the locals called them, were West Londoners. We listened to *Quadrophenia* swinging our arms around like Pete Townshend. Albert's mother yelled, 'Will youse lads knock it on the feckin' head. I'm tryin' te watch the tellie!'

'Why are they called The Who, Albert?'

'Dunno, do I. It's all about who you are i'n it. I mean the real you. Not just who everybody says you are.'

'I know what you mean. People are always trying to put you in a box - categorize you.'

'I'm working class and proud of it. Not upper class like you.'

'I don't have a class. I'm not English.'

'They like to think I'm stupid, that way they can forget about me - the teachers, my mum, everybody. They don't know who I am.'

'Who are you then Albert?'

'I am… a lighted match.'

I hadn't seriously thought about who I was until then. I was a member of my family. I was me, Eamon. We had moved house so many times that I never knew anybody outside the family for long enough to figure out what they genuinely thought of me. I wasn't aware of anyone judging me, deciding for me who I was. Until I failed the Eleven Plus, I guessed.

But then I remembered the Bloody Sunday demonstration, and that I was one of *them,* the problem Irish. Except that no one realised who I was. I had a foreign sounding accent, but people thought I was Australian or Canadian - not Irish. Unlike Albert, I was in disguise, unfathomable. As much as my teachers or other people in authority might try and pigeonhole me, they would never be able to figure me out. But who was I?

After a while, I made a few West Indians friends. One boy from from Barbados lived nearby on Queensgate Mews. His mother cooked ackee and saltfish for us. We listened to reggae, and he talked about cricket. He played a record called *Burnin'* by Bob Marley and the Wailers.

I liked the West Indian sense of humor and positive outlook. They had an extraordinary way of walking, half skipping and bouncing. Many of them had dreadlocks and wore black woollen hats that me and Albert called tea cozies, with all their hair stuffed inside. Walking down any street, you would be likely to see a hat bouncing up, and poking above other people's heads as the guy beneath skipped from his left leg to half step on his right leg back to a big bounce from his left leg.

Most of the teachers at Chelsea School had completely given up trying. The science teacher simply sat at his high laboratory desk in what remained of the lab, wearing a filthy grey top coat his arms folded in front of him on his desk, he muttered under his breath, 'You're all a bunch of worthless bastards, why don't you go out and mug some old lady … you make me sick …' as two boys held the nerd with thick glasses over a lighted Bunsen burner laughing fiendishly as the kid's skin blistered. After that incident, gas was no longer available in the science lab.

It was a challenge to walk around the school because you never knew what dangers lay ahead. It was unsafe simply to walk through a door. There might be books or a bucket of water perched on top, waiting to drop on you or some other booby trap. Albert and I walked down the corridor chatting, and when we came to a door we forced it open with a hefty kick. Then commando style we rushed through darting our eyes from corner to corner of the room to check that it was clear of any attackers. After a while I just did it without thinking, and it didn't disturb my rhythm.

We liked the English teacher, and tried to make it to his classes. One day he was encouraging a philosophy discussion. A West Indian kid said, 'Man, let me tell you 'bout Rastafarianism.'

'No, we're not going to talk about Rastafarianism. It's forbidden to talk about that here, never bring that subject up again!'

'Bleut clat!' roared the Rasta as he skipped out of the class room with is hair filled hat bouncing up and hitting the door jam. Wow, I thought, what's Rasta-fungalism?

The teacher didn't have any idea what Rastafarianism was. Like most white people, he assumed it was some militant black power movement to be discouraged.

On school days, Vincent was out of bed early before Mum had even brought me my cup of coffee, which she did every day. But I lazed in bed in the mornings. 'Errr....thanks Mum.'

'Time to get up, Eamon. You have to go to school, don't you?'

'Errr... I have a free period this morning. I'm meeting Albert, I mean my first lesson is at eleven ... or eleven thirty.'

Albert and I met at school and wandered down the King's Road to the caff. It was a greasy spoon opposite Granny Takes a Trip. We wiled away the morning eating runny eggs on white toast and tomato sauce washed down with tepid cups of weak tea. The customers sat around reading *The Sun*. The Lou Reed song *Walk on the Wild Side* was on the jukebox. I pushed in my 5p and played that one every day.

Just before lunch we meandered back to school to see if we could hustle 50p playing penny-up-the-wall or a few hands of blackjack in the school library that still had tables and chairs, but the books had long since disappeared. We then walked, back to my place where Mum made us a lunch of soup or sardines on toast, played a game or two of chess then headed out into the streets again. Mum assumed we were going back to school.

Humm, what to do next? 'Let's go up to the museums,' I suggested.

Albert and I walked down Old Brompton Road past Christie's to South Kensington and the Museums. We explored the numerous corridors and rooms of the V&A. Albert liked the Japanese swords and armour display.

'Let's go and have a look at the Natural History Museum, Albert.'

We crossed the street and up the steps of the museum to the giant Diplodocus skeleton in the huge atrium of the terracotta-tiled Victorian building. We found the connecting corridor into the Science Museum and went straight to static electricity machine. We electrocuted each other and made our hair stand on end for a while until we became bored.

'Oh well, 'ows about anover cup a tea?' Albert suggested. So off we walked, back down through South Kensington and along the Fulham Road past the grand buildings of the Brompton and Marsden hospitals, the expensive antique and furniture shops, and the ABC cinema which was showing the *Poseidon Adventure* in its one enormous theatre, to Saint Stephen's Hospital.

In the emergency waiting room, we made ourselves a cup of tea at the free dispenser, and sat on the waiting room chairs with junkies who were queuing to get their methadone doses. We listened intently to their stories about taking drugs and having sex with the nurses - maybe in their dreams.

Sipping my weak tea from a plastic cup with Albert talking to the drug addicts, I became depressed. Vincent was getting a top notch education and here I was bunking off school and hanging out with desperate people in a hospital waiting room.

It was hard for me to talk to anyone at Chelsea school without sounding like a know it all. My family had travelled the world and had been exposed to so many ideas and ways of living that I was like a walking encyclopedia - I knew just enough about most subjects to annoy people.

My real teachers were Mum and the TV news. No one at school especially not Albert had the faintest idea what was going on in the world. They barely knew who the Prime minister was. But I was deeply affected by current affairs, art and books. Like Vincent, I read voraciously, often the books that he had read and passed on to me.

'Eamon, here, read this, It's a terrific book,' he said flicking his copy of *The Naked Lunch* at me as he walked by.

I felt as if I inhabited two worlds. In the day time, I lived in the world of petty criminals and juvenile delinquents. At night, I went home to the educated and sophisticated world, where my family lingered around the kitchen table after dinner debating the meaning of existence, philosophy, religion and art. During the day, my life was about survival, how to avoid being attacked or arrested.

Our do-it-yourself education completed for the day, Albert took the bus home to return the next morning for another hard day of study. I walked home past my sister's school, down Gilston Road to The Boltons - a tree lined street that is divided into two crescents with communal gardens in the centre. Saint Mary the Boltons church sits in the middle of the gardens surrounded by trees and shrubs.

As I walked on by the bench in front of the stone church, I noticed a boy from school in the year above me, sitting with a girl. They were gazing at each other hand in hand. He gently touched her face and stroked her hair. They kissed.

My heart felt a pang of longing as I stole a glance at the romantic scene. They sat in the dappled light with the breeze whistling through the trees, the hand-like leaves of the plane trees flapped to and fro. It touched me. What a lucky boy, I thought and continued around the corner to home.

When Vincent arrived home from school, he disappeared into his psychedelic room, threw off his school uniform and let his hair down - literally, the Oratory was strict about appearance and Vincent had to prepare his long hair and tie and shove it up to disguise the fact that he was a hipster. Moments later, the Hiwatt amp cranked up, and Vincent belted out

'... Stop breakin' down, baby, please stop breakin' down
Stuff I got'll bust your brains out, baby, hoo hoo,
Yea, it'll make you lo-o-o-se your mind ...'

Keith Richard and Vincent on guitar, vocals, Mick Jagger and Vincent. After an hour or so, his door opened and, transformed, resplendent with auburn curls down to his shoulders, wearing patched jeans and a white collarless shirt, Vincent burst out of his room. 'Is dinner ready yet? I have to study tonight, so no one make any noise, get it?'

After dinner, he slammed his door shut, and his study light stayed on until the early hours of the morning.

From the age of about fifteen, Vincent always had a steady girlfriend. He had several of them - but only one at a time. He always treated his girlfriends like royalty. One night, he bellowed, 'My girlfriend is coming over tonight, so everyone has to keep out of the way. I don't want her being hassled by any of you, get it?' and slammed his door shut.

When his girlfriend arrived my sisters and me hid in our rooms. He took her to the psychedelic room and serenaded her. Periodically he dashed out to the kitchen to get something for her. 'Would you like more ice, baby? Ice, ice where's the ice?'

The Paris Pullman, a repertory art cinema, was just around the corner. They showed new avant-garde film releases and the old classics. On weekends, they played late night double features. Many of the films were X rated for over eighteen year olds, but I never had any trouble getting in.

Mum asked me why I wanted to stay out so late. 'It's for my education.'

'Well alright then, but you still have to go to school in the morning.'

I loved sitting in the dark, smokey cinema peering into the imaginary lives of other people. I was anonymous, neither the actors nor could anyone else in the cinema could see me. I was just a shadow, left alone with no one bothering me or asking me who I was.

I didn't mention to Mum that Vincent, and I also saw all the counterculture films including *Easy Rider, Woodstock, Monterey Pop, Mad Dogs and Englishmen* and perhaps the greatest film of all, *Performance,* with Mick Jagger set in Powis Square, Notting Hill.

These movies made me feel part of something at last. I was one of them - the characters being portrayed - a hippie weirdo, a member of the great counterculture.

I admired the filmmakers, especially the directors. I thought what fun it must be. Instead of people demanding to know who you are and what you think, the director gets to tell everyone who they were to be that day and how to act the part.

Albert and I started going into pubs when we were fifteen years old. For a year or so we could only manage a half pint or two of soapy fizzy beer. We usually drank Watneys Red Barrel. Albert said through a drunken haze after a pint one evening, 'Anyone who says they like the taste of beer is a liar.' Intoxicated, we stumbled out onto the pavement and smoked roll-up cigarettes.

The Hammersmith Odeon played different movies each week, and we discovered that late at night they showed X-Rated films such as *The Lusty Vicar,* humm. After seeing a picture one night, we thought maybe we should try and pick up some girls. We tried, but they said, 'Piss off you little twerps.'

In the evenings when I wasn't out with Albert, I hung around in the kitchen at home with Mum. She was an excellent cook and taught me - mostly by osmosis - how to prepare food and organise a kitchen.

'Eamon, you should always clean as you go. By the time the meal is cooked the kitchen should be all cleared up and spotless.'

I sat at the table and read the newspaper glancing at the news on the small TV in the corner of the room, but she warned me, 'Don't believe something just because it's on TV or you read it in a newspaper.'

'Why not?'

Because, you don't know why they are saying it. You don't know what their motives are or where they got their information from. If I told you the moon was made of green cheese would you believe it? When people see something on TV they tend to believe it no matter how ridiculous it is.'

I watched her chop vegetables and scrub the potatoes as I flicked through *The Times* and I didn't know what to believe.

'Eamon, you must use your judgment, discernment and knowledge to tease the truth out of a story.'

Mum was always reading racy novels and murder mysteries, and would invariably figure ou t whodunnit long before the end of a thriller movie.

My double life continued and by the end of April 1975 I had turned sixteen years old. I came home hungry one night, and wandered into the kitchen. The BBC news was on TV. The dramatic headline appeared

SAIGON SURRENDERS

The Vietnam War had been on TV my entire life. When I was a kid we watched *The Honeymooners, the Beatles Cartoons, The Wonderful World of Disney, The Monkees, Laugh In, Star Trek,* but the Vietnam War had always been there too, from my first memories until now.

Images of dead, burnt bodies, live people being thrown from helicopters, young girls burned alive, immolated monks, B52s dropping bombs, savagery committed by us, our side - America, Australia. The good guys, murdering, torturing, destroying, lying, making believe all the while that *God* was on our side. The hypocrisy and exposed false morality confronted me every time I looked at the TV. It went on for longer than I could remember - from before the death of John Kennedy.

Now it was over, and I felt old - as if I were one of the veterans looking over my shoulder at the devastation. 'Who started this shit anyway?' the veteran would ask.

'Ah, like in all wars, the ones who were so brave and reckless when they embarked on their demonic misadventure are long gone - rich or dead but, they left long ago,' the restless souls of the murdered ones murmured to my minds eye as I watched the shameful end to the horrific war.

I felt alienated, adrift from, and outside society. I don't want any part in this I thought. Our whole society is built on lies, it's a sham. Nothing is respectable, nothing is respected. I just wanted to bury myself in a fantasy movie, to run and escape.

Chelsea School didn't have a sixth year where grammar school kids take their A- Level university entrance exams. So after three years my sentence came to an end. During the final semester I took several O-Level exams. Amazingly I passed these and decided to go to a Further Education college the following September to take some more with a view to taking A-levels the year after.

I didn't have a sense of what I wanted to study or what career I would follow. Vincent was already at university studying law. I imagined myself in a barrister's wig and gown ... M' L'ud, only a sum no less than three million pounds would be sufficient recompense for my client's anxiety and distress caused by this injurious falsehood ...

No, that wasn't me, but what did I want to do? I didn't have a clue, First, I had to gain university entrance and that still seemed like a far off dream.

Towards the end of the final term, I was buying a sandwich for lunch one day in a shop on the King's Road opposite the school when I was shaken by a loud

KA-BOOM

A mushroom cloud billowed up into the sky and a raging fire burned. Kids rushed up to the flames to see what was happening. The English teacher tried his best to force the onlookers back from the Dantesque scene.

In the street outside the school, a deep hole had been excavated to carry out work on the gas main that ran underneath from the gasworks on Lots Road. There had been a small oil tanker parked there to provide fuel for the diggers and other machines.

The tanker had been blown across the street. It was twisted and warped, engulfed in flames and billowing smoke. Fire engines came blaring down the King's Road from the fire station near Chelsea Town hall, and the police arrived in force. I wondered where Albert was.

Later that afternoon, Albert who had been subdued since lunchtime, and I were lazing in the English class when marching boots came pounding up the hall. The door of the classroom banged open, and an enormous policeman snarled, 'Which one of you is Albert?'

Albert was dragged out of the room, and I didn't see him again for over a week. When I finally met him again at school I asked, 'Why did you do it Albert?

'Dunno do I. It was just there, a leaking oil drum. All I had to do was dip a hanky in the oil, light it, drop it in the pool of oil and off it went.'

'But why did you even think of setting fire to it?'

'Because I want to burn everything. The whole bloody lot. There's no place for me here. I mean, no one gives a shit about me. You're going to go to a fucking College, and what am I going to do? Go on the bloody dole, that's what.'

'Albert, what about the future? You'll find something to do, make a life for yourself.'

'The future? You must be joking, there is no future. Not for me.'

A few days later Albert and I went to the caff on the King's Road. A shop across the road had a new sign. It had been called Too Fast to Live, Too Young to Die and sold black leather jackets plus all the required paraphernalia of early 1960s English Rockers. The shop now had three gigantic letters stuck on the front.

S E X

They seemed to be made of foam covered in pink plastic and were six feet high sticking out about one foot. 'Cor, look, a sex shop has opened across the road,' said Albert.

After eating our runny eggs on white toast, and drinking several cups of tepid tea, we went to have a look. Too afraid to go in, we peered inside at straps, kinky leather underwear, and peaked leather caps like the ones the gay men who hung out at the Coleherne on Old Brompton Road wore. Rubber covered the walls and red carpet the floor.

'Bleedin' poofters,' I said.

'They'll try anything once, twice if they like it,' said Albert, and we sauntered off to find some other amusement along the King's Road.

Albert received a two year suspended sentence for setting fire to the oil tanker and causing the explosion. Luckily, no one was injured by the blast.

4

At the beginning of the new academic year in September, I took the number 22 bus from World's end across the river to Putney College. I selected the classes I wanted to take and joined the queue to enroll. People of all ages, races and immigrant groups were in line with me. The atmosphere was happy and excited. I felt like I was like going to a university, except that it was for secondary education, not tertiary.

Further Education Colleges provide secondary education for adults. However, judging by the large number of kids my age enrolling there must have been many substandard schools in London. The enrollment clerk handed me my student ID card and said, 'The common room is up the staircase over there,' pointing down the hall.

"What's the common room?" I asked.

'It's a free area for students to relax. Teachers never go up there. It's your community space. It has a jukebox and vending machine.'

It seemed like an ideal first port of call, and I headed over. I walked up the stairway into a large room with a picture window looking out over the tops of houses. Standing next to the coffee machine was a guy with a pleasant expression and bird's egg blue eyes. He smiled and nodded at me as he took a sip of his coffee, so I walked over to say hello.

'Oh, hello, I'm Tim. I just moved to Putney from Chichester. Ya, just moved in a week ago. My uncle has a flat around the corner. He had to go back to Switzerland, so I'm sub-letting it off of him.'

Tim was half English and half Swiss and spoke with an upper class English accent. 'I was a boarder at public school. I don't know how but I managed to get my A-Levels and went to the University of West Sussex.'

'What did you study?' I asked.

'Art, so I didn't have to do anything. Just draw squiggles every now and then. Anyway, I got kicked out, and that's why I've come up to London.'

'Why did you get kicked out?'

'Non attendance, I hardly went at all last year.'

'What are you doing at Putney?'

'My dad said he would support me as long as I kept studying, I've enrolled here so I could pretend to be taking another couple of A-Levels.'

'What subjects are you going to take?'

'I don't even remember. I ticked some boxes on the form and they accepted me. I'll find out soon enough I expect.'

Tim was short and slim, and like me his hair was long and bedraggled. With a pointy blond beard and moustache, he looked like a cavalier. I imagined him with a puffy collar, breeches and a sword by his side. He had an air of confidence and grace, catlike he seemed in control of his personal space. We didn't have any classes together, but from then on we met in the common room during breaks.

Most of the students at Putney only stayed one year, and each September, brought a new mix of people to the college. Civil war was raging in Lebanon, and many young Lebanese kids were sent out of Beirut to finish their education overseas. I soon made friends with some of them. In the canteen one day I asked a young guy, 'Are you from Lebanon?'

'No, I am Iranian,' he said. Concerned about the political situation in Iran he insisted, 'There is going to be a revolution.'

'Are you for the revolution?' I asked.

'No absolutely not. If the shah goes the extremists will gain control and my beautiful country will be ruined,' he said with fear and tears in his eyes.

I met an Egyptian Berber whose father was a mullah at the West London mosque in Regent's park. He spoke passionately about, 'The murderers who are trying to eradicate the Berber people - it's genocide!'

At any time, I could find at least two or three of my new friends in the common room or cafeteria listening to Bob Marley and the Wailers on the jukebox. Instead of going to classes we often stared dreamily out the large west facing windows of the cafeteria sipping weak tea from plastic cups. The college was directly under the flight path to the east-west runway at Heathrow Airport and most afternoons, the supersonic Concorde flew overhead on its way in to land into magnificent orange and purple sunsets. When the college day was over, we went to the Spotted Horse pub on Putney High Street.

When the weather grew colder Tim and I put on surplus Royal Air Force heavy, blue, ankle length, double-breasted greatcoats. They tapered in the middle and flared out at the bottom with enormous collars that we turned up to the wind. We wore them everywhere and slept in them when necessary. We looked like musketeers without swords, our huge coats and long hair flapping in the wind.

The year1976 was the bicentennial of The United States Declaration of Independence, and to celebrate this momentous anniversary, a large batch of acid tablets colored either red, white or blue was circulating in London. Soon these 'tabs' seemed to be available everywhere we went. One night Tim and I met someone who suggested we give them a try.

'Okay, never say nups,' I said. We went to the Spotted Horse and downed them with our beer. An hour passed, but nothing seemed to be happening. I bought two pints, and the barman asked for 40p. For some reason, I thought he was joking. I burst out laughing and stumbled over. He looked at me queerly then I noticed that his eyes were gargantuan like saucers and revolving. I tried to find 40p, but just looked at the money in my hand and had no idea which coins to give the man. He grabbed the money and went to serve the next customer.

I heard Tim's laugh and carried the pints mugs out to the back room of the pub. The room was full of the usual crew of bedraggled hippies with long hair and dirty jeans.

Tim was sitting on a bench curled up laughing uncontrollably. Someone said hello to me, and I jumped back in fright. He had enormous teeth that looked as if they were going to bite me in two. The faces of our other friends looked bizarre and ghoulish.

I grabbed hold of Tim and dragged him out into the street - for his safety, or so I thought. Outside, the pub's wooden sign, carved in the shape of spotted horse, seemed hilariously funny. We pointed at it, and laughed like a couple of monkeys, 'Chee chee - kee kee - hee hee!'

It took us several minutes to regain our composure until Tim said, 'Right, let's start walking before someone notices us.' We became serious and earnest. 'Yes,' I said, 'No one should see us in this state.'

We walked quickly towards Putney Bridge, which had taken on a strange purple color and was pulsating. Continuing down New King's Road, past my old school and down the King's Road, we came to a pub on the corner of Beaufort Street, and the King's Road called The Roebuck.

'Fancy a pint?' said Tim.

'All right, but we must act cool, real cool, no laughing.' I wagged my finger at him.

'Right', we said together and with determination we pushed open the door and in we went. It was quiet with just a few people supping beer at the bar. The barman was wiping a beer glass with writhing seaweed.

'Two pints of lager and a packet of crisps please.' That ought to fool him, I thought.

'Sixty pence.'

'Thirty p a pint?' shouted Tim, 'You must be joking, I ask you.'

'Chris, shsshhhh, this is Chelsea.'

The barman took a banknote from my outstretched hand and gave me back a hand full of gold and purple doubloons with pictures of Blue Beard the pirate on them. In the distance, I heard Tim laughing his lungs out. Oh crikey, where is he now? I followed the sound up a flight of stairs. As I walked up the falsetto West Indian voice of Junior Murvin rang out from the jukebox.

...Police and thieves in the streets, oh yeah!
Scaring the nation with their, guns and ammunition
Police and thieves in the stree-e-eet, oh yeah....

The room came slowly into view. First feet then legs until I finally had a full view of twenty or so laid back people standing around two pool tables. Some of them wearing strange clothes with safety pins holding them together, and I heard a mixture of London accents,

'Oh ya, rhally,' the Chelsea accent.

'Oy, giss a fag,' from Battersea.

Tim seemed to be getting along just fine, so I relaxed and watched the show.

He tried his best to play pool. Every now and then he burst into laughter at some hallucination. Once he miss hit a ball, and it went flying out the window onto the King's Road and the whole bar erupted into laughter. At least, I think that's what happened.

Eventually the pub closed, and we walked up the King's Road to Sloane Square then Sloane Street to Knightsbridge, up Piccadilly, down Whitehall, along The Mall to Buckingham Palace. I felt like a tourist in the city for the first time taking in the sights of London. The streets shimmered a like a Van Gough painting in rich vibrant colours unlike I had ever seen them before.

We pressed our faces the gates of the palace which loomed up into the sky as puffy clouds streamed overhead illuminated bright by the waxing moon, and our acid twitched brains. Then Tim said with a start, 'Cops, look out!'

'Yeah, lets get going before they hassle us,' and we headed back to the King's Road. As we passed Beaufort Street, I peeled off and found my way home and Tim continued walking back to Putney.

Unable to sleep, my closed eyes continued to see delicious colors and felt tantalizing sensations. My mind seemed to become strangely coherent. I felt as if I had gained some incredible awareness or knowledge. It was as if the whole of existence had exploded into tiny particles, but the particles all belonged together, so they coagulated back to their original form. However, they seemed to have gained something from their disassociation and had become enriched.

It made me feel special, like I was back in India with strange smells and sensations. However, I couldn't look at Mum the next morning. She brought me my coffee as usual. 'What's wrong with your eyes?' she said.

Sometime later I emerged from my room and went to the kitchen to get some breakfast. Mum was there, and she asked, 'Did you have a big night last night. You got home very late I think.'

'Er, a bit late. I was just out with my friend Tim. We walked all over the city.'

5

In June, Tim failed to make it to his A-Levels exams, finished at Putney and started looking for full time work. But after the summer break, I started my second year. However, Tim and I soon resumed our normal routine of drinking in pubs and walking around West London in our greatcoats. With nowhere else to go after the pubs had shut we ended up at Tim's place several nights a week to continue drinking and playing records. Usually a few of our friends from the pub came along as well.

Tim was into Led Zeppelin and Bad Company. Music Vincent described as 'apocalyptic rock' and the night wore on the music was turned up louder by increments.

We met a young Japanese guy who was studying English as a foreign language. He had only just begun the course, and we needed patience to understand him. We waited for him to flick through his pocket dictionary and construct a sentence word by word. It didn't take us long, however, to figure out that he had stopped off on his way to England. 'Ah so you were in Thailand, what did you do there?'

'Hai, Thailand has very good bu-da. Hai, very good.' Sitting on the floor of Tim's flat, he shared his bu-da with us and we rolled around laughing uncontrollably.

Eventually the neighbors complained to the landlord about the noise and Tim's uncle called from Zurich. 'Sod it, I have to get out of the flat,' said Tim.

He didn't seem to mind being evicted too much, but just smiled his wry smile and flashed his eyelashes. 'Rum do, what?' he exclaimed fatalistically, but he now had nowhere to live.

A few days after receiving the news from his uncle, I was in the Spotted Horse when Tim walked in. He had been looking for new accommodation and had found an empty terraced house that he thought would make a suitable squat. Many derelict buildings were spread across London, and squatting was common. It was difficult to get squatters out. Property owners had to go through legal proceedings that could take years.

Tim explained, 'There are a few places just across the road from West Kensington tube station and The Nashville Rooms. I've checked them out and a few of them are already occupied. There's one empty house in particular that's perfect. It looks like it's been vacant for years. I could live there on my own, I suppose, but ideally it would be good if at least two more people moved in as well. How about you Eamon, why don't you move in too?

'I don't want to leave home, especially not to move into some horrible place in West Kensington. I'm comfortable at home, and it's rent free,' I replied.

'Oh ya, I see your point I suppose. But I've got to go somewhere.'

Two days later I helped him occupy his squat. We met at The Nashville, a large pub and music venue, and nervously stared at our pints of beer until Tim said, 'Right, let's do it.'

'What's the rush anyway,' I said 'It's your round next.'

We sat in silence until we finished two rounds of warm beer to satisfy the drinker's code. Finally, mildly sloshed and filled with Dutch courage we walked up to the front of the empty house, gently nudged the door and open it swung. The interior was covered in dust but was otherwise in fair condition.

Bands played at The Nashville most nights of the week. It had a small public bar, and behind it a large music room with a stage, tables and a dance floor. They served a strong local bitter ale called Fullers ESB. When no bands were playing we gravitated to the public bar, and it soon became the unofficial 'common room' for the West Kensington squatter community. There Tim met other squatters who had friends that needed rooms, and he soon found other people to fill up his new home.

The house was so close to West Kensington tube station that we simply walked alongside the track and jumped over the back wall to the squat. When the Nashville shut we stumbled down the railway tracks and over the garden wall into the squat for late night parties.

It didn't matter how much noise we made. What were the squatter neighbours going to say - we'll call the landlord? In any case, fueled up with ESB we became so incoherent no one was able to complain about anything.

Tim had spent many years fending for himself as a boarder at public school, and had learned how to get along in shared accommodation. He was neat, self contained and kept his belongings in a box that looked like a pirate's sea chest placed at the foot of his bed. He rolled up his clean socks, shorts and shirts nicely before carefully placing them inside. He didn't like other people messing with his things - or looking in his chest.

His fellow squatters were the complete opposite. Their possessions were flung all over the house. They often spilled beer or broke glasses, and left the kitchen looking like a battle zone.

As time went by he became more and more tense. His soft smile changed to a frown, and his almond eyes screwed to hard squinting slits like a cat about to strike, until one day he seemed as if he were about to snap.

'Oh ya you guys, watch where you spill your beer, will you! It's disgusting man. You know what I mean.' He waved his hand in his characteristic upward, brushing gesture as if to shoo away a fly. To save an argument, I said, 'Come on, let's get out of here and go to the pub.'

We trudged out the kitchen door and jumped over the wall onto the railway tracks. 'These guys are driving me insane. I've got to get out of this place or I'll end up machine gunning the lot of 'em,' said Tim

I pushed open the door of the Nashville and a foul smell of stale beer and cigarette smoke hit me like a wall. It was still early afternoon and there were no lights on, just a grey dim light poking through the etched glass windows.

The Nashville was grotty in the cold light of day. In the evenings when it was dark with flashing stage lights and filled with people you could almost be convinced that it was a groovy place. Nevertheless, it was not a sign of success to play the Nashville.

As Tim ordered drinks, I noticed a poster advertising a band called The Sex Pistols. 'That's a good name for a band,' I said to no one in particular. A guy sitting on a bar stool said, 'They spit at the audience, and tell them to fuck off.'

'Oh, how absolutely gross,' Tim remarked. The guys in the public bar nodded in agreement and supped their pints of sickly, smelly bitter ale, which stuck to their beards and went rancid.

Living in a squat meant that you had to live 'the life', and that entailed drinking all the time instead of just most of the time. Every night had to be a party night. Somehow, this was supposed to bring you closer to the hippie goal of freedom and enlightenment. But I thought it was self defeating and destructive. For me, the time out of mind was purely an evening event. I didn't want to be intoxicated all the time. I often walked home to Royston Gardens just to escape the stupor and sober up.

Tim's mother owned a flat in Winburn Court, close to South Kensington tube station that she let out. It became vacant, and Tim, and his sister arranged to rent it together. He moved out of the squat leaving his drunken friends behind.

The Winburn Court flat soon turned into a party house with numerous young people coming and going looking for excitement. Tim's sister and her friends were different to the West Kensington crew. Like Tim, they were upper class, well educated and looked after by their parents. But Tim seemed out of place with them.

One evening his sister had some of her friends over, and we were all lounging in the living room when the door bell rang. Tim's mother was paying a surprise visit. As if someone had thrown a switch, his sister and her friends became cloyingly charming. 'Oh Mummy do come in, how marvelous to see you,' gushed his sister.

'Oh look everyone you must meet my ma-ma.'

His mother seemed to rise to the pompousness of the introduction and took on the air of a grand dame. 'Oh how charming to meet your delightful friends my dear.'

Everyone sat down and talked about their various country homes. 'Oh ya, oh absolutely amaaaazing... Oh do you rhally think so?... Oh you simply must come and stay at the house in Chalfont St Giles, oh do…oh mummy will be so pleased don't you know…'

Tim looked at me with a piercing glare. 'These guys are driving me bonkers. Come on.' He stormed out of the room into his bedroom. I followed him inside, and he slammed the door shut.

'Cor, it's just like being at school. I want to shoot the whole lot of 'em SPLAT.'

He slumped down on a chair at the table placed in front of his window. It overlooked a row of single story mews houses, and the back of the South Kensington Police Station. We could see police officers moving about inside. 'That means they can see us, too. Rum do, what?' said Tim.

'So your family annoys you?'

'What, are you kidding? They drive me insane, the whole bourgeois scene is pathetic.'

'Your mother seems very nice.'

'She means well I suppose. I just hate all this phony civilized crap.'

'You don't want to be civilized?'

'No, certainly not - all these false attitudes and delusions of grandeur.' They just think 'cos they have money they're better than other people. The older the money the better they think they are. I think the opposite.'

'Out of touch with common humanity?'

'Out of touch with life.'

'Are we in touch with life? I mean what's the purpose of it all?'

'I don't think there is any purpose, any meaning. You live, you die - puff, bag of shit.'

'So what's the point?'

'There is no point. That's why I don't want to waste my time on trivialities and niceties. I don't have any answers, but I can't stand the hypocrisy of people who think that they do.'

'But Tim you're one of them, upper class, rich, aren't you?'

'I don't have any money. My dad stopped supporting me when I left college.'

'Your family will always look after you though won't they?'

'That doesn't make me one of them. I'm not going to follow their code, their conventions. I don't believe in the divine right of kings. They weren't destined to be rich, or to be rulers, which is what they think. No, they just come from a long line of thieves. I reject their false moralising and bullshit lies.'

'So do you have any code or moral standards that you try and live by?'

'Of course I do the hippy code. Boom Shankar! You know what I mean,' and he waved his hand up through the air.

'What does that mean? How do you think we should live then?'

'The way our ancestors did before the last two thousand years distorted our perception of the world.'

'That a bit unlikely isn't it? You don't want to go hunting deer in the woods do you? You just want to go to the pub, and smoke bu-da, like me.'

'You're right I suppose. I'm just a bourgeois shit waiting for my inheritance. Let's go to the pub.'

It struck me that although I had lived in the wealthiest part of London for several years, most of my friends came from underprivileged backgrounds. When my family moved to London, we didn't know about the divisions in English society, and felt free to live wherever we chose. But England had so many divisions and barriers that working class people would not normally consider living in South Kensington or Chelsea. It seemed to me that the barriers were imaginary, a system, not real. My family wasn't part of it. We were outsiders looking in and the people trapped by their history didn't seem to notice us. If we had remained in Ireland or Australia we would have been trapped as well, like flies in amber. But we had left, and I sensed we were fortunate, liberated.

The feeling stayed with me, a sense of detachment as if I was an outsider looking into people's lives - as if they were actors in a movie and I was the audience.

A few weeks later I was at home watching an early evening news program called *The Today Show* on TV. My attention was grabbed by an interview with The Sex Pistols. The show's host, Bill Grundy, was interviewing the band with a few strangely dressed girls standing around. One of the girls had a Nazi swastika on her arm and another had short white hair. Grundy introduced the band by saying, '…they're not the nice, clean Rolling Stones…'

It seemed a strange thing to say, not least because the girl with white hair looked exceptionally clean. It didn't seem long ago at all that the Rolling Stones were portrayed as filthy and perverted by the mainstream media. So success and money make you clean, I laughed to myself.

Grundy went on to proposition the white haired girl and goad the band members into swearing at him. 'You dirty bastard…you dirty fucker…what a fucking rotter,' said a guy wearing a T-shirt with girls breasts printed on it.

A spiky haired bloke called Johnny Rotten said 'shit', and they accused the host of being drunk - it was hilarious. They played some footage of the band playing live in a club, and it was a terrific performance. The next day the newspapers described it as an outrage. Bill Grundy was fired, and the Sex Pistols gained instant fame - the Punk era had begun.

When I started at Putney College, I finally met kids - outside of my family - who seemed like me. I gravitated towards people with long hair who thought of themselves as hippies, but now, after only a couple of years, hippies seemed outdated - just a passing fad or craze. My sense of security, of fitting in that I had so longed for seemed to crumble before my eyes. Johnny Rotten described hippies as 'Old farts'. Old fart, me? I'm only eighteen.

My brother Brian had been living in the country, and one evening he arrived in London for a visit. 'Hey, Eamon, we're going to that new punk club the Roxy. Why don't you come along with us?'

'The Roxy, no way Brian, too heavy for me,' I replied taken aback at the very idea of my longhaired brothers going to a club where the bands spat at respectable hippies like me. The next day Brian said, 'You should have come along Eamon. We met Johnny Rotten and Sid Vicious. You missed a great night.'

In the evenings, I walked over to Winburn Court, and I just fitted in with whatever was happening. Tim always looked after his creature comforts and would only do things when he was ready. If you wanted to go out for a drink, and he didn't then you would have to wait. 'Hum, let's go out for a pint,' he would eventually say and off we would go.

As Tim and I were now living in the same neighbourhood, we started drinking at the pubs around South Kensington and World's End. One night we arranged to meet at the Roebuck, the pub on the King's Road where Tim and I had been hallucinating a year earlier. On the way there, I noticed that the shop called SEX had changed its name to Seditionaries.

I glanced in the window and was surprised by a mannequin dressed in trousers that had zips in strange places and a strap running between the knees holding them together. How are you supposed to walk in those? I wondered. I knew that The Sex Pistols had formed as a band while hanging out at that same shop back when it had been called Too Fast To Live Too Young To Die. The London punk scene had started there. The strange people that I had often seen coming out of SEX looked like the kids from school but wore the outrageous clothes sold in the shop.

I walked into the Roebuck, and as always several long haired hippies stood at the bar, but the new style was taking over. Intermingled were guys wearing the girls breasts T-shirts, with died, spiky hair and safety pins in their lips. The girls wore black tights and mini skirts with motorcycle jackets and slogans spray painted on the back. They too had pins and various things sticking into their skin and body parts. Several people wore the weird trousers strapped together at the knees, but they weren't like skinheads, they weren't into violence.

Some of them were posh. 'Oh ya, I died my hair pink because it's so cool - don't you think? I mean it's absolutely amaaaazing.' Others were working class from Fulham or further away. 'Ere, cop a load o' this. I've got MUM tattooed on me left buttock and a dagger on me forearm.'

The two pool tables in the upstairs bar were always full. The juke box played the Velvet Underground, and lots of Reggae. The other pubs we frequented seemed staid and uninteresting in comparison, so we mostly drank at the Roebuck.

A couple of months after moving to South Kensington Tim met a beautiful girl and they started going out together. Although Tim would still come out for a drink sometimes, I suddenly found my self on my own most evenings with no drinking companion.

6

In January of 1977, the year of the Silver Jubilee of Queen Elizabeth's accession to the throne, I met a small Welsh girl called Delyth at Putney College. She had long dark hair and wore full length skirts which gave her the figure of a girl from Flemish paintings - wide hips and narrow shoulders. She was quiet and soft spoken. However, she was popular, perhaps because she was so soft and even-tempered and a good listener. She looked at me in a matronly way her head tilted to one side, assessing me, trying to determine to which of her many friends I seemed most suited. 'You should meet Sarah, Eamon, you two would get on well together.'

One night I met her at a party in Tooting. We stayed up drinking, talking and listening to music until the early hours of the morning. Eventually Delyth curled up and fell asleep on the sofa and I stretched out on the carpet in front of the ineffectual gas heater, wrapped in my greatcoat.

In the morning Delyth and I left together and caught the same bus to go home. When the bus reached the corner of the King's Road and Beaufort Street, we both jumped off the open back of the Routemaster. She said, 'Look, there's my next bus. See you, 'bye,' and ran the short distance to the bus stop and jumped on a gleaming pure silver double-decker.

I was somewhat hung-over and thought I must be seeing things, and I walked straight into a lamp post. My head went 'bang!' and the silver bus chugged past with Delyth waving from the back. I then remembered the Jubilee celebrations and realized that the red bus really had been painted silver. I muttered to myself, God Save the Queen.

Delyth was an only child, and her parents were often away, leaving her alone. In their absence, she held parties in the family's large, rambling home at Parsons Green, just off New King's Road. Soon after bumping my head on the lamp post, I was invited to one of her parties for the first time. I called Tim to ask if he wanted to come along. He replied, 'The only reason to go to a party is to get a girl. I already have a girl, so there's no point in going.'

I arrived and rang the doorbell. 'Hello, Eamon. Come down into the basement,' said Delyth.

We clambered down a wide staircase into a large open room. It had a pool table at one end and a kitchenette with a variety of chairs and sofas arranged around it with boys and girls lounging in them, laughing waving their arms and talking.

'What a fabulous place! Where are your folks?'

'Oh, they've gone looking for some winter sun somewhere exotic, the Caribbean, I think.'

I noticed a girl sitting on the carpet, her legs folded sideways underneath her. She was dressed in a black leotard and pink tights - no skirt - and delicate black shoes with short stiletto heels. She had short brown hair with a dyed blue stripe up each side and was talking to a boy sitting beside her dressed in black with spiky hair. He seemed diffident and bored. She looked lively and fiery. Her arms were outstretched with her palms turning in and out and moving up and down in flamboyant gestures.

'Delyth, who is that girl?'

'Amanda? Oh, don't be silly, Eamon. But come, I'll introduce you to her.'

We crossed the room, and Delyth said, 'Amanda.'

Amanda's eyes flashed up towards her.

'This is Eamon,' she said nonchalantly and quickly walked away leaving me with the most beautiful creature I had ever seen.

'Eamon come and sit down. I won't bite, not unless you ask me nicely,' Amanda laughed throwing her head backwards.

I sat down beside her on the carpet. Spiky boy looked down his nose at me as if I were an insect, yawned, stood up and moved away.

'Who was that?' I asked.

'Oh, I have no idea at all. I don't think he was listening to a word I said,' she laughed again.

I stayed by her side for the rest of the night. Amanda told me about the Tennessee Williams play *Camino Real.* She had recently played the part of Camille, The Lady of the Camellias, in a school production.

She said, 'My ex-boyfriend, gave me camellias after the performance.

He climbed over a garden wall and picked them off a neighbor's bush for me. Wasn't that romantic of him?' She was animated as she spoke with a smile and a mischievous twinkle in her eye.

Amanda was seventeen years old, but she still had the air of a younger teenage girl. She was a delight to watch - coquettish with large blinking grey-green eyes and pouting lips covered in scarlet lipstick. She had a strong chin, broad nose and high cheekbones. Her father was German, and the striking Germanic looks showed in her face.

'Do you like art?' she said. 'I want to study art history. As soon as I finish school I'm moving to Kensington. Where do you live?' She continued, 'I don't want to be an actress, I just took the role because it was fun.'

'What do you want to be?' I asked.

'I want to be a great artist. What do you want to be?'

I had no idea at all. I did want to put my hand on hers and stroke her cheek. I moved closer and closer to her. Her hair smelled intoxicating. I waited for a moment that felt right so that I might kiss her. She looked at me once, as if she wanted something, but no, I didn't dare.

She continued talking to me and didn't seem bored. Maybe she just needed an audience? No, she seemed to like me. So we talked and talked. She listened to me and looked straight in my eyes.

We eventually found our way up to the living room on the ground floor and talked until the first light of morning turned the dark of the night to dim grey. Her fresh complexion and ruby lips looked even more alluring as the light poked in through stained glass lead lights and net curtains. Like vampires retreating to sleep for the day the party goers filed out through the front door and Amanda and I stood at the front gate.

'Well, Amanda, it was…'

'Eamon, you're so nice,' she said. 'I enjoyed talking to you so much.'

She hesitated for a moment, saying nothing, hanging frozen in time leaning slightly towards me. Like a zephyr, the moment passed, and the intimate mood evaporated. She sighed, leaned back and said, 'Goodbye, Eamon. I have to go home to Wimbledon.'

She turned on her heel and left me. I watched her totter away on her black stilettos in her short plastic coat that only just covered her delightful behind swishing around her trim thighs.

I walked home alone to Royston Gardens. Delyth was right, 'Oh, don't be ridiculous, Eamon. Ha ha ha, you and Miss Universe Amanda?

She could never be with a foolish little boy like you.' A fool like me, a fool like me.

About a month later, Delyth threw another party. I arrived quite late, long after the pubs had closed. I found my way into the dark living room which was full of party goers jabbering away with loud music blaring. It didn't look promising. People were falling around, talking loudly and seemed too far gone.

I saw through to the far side of the room where draped in an arm chair was Amanda. She was wearing black footless tights and a long sleeved men's collarless shirt. The top buttons of her shirt were open, and she was not wearing a bra. She had the same luscious red lips and gave me a small, intimate smile. She shone through the room like a movie star. As if in a movie, the focus pulled in, and I could see only her, bathed in light. The music seemed to slow and fade, all I could sense was her. I pushed my way through the crowded room and fell onto her waiting, parted, moist lips. We kissed and kissed.

After a while without speaking we left so we could find somewhere to be alone. We walked down the King's Road entwined in each other's arms past Seditionaries and wound our way through the streets to Royston Gardens, kissing all the way. At home no one was awake, and we snuck into my bedroom.

In the morning we went to the Ice Dream Parlour on Fulham Road for brunch. Amanda talked animatedly, smiling, laughing and giving me knowing looks. 'Have you ever seen 'A Streetcar Named Desire'? I love Blanche DuBois.'

'You like Tennessee Williams a lot?'

'Of course I do. I love high tension, opposites pitted against each other. Have you been to the Tate recently?'

'Not recently but I used to spend time wandering around the V&A'

'I love the clothes in the V&A, all the old fashions especially the early twentieth century stuff.'

We drank Bloody Marys with our bacon and eggs. 'One more drink and I'll be under the host,' she laughed.

What a lovely laugh, I thought. I could have sat for hours just watching her lively face and smiling eyes. After brunch, I took her to the bus stop on Fulham Road opposite the ABC Cinema. We kissed, and I buried my face in her blue hair. She smelled of musk and spring flowers. 'Amanda, I'll call you, what's your phone number?

She hesitated and said 'Give me your number.'

The bus came and off she went on the red double-decker. I felt as if it had all been a dream. I gave her my number, of course, but didn't believe that she would ever call me. How could such a beautiful, entertaining, desirable girl have any interest in me?

I was swooning inside with the exquisite memory of our night together. It was sweet torture to think of her wrapped around me. When would we be together again? Would she ever call, would she?

Three days later she did call.

'Amanda, you called me!'

'I said I would call, didn't I?'

'You said you might ...'

That evening we met again and were rarely apart from then on - except that I was living with my parents, and she had to go to school in the daytime. I lost interest in and rarely went to college. Instead, I waited patiently until the evenings came when we could be together again.

During the day, I could think of nothing but her. The sound of her voice, her loamy smell, the feel of her body entwined with mine. I was desperate to see her and like an addict my body writhed in pain unable to expel the memory or thought of her. I called her as soon as I thought she would be home from school.

'Amanda...'

'Eamon... I'll come over right away.'

The time passed like a glacier sliding until the doorbell rang and we were in each other's arms again. One evening lying in bed exhausted, we stared into each other's eyes, and I said, 'I love you.'

She said, 'I know, I love you too.'

Amanda was a punk, and I was a hippie. We made an odd-looking couple walking down the road with our arms around each other, Amanda wearing a brown plastic mini skirt, black or red tights and stilettos. She had rather short brown hair with blue streaks, flaming red lipstick with red earrings and plastic bracelets. I wore patched jeans, cowboy boots and a plaid shirt with my hair hanging well below my shoulders.

Walking down the King's Road, the centre of London fashion where the avant-garde went on parade, we seemed a shocking sight. I was amazed at the reactions we provoked. As we passed by people their eyes widened, and their heads swivelled to keep track of us. One couple stopped and shouted at us, 'No, disgraceful!' and 'Shame on you!' It was like the reaction some people have to a mixed race marriage. Hippies and punks were supposed to be enemies.

'How do you like it Amanda, causing a disturbance just by walking down the road?'

'The King's Road, Chelsea. I love it Eamon.'

Amanda's mother was twenty or so years younger than her father, and they had never married. 'I'm a love child,' she boasted.

'Do you have any brothers or sisters?'

'I have a half brother. My parents split up when I was ten and mum married another man, and had a son.'

'Do you live with your mum now?'

'No, with my dad. When they split up they asked me who I would prefer to live with. I opted to stay with my father in Wimbledon.'

'You didn't want to be with your mother?'

'She didn't have anywhere to go. She was just going to see where life took her. Dad kept our flat. It was more sensible for me to stay with him.'

'That was a heavy responsibility to place on you when you were so young.'

'It made me grow up fast. No point being too sentimental, you have to be practicable about things.'

'Did your dad find someone else?'

'No, he never did.'

'Has it been hard for you Amanda, being brought up by an old man?'

'Oh no, I never missed my mum too much.' Her eyes darted to-and-fro, not knowing where to look as she answered me.

Amanda liked to take me shopping. She was always looking for 'inspiration'. Many fashion boutiques had opened on the King's Road mimicking the punk styles that Seditionaries had pioneered. A shop called Boy, sold copy-cat designs, and the Antiquarius arcade was full of stalls selling quasi-punk gear. At Worlds End, the 20th Century Box sold old clothes from the 1920s to 50s, and that is where we usually ended up.

'Eamon, who do you want to be today?'

'I want to be ... me.'

'Don't be so boring, try these on - you'll look so much better in a pair of pegs than in horrible old jeans, and look at this Prince Edward check jacket.'

'I thought you liked it that I was different to you,' I said.

'Yes, but you can't stay that way forever, you have to grow up sometime.'

She took me into Seditionaries and made me try on a pair of Bondage Trousers. 'Amanda, I can't wear these! They have a strap between the knees. How will I walk?'

'Oh, come on, Eamon. Nothing wrong with a bit of deviation.'

Amanda liked Art Nouveau, Art Deco and the author Dorothy Parker, 'That woman speaks eighteen languages, and can't say no in any of them,' was one of her favorite Parker quotes. She gave me a copy of the Christopher Isherwood book, *Goodbye to Berlin*. Of the central female character in the book, she proclaimed, 'I love Sally Bowles. She's independent, leading her own life. But just because a woman makes her own way, it doesn't mean she has to be like a man. She can still be sensual, beautiful and feminine, vulnerable too. But one thing a woman should always be is well presented. The right clothes and make up. Appearances are more important for a woman than for a man.'

In the evenings, we listened to David Bowie's *Heroes* and the Stranglers album *Rattus Norvegicus*. We saw the film *The Man Who Fell to Earth*. The main character was Newton - he was a visitor.

One night Amanda said, 'I want to take you to a club in the West End.'

We hailed a taxi, and as it whirred down Oxford Street to Tottenham Court Road Amanda took out her red lipstick and black eye shadow. 'It's like you're putting on your disguise,' I said.

'It is my disguise Eamon. I want people to think I 'm some exotic creature. You should try disguising yourself too.'

'I'm in disguise alright. My clothes are just a uniform. I'm just trying to fit in.'

'Ha ha, I wonder what they'll make of you in this club.'

The taxi pulled up in front of a black door next to Tottenham Court tube station. Amanda pushed open the door and rushed up a flight of stairs with me following. A bouncer stopped us at the top and said, 'Ere, Manda, wot you doin' wif a bleedin' hippie?'

'Don't worry Toad, we're going to a fancy dress party later,' she said and breezed past him clutching my hand. We entered a dark room crowded with people dressed in black with white or pink hair. Hours later we emerged and took a taxi back to Royston Gardens kissing all the way.

Punks were a modern version of 1920s Berlin decadence - or so, they liked to think. They said they believed in nihilism, nothing-ism, the idea that life is without any meaning, purpose or intrinsic value. Bondage and unusual sexual practices, at least as inspiration for fashion accessories, were central themes.

Punks wore plastic and rubber garments, tied up various parts of their bodies and cut revealing holes in their clothes. Safety pins pierced through their skin in odd places. 'You gotta be kidding. Stick a pin through there?' I demurred.

Whatever mainstream society shied away from, everything horrible, grungy, secret and hidden they wanted to bring out into the open and put on display.

'Are you into all this kinky stuff Amanda?'

'I just like the fashion, the body as art, life as a tableau.'

To celebrate the Queens Jubilee, parties were planned across the country from the middle of May onwards, bunting and flags were put up all over London in preparation. One evening in late May, a friend played a new Sex Pistols single called *God Save the Queen*.

'Can you imagine what normal people think of this song Amanda?'
'Oh it's so funny, I can just see mums and dads wincing,' she laughed.

Johnny Rotten, belted out the lyrics in a mocking, ironic tone, but the theme of the song went straight to the heart of English society.

'... God save the Queen, we mean it man...
...When there's no future, how can there be sin?
We're the flowers in the dustbin ...
... No future, no future, no future for me ...'

All the radio stations refused to play the song, and it was officially banned on the BBC. But it blared out from the shops on the King's Road and we heard it everywhere we went.

The main Jubilee day was in early June, and neighborhood streets across England were closed off, tables were laid out with food and drinks and most people were very merry. Tens of thousands of people lined the streets waving flags and cheering as a procession led from Buckingham Palace to St Paul's Cathedral.

That evening Amanda and I were in the upstairs bar of the Roebuck. A small TV hung from the ceiling in the corner, and the news was on with the sound turned down. The bar was full of young punks and assorted long haired freaks as usual. A guy with a mohican hair cut - both sides of his head shaved and the remaining strip of hair in the middle combed upwards into a ridge - said, 'Oi, shut it will ya, cop a load of this,' as he turned up the volume on the TV.

Police boats in the twilight with lights flashing were milling around Westminster Pier with the Houses of Parliament in the background. Some policemen clambered aboard a boat docked on the pier. Many other craft circled around churning up the river as policemen emerged holding people by the shoulders.

A reporter's voice crackled saying that The Sex Pistols had chartered a boat and were performing *God Save the Queen* while sailing down the Thames as it passed the Houses of Parliament. The event ended in chaos when their boat was surrounded by a flotilla of police launches and others filled with press photographers. The police forced them to dock, and their manager Malcolm McLaren, Vivian Westwood and many of the band's entourage had been arrested.

The bar burst into a chorus of cheers and laughter. Arms flew upward throwing crisps, cigarettes and beer at the TV. The guy with the mohican shook his head in amazement, 'What do they think they're up to? Bleedin' mad they are.'

I felt elated, like I had finally gotten into the spirit of the day. I had felt like an outsider most of the time I had been in England - I was an outsider now - I wasn't a punk. But this made me feel connected, at least to the people in the room that night. It was as if midnight had just struck on New Year's Eve. Immediately, we all became friends, hugging kissing, buying each other drinks. What a glorious gesture I thought. What an act of political theatre.

The next day the newspapers and airwaves were filled with indignant outrage. Nevertheless, the record was a big hit. The authorities had to twist arms to stop the single from being declared Number 1 in the British charts, which everyone knew it was.

When asked in an interview about the reaction to the song, Johnny Rotten said, 'I don't understand it. All we're trying to do is destroy everything.'

Punks wanted annihilation, to tear the whole putrid house of cards down around everyone's ears.

It seemed to me that the divisions in English society were made undeniable and laid bare for all to see by the punks. An underclass of disaffected youth across the country was seething with resentment at the society that they felt excluded them. They imagined no future for themselves and wanted to destroy everything.

'They don't actually want to destroy everything Eamon. I think they simply want to express themselves in a different way, and they have a taste for the bizarre,' declared Amanda throwing her head back.

I didn't believe in annihilation or nihilism. I sympathised with their feelings, but my inner voice drew me back to India, to visions of the sun setting into the ocean, dissolving into myriad colours.

A few months after I met Amanda she finished school and moved into a bedsit just off Kensington Church Street. My two years at Putney also came to an end, and I faced a terrible reality. I had wasted my opportunity. I had few academic qualifications and had not gained university entrance. Now, both Maranda and I needed to find work. We were now among the one in ten, the 10% unemployed.

I went to collect my unemployment card, called the UB40, at the dole office on Fulham Broadway. On the way in I bumped into Albert who I hadn't seen since I left Chelsea School two years earlier.

'Ere, Eamon what are you doing signing on? You were always the clever one.'

'I finished at Putney College so now I need to find a job. How about you Albert, have you been out of work long?'

'Been out of work long? Never been in work have I,' he laughed.

'Are you still working at your mum's shop?'

'I help out but it's not exactly work. She doesn't pay me.'

'Are you living at home?'

'Er, for the time being I am. I had to stay at home in any case while I was on probation. I've finished that but ...'

'What's up Albert?'

'Ain't you heard? You must have heard about it?'

'What? I haven't heard anything.'

'Well it's just that there was a fire, at a bus station, and t burnt to the ground. I've been convicted for doing it, and sentencing is next week. I could be looking at nine years in inside.'

'Albert no, that can't be!' I exclaimed

'The judge said that due to the seriousness of the crime I should prepare myself for a lengthy custodial sentence. You can come and visit me. Look, I've got to go. I have to sign in at the police station every day or they'll come after me. See you sometime, Eamon, it's a shame about me, i'n it?'

He disappeared down the road. I was stunned to think that my friend Albert could be put in gaol for nine years.

I joined the end of a long line of forlorn people, young and old. They shuffled their feet as the line inched forwards, smoking Number 6 cigarettes and reading newspapers or trying to pick horses in *The Winning Post*. The mood was depressed, numb. People's eyes focused on the ground in front of them, and their heads shook slowly from side to side.

Oh my, so this is what it's like to be unemployed? The news was always filled with how terrible the economy was with double digit inflation and rising unemployment. I asked a young guy ahead of me in the queue, 'How long have you been looking for work?'

'I'm not looking for work. There isn't any work to be found. I gave up months ago.'

'How long have you been on the dole?'

'Since I left school about a year ago.'

The line shuffled along interminably until I was finally beckoned to approach a woman sitting behind a plate glass window. I attempted to sit in a chair near the window. However, it had been bolted to the floor just a bit too far away and offset to one side. I half knelt and strained forward to get within shouting distance of a little perforated speaking hole in the glass. It was as if they were deliberately trying to make the experience as unpleasant as possible. 'I want to sign on,' I yelled through the hole.

'Have you registered for unemployment benefit previously?'

'No I haven't.'

'Then you will have to go and queue up over there and fill in a form.'

The woman pointed to another line of miserable looking men, boys and girls on the other side of the room. Oh no... I queued up for another hour before I finally received my UB40.

I asked, 'How much money will I get?'

The dole officer replied, 'Sixteen pounds every two weeks.'

I though it's hardly worth it, as I traipsed back home down Fulham Road in the drizzling rain.

Luckily, Dad knew of a vacancy at a roofing company and, I soon had a job. It was dangerous work - climbing on roofs and painting them with waterproofing goo. However, the pay was £50 pounds a week. As I was living at home, had no car and no expenses, I was able to spend all my money having fun with Amanda.

She took me to the Tate Gallery at Millbank. Amanda loved the Francis Bacon paintings. To me the contorted figures looked like tortured, twisted creatures trying to burst out of their skin, and shake themselves free from their bodies. 'Why do you like them Amanda?'

'Because that's how we truly are, inside'

Is that really how we are, I asked myself? Tormented insane beings, lost in a wilderness of pain? My heart felt wrenched at the thought of Albert, his life thrown away, consumed by his pyromania. He actually did want to burn the house down and destroy everything.

I looked back at the writhing figure in the painting and shuddered. I didn't even have to be unemployed for more than two weeks, that's how lucky I was. No need for me to hate society. I better count my blessings. I think I'll cut my hair, enough of this childish behavior, I better start acting grown up, I thought.

'Amanda I'm going to cut my hair.'

'Because of the Bacon paintings?'

'Yeah I guess so. I don't want to end up like that - inside.'

'Afraid and regretful?'

'That's right Amanda, I don't want to live in fear.'

In the evening, I walked to High Street Kensington to meet her near her new bedsit. My route took me down Ashburn Place, past the back of Gloucester Road tube station. The area around Gloucester Road had so many Arabs dressed in flowing thawbs and agal headdresses that it was known locally as Saudi Kensington. The brick walls of the station were covered in Iranian graffiti - dozens of squiggly lines of Farsi and at the end were the words written in English

DOWN WITH THE SHAH

I crossed Cromwell Rd, passed the large hotels that teemed with tourists from all over the world, and wound my way through the elegant Georgian and Victorian back streets. When I reached Kensington High Street, at the entrance to Kensington Gardens, I turned left and continued past the Kensington Market, Barkers and the Art Deco Derry & Toms building and met Amanda on the steps of the newly built Town Hall on Hornton St.

We sat on the red brick wall by the fountain, talking and canoodling in the apricot light of the long summer evening with the sound of water tinkling and splashing behind us. I felt exuberant, in love, moistened by the spray of the fountain with Amanda in my arms. 'I wish this moment would last forever, don't you?'

I caught a fleeting glimpse of temporal emotion in her eye and she replied, 'Nothing lasts forever, not even love.'

As the summer drew to a close, darkness enveloped the city, and we spent more time in dark clubs and venues with people all dressed in black. One night I arrived home from work exhausted, filthy and covered in red roofing paint. I was desperate to see Amanda, and I called her straight away before I had a shower.

'We're going to a party in a dungeon near Charring Cross. Come over and we'll all go on from here,' she said.

Amanda shared her bedsit with a young gay punk. As I walked up the stairs I heard chatter and laughter. The tiny room was crowded with a group of punks and an assortment of gay men, lesbians and strange people.

I stood sheepishly in the corner, keeping my back to the wall. But Amanda's flatmate said, 'Eamon, he's a dabbler. He'll try anything once, twice if he likes it.' He also said that I was attractive and that boys fancied me. I clung onto Amanda's arm.

We piled into taxis and arrived at Charing Cross. To my horror, the venue genuinely was a dungeon. We went down a flight of dark, wet steps into a dank, cavernous cellar lined entirely in bare, wet bricks. The low ceiling was arched, as if under a railway bridge, and various corridors led into windowless chambers. The party was full of bikers like the men who hung out on the street outside the Coleherne. It soon became obvious that groups of semi naked men were having sex with each other in the various chambers. The punk girls thought it was most amusing, so did Amanda. Guys came up to me and tried to engage me in conversation. I twitched and stammered. My eyes rolled around desperately avoiding the stare of the bloke chatting me up.

After a while, Amanda saw my discomfort, 'Are you alright?'

'Ye-ye-ye sure, just not used to blokes smiling at me like that, as if I'm a juicy peach ready to be eaten. Now I know how girls must feel.'

She took me to a quieter room with a bar that I could prop up. We chatted to Sue Catwoman, and other heterosexual punk girls and I felt more comfortable. In the early hours of the morning, our group left the dungeon party, and walked back to Kensington.

As the months went by my style of dress gradually changed. Amanda changed too. She transformed from a punk into an impeccably dressed beautiful young woman. As Coco Channel said, 'If a woman dresses beautifully, people notice the clothes, if she dresses impeccably, they notice the woman.' People noticed the woman in Amanda.

One day she said, 'Let's visit my mum in Brighton for the weekend.' The train from Victoria Station took only one hour. Her mother was elegant and shared Amanda's shining eyes. She lived with her husband and Amanda's half brother above a newsagency that they owned near West Pier, a beautiful Victorian wrought iron and wood construction – now washed into the sea. It jutted out into the English Channel like a jewel encrusted pendant.

Brighton beach is covered in large pebbles and backed by a wide promenade. In the stormy winter night, we clinked our way through the stones grasping each other to brace against the gale winds and stood under the rusting metal pylons and creaky wooden decking of the wedding-cake pier. The waves crashed into the pebbles and made a rumbling sucking sound as the stones jiggled together when the waves withdrew. The wind howled, and the rain washed our faces.

Amanda wore a black French style beret and green trench coat. She now had long flaming red hair, dyed with henna, and as always, scarlet lipstick. The waves sucked, the wind whistled and our hearts soared. Amanda cocked her head and shouted at me through the din, 'I love you.'

I stared transfixed by her eyes, burning bright through the darkness. It was as if the whole world had been engulfed by a terrible hurricane, but Amanda and I were immovable, captured in each other's orbit, impervious to the maelstrom around us.

In early 1978 Amanda got a job as the assistant stage manager at the Country Cousins, a cabaret club in Lots Road opposite Chelsea School. It was essentially gay, but the clientele were an eclectic mix. Many famous people went there including some prominent politicians who were not 'out'. She worked in the evenings and usually didn't finish until two in the morning.

'It's brilliant fun. Holly Woodlawn, the transvestite from the Andy Warhol film, *Trash* is on this week, and I'll be working late.'

'When will I see you?'

'Next week I have a few days off, but I have so much to do.'

I was still painting roofs during the day and was once again I was on my own in the evenings. Amanda was meeting new people and being invited to openings and parties. 'You can come along if you like, Eamon, but I'm not sure you'll enjoy the company.'

It was true, her new friends were different to the punks that she used to go around with. They were much older than us and seemed wealthy and successful. I was just a boy, and they had no interest in me, but she was a beautiful young lady.

'This is Eamon.'

'Charmed, I'm sure. Now come, Amanda, I want to introduce you to somebody.' She was whisked away, leaving me with a canapé half in my mouth.

Alone with nothing to do I was walking on by the Water Rat pub at Worlds End. I glanced in the window, and Amanda was sitting at a table with a man. I thought she was at work. I walked in and sat down beside her. I glared at her, my eyebrows furrowed, my fingers twitching.

'Eamon, what are you doing here?'

'What am I doing here? This is my local pub. You're supposed to be at work.'

'I'm not supposed to be anywhere. I decide where I go and when I go there.'

My hands felt as if they were on fire. She was sitting with some old man who looked as if he could have been thirty years old. 'What do you see in this old geezer, Amanda?' I said, nodding my head in his direction.

'This is Michael. He happens to be rather successful, unlike you.'

The old chap interjected in a slobbering public school accent, 'Now look here, you little sod, clear off, why don't you? I mean rhally, can't one have a quiet drink. You just leave this young lady alone.'

'Young lady? She's mine, you old bastard!'

'Eamon, I'm not yours, I'm not anybody's.'

'Well, fine.' I stood up shaking. 'But you're coming home with me now.'

I grabbed her by the hand and pulled her out of the pub. As we left I heard the old man protesting, 'Outrageous. Who is that chap, what?' But he didn't give chase.

We stomped up Beaufort Street, both of us enraged. I headed in the direction of Finch's pub. We sat in the back room and glowered into our drinks.

'Who was that guy?'

'I told you, that was Michael. We were just having a drink.'

'Oh yeah, sure.'

'Look, we're not married. I can do what I want and have a drink with whoever I wish. We need an open relationship.'

'You must be joking, an open relationship? I' m not going to share you with anyone. I should be enough for you.'

'What, forever, just you and me, like Adam and Eve? You're so immature Eamon. You have to have some trust.'

'I love you Amanda.'

'I know, I love you, too.'

From then on I was consumed with jealousy at the thought of her at work or with her new friends. I wanted to possess her, mentally and physically, to crawl in under her skin. More than that I craved to merge with her being, to know her every thought and feeling as if it were my own, willing her to think of, want, and love me alone. These feelings were destructive, insane even, but like an addict I couldn't control my thirst, my desire.

Amanda began to look at me strangely - side glances - as if she didn't know me.

'Amanda I love you so much.'

'I know Eamon, but I can't be with you all the time. I wonder what you're like when I'm not around?'

'I just wait to see you again. I feel empty when you're not with me.'

'It's funny Eamon, when we were in Brighton visiting my mother she said to me, 'You two don't talk much. I thought at your age you would never stop talking to each other - trying to get to know one another.'

'I want to know you Amanda.'

'Maybe you just want to control me. Sometimes I think you have no idea who I am or what I want.'

I felt betrayed - how could I not know what she wanted? I spent my whole life trying to please her. It was she who didn't know me or how much I loved her.

The following week she had a few nights off work. We went to Tim's place for a drink, and a guy I had not met before said, 'Try these.' He handed me two little bits of paper. I gave one to Amanda, and we swallowed them.

Sometime later I started to feel strange. I was seeing unusual and inexplicable movement in the wallpaper. Amanda became annoyed with me. 'What's the matter with you? I don't feel anything,' she snapped and went into the bathroom slamming the door.

I was fascinated by the wallpaper which seemed to be alive with strange insects crawling over the surface. After what seemed no more than an instant Tim said, 'What's happened to Amanda? She's been gone for ages.'

I jumped up with a start, 'Did she go out?'

I hurried to the bathroom and pushed the door open. Amanda was sitting there, her eyes like saucers. 'It's incredible,' she said 'It is like the scene in *The Man Who Fell to Earth* where Newton is making love and all covered in liquid, it's so beautiful.' Suddenly I felt sure that I was experiencing the same sensations as she was - floating in the dark, awash with my lover's essence - Amanda's essence.

'Come my love, come outside.' I took her by the hand. She seemed like the young girl I had first met, wide-eyed and tremulous. I could feel her vulnerability. She was like a trembling kitten, looking around, fascinated but fearful.

For a long time, we sat facing each other in chairs on opposite sides of the room, our legs crossed, and hands draped over the arms. We gazed into each other's black-pool eyes. In my mind, I heard shifting music, lilting and wistful. It was as if we were transported from a dark room in London to an exotic garden in Japan with a little waterfall. Beautiful birds singing, damp verdant moss, pebbles, exquisite trees with long dappled leaves and little goldfish in a gentle, translucent tinkling stream.

We were in complete peace. Amanda took on the ethereal appearance of an enlightened being - serene, in permanent existence, but not here, somewhere else.

Eventually we went out for a walk and found ourselves on the embankment sitting on a bench under a statue of the painter Whistler, staring at the Thames in the pale dawn light.

For the next few weeks, we were happy together. She was tender and loving. She looked at me with longing in her eyes, almost tearful as if her emotions were just bubbling beneath the surface. One evening at the end of summer, Amanda said, 'Let's go for a walk.'

We strolled around the corner from Royston Gardens and sat on the bench in front of Saint Mary the Boltons. The plane trees were blowing gently, laden with a full burden of large hand-like leaves showing the first tinges of autumn brown. The sunlight pushed through the leaves and fell on us in twisted shapes. I looked at her as shadow, then light, shimmered across her face, and tried so fathom her thoughts. She looked sad but untroubled, resolved.

'Eamon, I cannot take responsibility for this relationship any longer.'

'What do you mean?'

'We can't stay together forever, Eamon.'

'Why not? We're in love.'

'Because we're too young. Imagine us at forty. We would have been together for more than twenty years.'

'That sounds perfect to me.'

'Eamon listen to me. You need someone nice and sweet, not me. I'm not the one for you.'

'But I love you Amanda, no one else. You're the only one.'

7

Capital Radio 'one... nine ... four' as the deep-throated voice-over intoned was the first commercial radio station in the United Kingdom. Located in a tall building on the Euston Road, Capital offered a free jobs board where advertisers could post ads aimed at young Londoners like myself. The overall unemployment rate may have been 10 per cent, but for people under 25, it was over 20 per cent.

Soon after Amanda left me, my roofing work came to an end, so one day I went to Capital see if any new jobs had been posted. My eye was caught by one for a projectionist at the Institute of Contemporary Arts, the ICA. I applied and was interviewed by a short guy with stick-up hair and large, rimmed glasses called Gene. He offered me the job, he subsequently told me, on the basis that as far as he could tell there wasn't anything wrong with me.

The ICA is on The Mall, just up the road from Buckingham Palace. It occupies Nash House, one of a row a Georgian terraces designed by the eighteenth century architect John Nash that line the northern side of The Mall. Across the road is leafy St James's Park, and across the park the back route to Downing Street, Whitehall and the Palace of Westminster. Behind Nash House are Pall Mall, St James's Palace, Piccadilly Circus and Soho.

I was employed to show films in the repertory cinema and light static art exhibitions in the galleries. The institute also had a theatre and various lecture rooms. Gene was the head projectionist and he set about training me. He was meticulous and slowly, patiently taught me how to load the projectors and screen films.

The ICA was a repertory cinema, and we showed dozens of films each month at morning, afternoon and evening screenings. On a typical day, at least three different films were shown, so that in a normal week many different films would be screened. I usually worked the evening shift and finished around 11:30 at night.

We screened seasons of a particular director's work such as Buñuel or Fellini. I was paid to see many of the great classic works of cinema from Un *Chien Andalou, Cet obscur objet du désir, Le Grand Bouffe, Aguirre der Zorn Gottes* and even *The Wizard of Oz.*

Perhaps because I saw the same films over and over again, I came to like the ones where nothing was clear, but obscure, hidden, unexplained. Why do movies to have a beginning, middle and an end I wondered?

I found that I liked films that were more like paintings where my eyes could roam around and take in the visual spectacle while my emotions were pulled in different directions and my intellect unraveled new aspects and sub-plots.

Most films and books conform to a predictable order, designed to be easy to follow. But I preferred the stories where everything was disjointed, out of place, leaving me to figure out what the author was trying to say. I didn't like being spoon fed to make everything obvious.

I grew to love the films made by directors such as Antonioni, Buñuel, and Godard, where I never knew exactly what meaning they were trying to convey. I watched their films over and over, and it was a new experience every time.

I sat in my smoke filed box with the heat and flashing lights of the projectors, peering through the viewing hatch. I felt shielded and isolated from the rest of the world. There were only me, and the filmmakers.

I felt lucky I had a job to go to - otherwise I would have shrunk into a cocoon of gloom and misery. When I woke each morning, I felt sick with an empty longing, a feeling that something was missing. Like a dog looking for his master, I moped around looking everywhere for my lost heart.

I called Amanda and she agreed to see me. We met for a quick drink in the pub, but after a few minutes, she said, 'Must dash.'

'Amanda, you're going so soon?'

'I'm going out this evening. It was good to see you though.'

I called her again a week later and she said, 'Eamon I think you should stop calling me.'

'Why, can't we still be friends?'

'Maybe someday, but not now, it's too soon.'

'But Amanda I have to see you or I'll go mad.'

'Look Eamon, don't call me any more alright? I don't want to see you or talk to you. Not until ... until you've met some nice girl. Someone who can take care of you,' click.

I sat with the phone in my hand, perched at the kitchen table staring out the window for what seemed an age. Eventually Mum came in and said, 'What's wrong with you Eamon you're so depressed, listless.'

'I feel lost Mum. I don't know what to do with myself anymore.'

'What about your job, you must like seeing so many movies?'

'Yeah sure.'

'Are you sad about Amanda?'

'I love her Mum, inside I'm on fire with love for her. She just doesn't care how I feel.'

'Eamon, it's not just about how you feel, but how you make the one you love feel. Your love has to go outside yourself and do something for her. Love is giving, not taking.'

'But she dumped me Mum. How can I ever forgiver her for that?'

Tears welled in her eyes with a far away look as if she remembered something from her past. She said, 'Well you must forgive her. You should forgive everyone who wrongs you. It's a terrible thing not to be forgiven, a terrible thing.'

I felt my mother's sadness, and asked her, 'Did someone not forgive you?' She didn't answer but just turned away and lit a cigarette.

She was right. Had I ever given of myself to Amanda? She made me come alive. When I was with her every cell of my body tingled. She made me feel handsome, strong. She taught me about art and opened my eyes to a sensual world of love, and I had repaid her with mistrust and suspicion. As Mum spoke in her soft caring voice, it dawned on me how I had squandered Amanda's affection. Now she was gone, and I was abandoned, forlorn.

A terrible sadness took hold of me. The next morning I just lay in bed, inert unable to stir myself and face the day. Mum brought me a cup of coffee, as she used to when I was late for school. 'Eamon, don't you have to go to work today?'

I did have to go to work, and I had to be on time. So I rushed to Gloucester Road station and caught the tube to Piccadilly Circus. I walked down Waterloo Place, crossed Pall Mall, and passed by the grand Athenaeum gentlemen's club with its neoclassical bas-relief frieze, and the Duke of York Memorial column on Carlton House Terrace straight down the long delivery ramp at the back of Nash House into the projection box.

As part of my ongoing training, Gene and I were both scheduled on for the same day-time shift. It was Saturday, and the Queen was holding a garden party at Buckingham Palace. The Mall was closed to traffic and turned into a long car park. Standing out at the front of the ICA, Gene and I watched as the guests clambered from their Rolls-Royces, pulled their outfits straight and tamed their eyebrows with licked fingers before making their way to the front gates of the palace.

An endless list of names poured out from a PA system calling the realm's finest citizens to join the queue to be presented to the Queen. Most of the guests looked as if they hadn't had to walk so far in decades. The wind blew the gentlemen's tailed coats and the ladies' floral dresses. We laughed out loud, wagering whether they would be able to complete the half mile walk. It occurred to me that The Mall is the Monarch's Road - the King's Road.

Our shift finished in the late afternoon, and Gene said, 'Let's go for a quick drink in Soho.'

We wandered up to bustling Piccadilly Circus and pushed our way through the crowds, edged our way through busses taxis stuck in traffic, to Shaftsbury Avenue, Great Windmill Street and through the quiet Berwwick Street market to the Crown and Two Chairmen pub on Dean Street.

Gene was in his mid twenties, with a round face, dark complexion and was from New Zealand. He had been working at the ICA for five years, ever since he first arrived in London. I took him to be a highly responsible, sober and upright person. After all, he was my boss and was training me to be a projectionist. I soon found out, however, that he was impressionable, like a blank page, or maybe, like me, he was still growing up.

Gene had gone steady with the same girl from the time he was sixteen years old. The two of them left New Zealand when they were nineteen, but only a few months earlier, after eight years together, she had asked him to marry her. As soon as they were wed they realized their mistake and split up. Now Gene he was free for the fist time in his adult life.

'Why did you say yes? I mean why did you agree to marry her?'

'I had to make something happen. Otherwise, it would have just gone on and on forever.'

Now, he seemed to want to make up for lost time. On our nights off we went out drinking. No matter what I suggested, he always said, 'Yup, let's go.' He was up for anything, he never hesitated and would try anything once, twice if he liked it.

Gene was a car freak and drove an MGB roadster. He was brought up around cars, knew how they were constructed and how to fix them, they were in his blood. I didn't even have a driver's license. 'What do I need a car for? You can't park anywhere, and it's quicker to get around on public transport than driving,' I tried to convince Gene.

However, I soon realized that getting around by car had one considerable advantage, especially when you have a chauffeur to go with it - you can go much farther a field. Gene drove us all over London going to pubs, parties and gigs.

We went from the Rainbow in Islington to the Ritzy cinema in Brixton and to clubs in the East End. We drank too much, but Gene drove us home all the same. For Gene, a car represented freedom, and he didn't want his freedom restricted. Leaving his car at home would have been giving in.

Gene had a useful knack for parking. If you arranged to meet somewhere, he would roll up and park right out the front. Other people would arrive late, complaining that they spent twenty minutes looking for a spot. It was a worthwhile talent. After all, what's the point of having a sports car if the girls don't see you get out of it?

He wore glasses and dressed like a nerd, but in his car, he was the boss. It was his world. The MG had an expensive stereo system, and the first thing Gene did when he got into his car was reach for a cassette to play. He liked hard-driving rock 'n' roll.

One night I said to him, 'Let's drive to King's Lynn.'

'Why?' he asked.

'We've never been there before - come on it'll be fun.'

'What'll we do when we get there?'

'It'll be great, don't worry. Let's just be crazy and jump in the motor and do it right now.'

'Right oh,' said Gene. We set off at 3 am, vroom in the MG.

'Put the top down.'

'It's cold,' Gene yelled.

'Turn the heat up,' I yelled back.

Off we roared up the A1 with the top down into the darkness of the flat countryside and drove into the dawn, the two of us swigging beer with Dave Edmunds blaring from the stereo.

… I knew the bride when she used to Rock 'n' Roll,
OH, I knew the bride when she used to rock 'n' roll …

King's Lynn is in East Anglia, on the Wash, the square chunk of water that sticks down into England from the North Sea. We arrived soon after dawn and drove straight up to the sea front. The sky was a uniform grey. It was drizzling, windy, cold and miserable. The sea looked like used dishwater. Filthy little waves rolled in and a seagull shat on us. No shops were open which was just as well - this place looked horrible. Gene looked at me with a Laurel and Hardy 'another fine mess you've gotten me into' stare. We both felt sick and hung over.

'Let's go to Wales!' I beamed.

'Wales?' said Gene.

'Yea, it'll be great, they have mountains and all kinds of stuff there.'

Vroooom, off we went with the music blaring.

… crawlin', crawlin', crawlin' from the wreckage into
a brand new caaaaaaar …

We sped across England through Peterborough, Leicester, Telford and on into North Wales. When we finally reached Snowdonia, I was relieved that it actually was mountainous and beautiful. We climbed hills, ate cream teas, drank beer and had a lovely time. Then the next day, we jumped in the car and tore back to London. Vroooom

...PUMP IT UP! until you can feel it
PUMP IT UP! when you don't really need it....

Gene lived in Willesden, just north of the Royal Borough, with several New Zealanders, and one of his brothers. I took the bus over to visit them. When I arrived we clambered up the dilapidated staircase and into the freezing kitchen. It was lit with a bare bulb and smelled rancid. We grabbed a beer from the fridge and walked up the tiny hallway to the sitting room where there his brother was lounging on the floor in front of TV and a gas heater. We lay down on the carpet beside him.

'Wha'cha doin'?'

'Nuthin'.'

'D'ya' wanna go out?'

'Nah.'

The two of them smoked a few cigarettes and stared at the fire. After a short while I reached my limit. 'Gene, let's get going!'

Vroom, off we went in the MG looking for action - any action.

Later in the pub I said, 'Gene, you seem so laid back until you get behind the wheel.'

'Yea, I need something to occupy my senses otherwise I tend to lie around - it takes a big prod to get me going.'

One day, after I'd been working at the ICA for a few months, Gene announced that he was leaving. He had been offered a job in a studio in Soho that mixed the sound for TV commercials and films. He was going to work in the transfer bay loading machines with recording tape. It seemed to me that he was leaving a place where he was the boss for a fairly junior position.

'Gene why are you leaving? I thought you were well entrenched here.'

'I've got to try and make my mark in this world. I've got to keep moving forward.'

'Yea, but you're the top dog here. There you'll just be one of the back room boys.'

'Eamon the prospects at the ICA are fairly limited, and I'll never make any decent money. Something happened a few weeks ago that made me determined to find another job. I went to see the manager at the bank up the road to get a credit card and a personal loan. Since splitting up with my wife, I'm kind of broke. Anyway, he approved the loan with no problem, but on the way out he said to me, 'You'll never actually have any *money,* will you?' It shook me up.'

'What did you say to him?'

'I said, I don't know, maybe I will someday. I realized then that I had to move on.'

To my surprise, I was now the senior projectionist and head of the department. A few freelance projectionists worked shifts, but I was the only one in full time employment with the ICA.

Not long before Gene left, we took delivery of a mixture of 35mm and 16mm films representing the collected works of Andy Warhol and Paul Morrissey. A Warhol film season was scheduled to coincide with an exhibition of his screen prints organized by Sarah Kent titled Andy Warhol: Athletes.

I now had a couple of dozen Warhol films in my care. I was astonished. It was like someone had delivered a box of Picassos and said, 'mind these for a while'.

There were many films including Kiss, Haircut, Screen Tests, 13 Most Beautiful Women, The Velvet Underground and Nico, Chelsea Girls, Flesh, Heat, Trash and others.

The film 13 Most Beautiful Women is a single camera shot against a white background. Thirteen different women sit in the frame for fifteen minutes each. The camera doesn't move. It's a head and shoulders shot with no sound. The women smile and blink and act naturally, that's it, nothing more. While showing the 16mm film one day it broke in the projector. I quickly spliced it back together and continued the screening. The perforations on the side of the film that fit into the sprocket drive mechanism were torn so I had to cut the bad piece of film out. I was left with 18 frames, or ¾ of a second, of film of a woman called Sally Dennison.

Warhol came to the exhibition opening party in July as well as a number of celebrities. While Andy was talking to the artist David Hockney, I approached, held out my hand for him to shake and said 'Hello, Andy, could you sign this for me?' He had the limpest handshake I had ever felt.

He signed the piece of film with a quizzical look on his face. 'Who are you?' he asked.

'I'm the projectionist, that's all,' I replied.

Hockney said to me, 'You're a very clever boy.'

At the end of the season, we received notice that Warhol was in a dispute with the films' distributors. We were requested to keep hold of the prints and not return them. They were only released after a further six months and in quiet times, I showed them to myself, over and over again. I particularly loved the Warhol films as few of them had any plot at all.

At first working as a projectionist was exciting, but it was lonely and boring working in the projection box all by myself. I could only endure watching *Celine and Julie Go Boating* so many times.

Tim and his girlfriend went travelling. 'Eamon we're off to India.'

'Wow, Tim, how long will you be away?'

'Six months, maybe longer. We'll have to see how the money goes.

We're going to go through Turkey, Iran and Afghanistan.'

'What will you do when you get back?'

'We're not coming back. We're going to live in Geneva.'

'Geneva! Why go there?'

'Because I'm Swiss and I can make more money there for sure. I can speak some French, but no German, so I figure Geneva is the place to go. Anyway that's the vague plan. We have to get to India first, you know what I mean.'

As time passed my heart felt sadder and sadder. I felt lost and alone without Amanda. At work each night I sat in the box with the film whirring though the gate in the heat and bright light with no one there but me. Once I fell asleep while a film was showing. I heard a bang on the door, 'Eamon, what's happened to the film?' an anxious voice shouted through the locked door. I woke up to see the finished reel flapping around in circles.

On another occasion, *Celine and Julie* was scheduled to play again - oh God, not again! I wondered if anybody would notice... no, it's such a long and tedious movie. No one would sit through it more than once. So I left a reel out. Once again, someone came banging on the door. 'Leave me alone, I'm busy!'

I decided I had to find something else to do. Like Gene, I determined, I must keep moving.

8

An American girl turned up at Tim's place one day, and I invited her over to Royston Gardens a few days later. I opened the door and she was standing there with a tall, skinny guy wearing tights. At least they looked like tights. 'What?' he exclaimed in disbelief at my ignorance, 'It's my cycling gear.'

It was unusual attire for London in 1978. He grabbed a bicycle from the lift and started to wheel it into the apartment. 'Oh, you want to bring your bicycle inside do you?' I said.

'Sure, ya, I don't want it to get stolen. It's an expensive bike. D'ya mind? I'm Bart by the way,' he said in a broad Californian accent.

Bart was over six feet tall, very slender with dark curly hair and a swarthy complexion. He spoke in a weird way. Well, it seemed weird to me, but I had never been to California. He wanted to party.

'You want to go to a party?' I asked.

'Hey, I thought we could party here,' he replied.

So we began to party. It took me quite a while to realize that he was using party as a verb. I was used to using it as a noun. My understanding of, party, was going to someone's house, full of noisy people shouting above the din of too loud music and hanging around in the kitchen gulping beer forlornly hoping to meet a girl. To Bart, 'party' meant any gathering of more than one person engaging in any activity together - yes, including sex. Humm, so you can ask a girl to party...

After that day, Bart and I seemed to be partying all the time. We partied at my place, at his place, at anybody's place, if they let us in the door. The legal age for drinking in California is 21 years old, and the law is strictly enforced. So Bart didn't come from a youth drinking culture, and had no interest in going to pubs or any of the places that Londoners usually went to party. His idea of a good party was sitting on the sofa at home with a friend or two listening to Al Di Meola.

'Turn off that Al dee-mi shit and put on some rock 'n' roll.'

'Man, you wouldn't know good music if it bit you in the ass. Al Di Meola is choice, the most excellent sound reverberation pleasure there is, man. I just bought a new stylus for my stereo today, and the sound is sooooo sweet, dude. Here, have some organic carrot juice. I wish we were in California, man - we would have some top grade sinsi, humm, sinsi. I am sooo there…humm.'

He was obsessed with 'choice' stereo equipment and other 'most excellent' things. Bart was from Palo Alto, Silicon Valley, in the San Francisco Bay Area. He lived with his mother and stepfather in a big apartment on Flood Street, one block from the King's Road. Bart told me all about the Bay Area or, 'Bear-ea', as he pronounced it and Palo Alto or, 'Pow-alto'.

'Man, the weather is so much better there than in London. Warm sunshine, clear air, and the fruit is so abundant and delicious - apricots and peaches- humm.' He was also obsessed with fresh fruit and vegetables.

In California, he liked to go mountain biking with his buddies and rode bikes to taco stands and imbibed, '…the best, most glorious sinsi, humm...'

One night over at Bart's place we watched the movie *Cabaret* on video. I had never seen it before. The Sally Bowles character with her green nail varnish reminded me of Amanda, and I grew melancholy. I had met some girls since Amanda and I had broken up, but nothing more that a one night tryst ever came of it. Bart said, 'Man, I'm going to California for Christmas with my mom, you ought'a come with me.'

'Oh yea, what would I do in California?'

'We'll party with my old buddies, have some fine sinsi and have a wild time dude. It'll get you away from here and you'll forget about Amanda.'

'Where would I stay?'

'Our house in Pow-alto is being rented out. So we're going to be staying in the Hilton on El Camino.'

'What's El Camino?'

'El Camino Real, it means the King's Road in Spanish. It goes all the way from San Francisco, through Los Angeles and into Mexico. We'll be staying on El Camino in Pow-alto. The girls in California are soo nice, sooo mellow, soooo cool,' he said.

'Do you think I'll meet any girls?'

'Maaan, are you kidding?'

I wasn't sure what his last answer meant, but the next day I called a travel agent and bought a ticket to San Francisco.

As the airplane from London to Newark flew over Greenland, I looked from my window down onto the expanse of icing smooth snow, while mountains in the distance emerged like molars. Soon the frozen land was left behind, and we crossed a desperate sea filled with craggy icebergs.

Although I already felt like a world traveler, until now I had always been with my family. This was the first journey I had taken on my own. I was glad to be out of the cauldron of London and to at last be able to forget about Amanda - for a few moments. I couldn't remember when I had ever felt free from myself, not trapped in my skin. I stared out the window and dreamed. Maybe I'll meet a girl from Alaska, and we can live in an igloo, or an Australian who will take me home. Ah, but home is where mother is.

Baseball diamonds in myriad towns passed by the engines and disappeared under the wing as we crossed the vastness of the USA. We arrived at San Francisco International Airport in the mid afternoon. Palo Alto is south of the airport in the opposite direction to the city, and I had decided to spend a couple of days in San Francisco before going to see Bart.

I found a cab, and the driver asked me, 'Where you goin' bub?'

'I don't know, the centre of town where the action is.'

'Ohhh Kayyy, no problem,' and the big yellow taxi purred down the freeway.

The cab dropped me on the corner of Polk and California Streets. I stood on the sidewalk and it was as if I had walked on to the set of a movie. A black and white police car was parked across the street with a cop wearing an enormous gun leaning on the hood. It was sunny and warm, and a disheveled black man shuffled past me.

I walked around until I found a cheap motel. When the afternoon turned to evening, I ventured out to find something to eat, and a cocktail, hmmm, cocktail. I was gasping for a drink. I asked the clerk in the lobby, 'Where around here should I go to find a little action?' He looked me up and down and asked me, 'Straight or gay?'

I was slightly taken aback and said, 'Er, whatever.'

'Well if you walk in any direction there are gay bars all over the place. If you are looking for straight, I have absolutely no idea.'

'The girls in California are sooo cool', I thought.

The clerk was right. As night fell, the lights came on inside the bars, and they all looked pretty gay to me. Disco music was pouring out into the street.

… Y - M - C - A, it's fun to stay at the Y - M - C - A - A …

There wasn't a female in sight, but what the hell. Two nice young men stood outside a likely place. It didn't have any doors, and I could see a long bar inside with a mirror running along the length of it and all manner of alcoholic drinks stacked up. This is the place for me, I thought and started to walk in. The nice young men stopped me, and one of them said, 'Got ID, kid?'

'I beg your pardon?'

He looked puzzled and said, 'License, license.'

After a bit of discussion, I realized that he wanted to see some proof that I was 21 years old, or I wasn't going to get any booze. In fact, they weren't going to let me in at all.

I was dressed in a charcoal grey blazer, black neatly pressed pegs, black and white two tone shoes, black shirt with silver cufflinks. I was nineteen going on twenty years old. In London, no one would ever question my age or my eligibility to enter any class of establishment. The two nice young men were wearing tiny satin shorts that looked most uncomfortable, white T-shirts and shiny, short, puffy down jackets, bovver boots with white socks and sporting handle bar moustaches. To my eyes, they looked ridiculous.

I put on my best posh accent and said, 'Look, I'm *awfully* sorry, but I have just arrived from London don't you know. Dash it, I am still jet lagged and my *'otel*, the Hilton on El Camino is quite far away. I *really* don't suppose that I have my license with me, only my credit cards and cash.' I pulled out my wallet, which had a wedge of US bills, that I hoped would be enough for my whole trip.

'Oh, you're British. How are the Bobbies and the fog? I'd love to go to England. All right, go ahead, but next time, remember to bring your license with you.'

Phew! I was in. I sat down at the bar and ordered a drink. Hmm, a license, I didn't have one of them. Worried that I might have more trouble elsewhere I thought I'd better stay for a while.

After a few drinks, I began to rather like 'The Polk', as some other nice young men in the bar told me the district was called. I stumbled out onto Polk St, which by now was lively with a real carnival atmosphere. Music flowed from every bar.

Everyone seemed to be having a grand time. Young men from all walks of life in their work clothes paraded down the road. Among them were sailors, construction workers, cowboys, kung fu fighters, bikers. Then I saw two men who were wearing cowboy chaps but no trousers - or underwear. Right I thought, enough of this. There MUST be somewhere else to go in San Francisco!

I wound my way down to the North Beach area where things were a bit more to my liking. In the morning, I was woken by fog horns. I peeked through the curtains of my motel room and sure enough, the city was shrouded in a grey mist. I walked up Telegraph Hill to Coit Tower where I caught a glimpse of the top of the Golden Gate Bridge poking through, with the lower half and the bay itself still covered in a blanket of fog. That evening I found a jazz club in the Fillmore district where no one said, 'Got ID, kid?'

I called Bart the next morning, and he told me to come on down to Palo Alto. I walked to the Southern Pacific Depot in the South Market warehouse district to get the train. I arrived in Palo Alto and found my way to the Hilton on El Camino. 'Eamon, wow, you made it man, that's great! Where are you staying?' asked Bart.

'I only just got here, so I've no idea.'

Bart hadn't promised me anything but, I had rather hoped, even expected, that he would have arranged for me to stay with one of his friends. I hoped that I would spend my time in the Bear-ea partying with his buddies and their young lady acquaintances. Bart seemed edgy and ill at ease.

'Is everything okay with you, Bart?'

'Man, I've got all kinds of family issues to deal with here. My real father is in town, and he and my mother are arguing. You don't want to know about it.'

Bart suggested that we go mellow out with some of his friends and maybe one of them would have a place for me to stay. Bart's mother drove us to a house not far away in residential Mountain View.

We were welcomed into a large, single-story family home by a young guy in a top hat. 'Hey dude, so you're from England, cool. His mother came out of the living room and said, 'So Bart, you hang around with punk rockers in London?' She looked rather distressed and disappeared into the back of the house.

Bart asked his friend if I would be able to stay with him, but the answer was no. 'My mom is just not cool. Sorry, Eamon dude.'

Bart's friend took us into the garage and fished out a couple of bicycles and a skateboard. 'You guys ride the bikes, I'll take the board,' he said.

We rode all over Pow-alto visiting Bart's friends. By the early afternoon, I was exhausted. We had found nowhere for me to stay, no one had any most excellent sinsi, and not one of Bart's friends were girls.

'Bart man, I'm gonna go back to San Francisco. Maybe I'll come back down to Pow-alto in a few days.' Bart didn't complain too much. I took a taxi back to the station and caught the train to the city.

On the train back to town, I had pondered what I should do now that my most excellent visitation experience to the so cool Pow-alto was cancelled. San Francisco was picturesque, but there seemed little chance that I would meet a girl in this town. What was I going to do for two weeks? I know, I'll hitch hike down to Los Angeles, why not? That's what hippies do. Take to the road and experience the real America. There would be lots to see on the way, and I could go to Hollywood.

The next day I took the subway, strangely called BART (Bay Area Rapid Transit), to the end of the line at Daly City and asked where the road to Los Angeles was. The station master said, 'El Camino starts right out side and it goes all the way to LA.'

An inscription described how Spanish priests had built a series of missions from San Diego to San Sonoma north of San Francisco. The road that linked them all together was known as El Camino Real, the King's Highway and that the route began right here.

What better place, I thought, to start my journey. I stuck my thumb in the air and got a ride almost straightaway in a small truck. We drove down the peninsula to San Jose. There, El Camino became Interstate 101. The driver was going to a town called Gilroy to pick up a load of garlic. As we entered the town, a road sign declared

GILROY GARLIC CAPITAL OF THE WORLD

My next ride was in a woody station wagon. The driver was going to Monterey. 'Where are you goin' dude?' he asked

'I'm travelling down El Camino Real to Los Angeles.'

'Far out. Actually, Monterey is not on El Camino. Highway 101 goes straight down the middle of California. Have you though of going down Highway 1? It's the coast route, much prettier - very beautiful, in fact.'

So I decided to go to Monterey and see where the next ride took me. By late afternoon, I had reached Monterey. It was winter, and the sun went down soon after five in the evening. I found a Motel 6 and checked in. I woke up early and walked down the road to find breakfast. The downtown area of Monterey was crowded with lots of young people. Some looked like surfies with long blond hair, floppy T-shirts and sneakers. Most people were wearing brightly colored clothes and everyone was smiling. I looked at my attire in a new light. Standing in the bright sunshine I was wearing a black shirt, black trousers and a stuffy grey English jacket. I must look like Lurch from the *Addams Family*, I thought. It dawned on me that I was the one who looked ridiculous.

Embarrassed, I found a clothing store and changed my persona. I emerged out on the street in a plaid lumberjack shirt, Lee Cooper jeans turned up at the bottom and a pair of Converse All Star Hi-top sneakers. I smiled at everyone I passed, but after a while, the corners of my mouth began to hurt, and I had to stop. I checked out of the motel and stood by the side of the road and stuck my thumb out.

Soon I was soon zooming down the highway in a Porsche Carrera. The driver was in 'the business' - the movie business, that is. The soft top was down, and the wind blew through my hair as we accelerated around corners and curled along the windy road. He pulled a cloth pouch out of the glove box and said, 'Here man, put one together will you - top grade sinsi.'

The road twisted and turned hugging the rugged coastline the piercing sun flickered through the trees, the sky and ocean were a brilliant blue. Eventually we turned inland to the town of San Luis Obispo and rejoined El Camino Real. As the sun was setting we crossed Malibu Canyon and soon the giant city of Los Angeles twinkled in the wide valley below the hills.

'Where do you want to go? LA is a big place.'

'Downtown, I guess, if that's convenient for you.'

'No problem.'

I walked down the off ramp from the freeway and saw a Spanish style church at the bottom and a sign that read

PUEBLO LOS ANGELES

The sign had a paragraph of text that told the history of the church and surrounding area. I was in the heart of the sprawling megapolis, where it all began as El Pueblo de Nuestra Señora la Reina de los Ángeles, The village of Our Lady the Queen of the Angels, which was also the name of the church.

The decorated wooden entrance to Chinatown was across the street, while the skyscrapers of the city lay to the south. A priest walked out, and I asked him where I might find a cheap hotel. He pointed south down Main Street. 'About seven blocks down the road is the Cecil Hotel. It is cheap and has lots of rooms. I am sure you will find a room there,' he said in a broad Mexican accent.

I found The Cecil and as I passed through the grand entrance, my ears were engulfed by trumpets, guitars, singing, shouts and whoops.

'... Guadalajara, Guadlajara
Tienes el alma mas Mexicana!
Ay, ya, ya!'

A large band of over a dozen Mexican Mariachis was playing in the lobby. All around were men in suits and elaborately dressed women with children running around. At the end of the room, looking embarrassed and happy at the same time, was a wedding couple standing arm in arm.

The entire band was dressed in silver studded suits with wide-brimmed hats. The sound reverberated around the large art deco lobby and when the song finished everyone shouted and cheered. I squeezed my way through the Spanish speaking crowd to the front desk and shouted at the clerk, ' Can I have a room please.'

'That'll be twenty dollars in advance.'

I made my way to the elevator and up to the tenth floor. I put my bag down, had a quick shower and went back out into the night. I walked down W 7th St and felt I was in Mexico. Instead of gringos, the street was crowded with hispanoamericanos. As well as many Mexican,

Guatemalan and Salvadorian restaurants, street vendors selling tamales, boiled corn cobs, enchiladas and tortillas were on every corner. Families strolled by enjoying the evening, chatting animatedly. Grandmothers linked arms with their middle aged daughters surrounded by children dressed in colorful clothes. Many people were wearing T-shirts printed with the word

SANDINISTA

I sat down in a restaurant and ordered enchiladas verdes and a Corona. Spanish was the only language I could hear. After diner, I ordered a tequila, then another one - no one cared about my ID here. I felt a certain freedom not being able to understand what people were saying, not being forced to be a part of anyone else's life. I was just an observer, like a cat. Not knowing what people were saying made their conversations seem intriguing and vital.

I wandered around the streets and had a drink in a few bars. Eventually I found my way back to the Cecil. The next day after breakfast, I wound my way through the streets back to el Pueblo and Our Lady of Los Angeles. Midday mass had just started.

The church was packed, and an usher made some people shove up, so I could get a seat on a pew. After a few seconds, the congregation stood up and started to say the Confiteor. I couldn't understand the words, but I knew what it was when the congregation beat their closed right hands on their hearts and said, 'Mi culpa, mi culpa, mi gran culpa.'

I was head and shoulders over everyone in front of me and although I was about twenty rows from the altar I had a clear view of the priest I had spoken to the night before.

On the right hand side of the altar, facing where I was sitting, was large a painting of the Virgin Mary surrounded by beaming sun rays.

The priest gave an impassioned sermon waving his hands and contorting his face. I could make out a little of what he was saying. He mentioned refugees, injustice and compassion many times. When he finished I wanted to clap.

I lined up to receive communion but was so much taller than everyone else I felt like a giant. The priest noticed me from half way down the church as I towered over the people ahead of me.

After Mass, the congregation filed out into a large courtyard lined by trestle tables with doctors and nurses sitting at them. People formed lines that snaked around the courtyard as the doctors poked in children's mouths with sticks and put stethoscopes on their chests while nurses prepared and passed out packages of medicine. At other tables lawyers were giving free immigration advice.

The priest came out and talked to people and patted the children's heads. I approached him and said, 'Hello, Father. I want to say thank you. I found the Cecil Hotel.'

'You are most welcome. I hope you enjoy your stay in Los Angeles.'

'Father, what is happening here?'

'Most people here are refugees or immigrants without papers. There are many people fleeing violence in Nicaragua where the Sandanistas are trying to overthrow the government. They have nothing, no money. They can find work here in Los Angeles, but they need help. We do what we can for their material needs and assist with immigration advice. This is their sanctuary.'

'So the people wearing Sandanista T-shirts are from Nicaragua?'

'Most of them perhaps, but there are many people fleeing El Salvador and Guatamala as well. They all hope that the Sandanistas will win.

'What about you Father, are you for the Sandanistas?'

'I believe that Jesus came to free us from sin, and slavery is a sin. I try to follow the teaching of Jesus.'

'Well, thank you for your help and hospitality Father.'

'Go in peace my son, adiós'

After a week or so I hitched back up to San Francisco and returned to freezing London.

9

I went back to work at the ICA, but after my experience in the USA, I felt unable to settle in again.

Gene gave me the number of a recording studio that needed a tea boy. 'In on the ground floor Eamon. Stick at it, and one day you'll be a record producer.'

I was offered the job and resigned from the ICA. The studio was located on Little Russell St in Bloomsbury, just one block from the British Museum. The entrance was down a flight of steps in a courtyard. Three recording studios and a billiard room with refrigerators and a television on the wall were squeezed into the dungeon like space.

Marianne Faithful was making her album *Broken English*. One day Marianne, Steve Winwood and I were playing billiards during a break in recording. The Iranian Revolution was on TV. Plonk, went the billiard ball, click, as the queue struck the next ball. We watched trucks on fire filled with bodies and crowds of wild-faced people running through the streets of Tehran. One man approached the camera waving his hands frantically trying to stop the crew from filming the chaos and bloodshed. Hmm, Tim must be in India by now, I hoped. There seemed to be revolutions happening all over the world I thought.

Upstairs above ground level, a photographic studio occupied a large, two-storey atrium in the middle of the building. One night, they held a party with a DJ and light show and I was invited. I walked from the main room into a dimly lit studio and almost bumped into Amanda. 'What are *you* doing here?' she asked, as if I were a janitor who had strayed into the wrong area.

'Just hanging around. Are you here with someone?' I said

'Oh Eamon, of course I am.'

'Are you in love with him?'

'You don't mince words do you? It's none of your business who I'm in love with,' and she walked away head high in the air.

In the small hours of the morning, I took a mini cab home alone. The radio was playing, *When You're in Love with a Beautiful Woman.*

I felt stupid, like a little boy. What I had wanted to say was, I'm fed up with being all alone, can we get back together again now please? What a missed opportunity. Maybe I should call her, I sighed out loud.

'Vhat did you say sir?' shouted the Indian taxi driver looking at me in his rear view mirror.

'I said turn that bloody music down!'

A few days later at home, I sat at the kitchen table looking out the back window across to Blakes Hotel as Mum cooked dinner. It was dark and looked cold outside, but a light was on in the hotel's penthouse, so I watched to see if anyone famous would come out onto the balcony.

Mum asked me over her shoulder, 'How is the job in the studio going ?'

'Oh, okay I guess. I don't know, to tell the truth. I took the job because I thought a ground floor job in a recording studio would be a way in to the industry.'

'I hope you can make this job last,' she said.

She was right to think that I had left the ICA a bit hastily, my new job wasn't going that well at all. *Broken English* had finished recording and the studio didn't have any new projects to work on yet. My job title was tea boy, but there were no musicians to make tea for or play pool with. I spent most of my time just sitting around.

I fancied myself as a record producer stretching back in a swivel chair with my feet on the mixing desk. Now that fantasy seemed like just another mirage in a smoke-filled room.

'I'm sorry Mum. I have made a mess of things.'

'Don't worry Eamon, we still love you. But I hope that you can settle down for a while.'

'You're right, Mum. I've been neglecting you all, especially you.'

'You're never at home at night. I worry about you.'

'I'm at loose ends, since I split up with Amanda.' I felt abashed even mentioning her name to my mother. What had I put her through during all these years? She never scolded me or tried to force me into anything. Dad said that he realized when I was about thirteen that it was useless to tell me what to do. I was such a hard-nosed know it all no one in the family dared say 'boo' to me.

Mum was in her mid-fifties now. She had devoted her life to the family - after all, she had seven kids. It seemed as though she provided the only stability the family had. Although we had actually been living in the big flat for about six years, the longest time the family had ever been in one place, I still felt it was only temporary.

'Sometimes I think you're like a stray cat, Eamon. You need to think about helping others for a change. At the moment, you're not even helping yourself.'

I thought of the pain she must feel inside, her fears for the family and hurt she felt at my neglect. I never asked her how she felt or if she were happy, never mind about her own desires, weaknesses, loneliness. She had seven children, yet she was lonely. I took her love for granted, and gave precious little love in return. I was never the friend to her that she had always been to me. She was always loving and helpful. Her anger never lasted more than an instant. All the family knew we that we could depend upon her, that she was on our side, one of us.

'When you were a young boy, you were always laughing and smiling. I worried about you when we went to India without your older brothers and sister to look out for you. I think that made you grow up too fast. You've been so serious since we came to London.'

'We've been in London for half my lifetime now Mum.'

'I know, but all the moving house when you were young and change of schools. I think it made you restless inside.'

'I'll try and be good Mum.'

'You won't let us down will you?'

'Of course not Mum, of course not.'

A running, tumbling noise came down the linoleum tiled hallway. It sounded like a roller coaster, little-girl-shrieks and all. My three sisters charged into the kitchen quickly followed by Charlie the dog and our two cats.

'MUMMY is dinner ready yet?'

Vincent strode in after them. 'I'm going out, so I hope dinner is going to be soon.'

My job at the studio lasted another few weeks until one day the owner said, 'Eamon, let's go for a walk.' He explained that they simply didn't have enough work to keep everyone busy, and I was unemployed once more.

My situation was now more serious than when I had been out of work previously. When I had finished - failed - college I had just wanted a job, any job. All I wanted at that point was to earn enough money to keep me and Amanda entertained, nothing more. Getting the projectionist position at the ICA was a stroke of luck, and I had squandered the opportunity. Now I wasn't on the ground floor of any career. I was in the basement. I scoured the *Evening Standard* jobs section looking for something that I could imagine doing. One day I saw an ad with the heading

PUBLISHING

That sounds like me, I thought. Yes, humm, that swivel chair I wanted. I imagined my feet resting on a pile of books on my desk while the delightful Miss Ringrose took my dictation. '... and to conclude, Mr. Prime Minister, this august publishing house, will never, I say *never,* be bullied into withdrawing a book from distribution - not for the pittance that you've offered in any case...'

'Eamon, what are you doing? Your eyes look glazed, and you're mumbling to yourself,' my worried mother asked. I took my feet off the table and called the number in the ad.

My new job was selling advertising space on a trade publication for Haymarket Publishing. Several people had started at the same time as me, and our first week was spent in basic training.

We congregated each day in the boardroom on the first floor of the Wardour Street office in Soho and sat around the board table with the trainers. I grabbed the position at the head of the table and kept it for the whole week.

At the beginning of May 1979 Margaret Thatcher and her Tory party, won the general election and she became the new Prime Minister. She appointed the founder and CEO of Haymarket Publishing, to her cabinet, which meant he had to give up his executive role at the company. Sitting in his seat at the head of the boardroom table, I looked straight out the window across Wardour Street to a Korean restaurant where a blue plaque on the wall stated

KARL MARX LIVED HERE

Very appropriate, I smiled to myself.

'Are you listening Eamon?'

'Oh, yes, eh-erh, of course...'

The next week I was allocated a desk in the Frith Street office. I walked into the large open plan room filled with people on telephones. The office manager said, 'Go sit beside Bernie over there, he'll show you the ropes.'

At the end of the room, at a bigger desk than anyone else's surrounded by neat piles of books and magazines, sat a bearded man. 'I'm Bernie, I'm from Yorkshire,' he said.

'Hi, Bernie, what should I do?'

'Pick up the bloody phone and sell some space,' he barked.

Bernie shared a house in Hammersmith with several other people, 'Come over tonight, and we'll go for a pint,' he said as we left the office for the day.

Later that evening when I arrived, he opened the front door and said, 'I must grab my hat. Come up to my room for a minute.' As we walked up the stairs I heard a girl moaning and shrieking, and the noise grew louder as we approached his room.

...aragh...oohhhhh...ahhh...oh ao, oh ah...

I couldn't tell whether she was in pain or ecstasy. He opened the door to his room, and a waft of incense floated out. The lights were red and green, and a lava lamp in the corner tumbled its orange plasma up and down the sealed glass vase. Then I heard an unmistakable, deep drooling voice, singing about dungeons and torture with a woman's voice moaning and screaming in the background.

... Flies all green and buzzin'
In this dungeon of despair ...

Bernie was a Zappa freak. He was a few years older than me, quite tall and athletic looking with curly brown hair and a full beard. He put on a cowboy hat with a headband of flashing green and red lights. 'Let's get going, off to the pub we go.' He stuck out his chin and led us back down the stairs.

In the pub we clinked our beer glasses and Bernie said, 'Humm, sup it down lad. Ee, that's good. Not as good as a pint of Tetley's, mind you, but not bad for a London beer. After a few pints, let's say we go for a curry?'

Bernie was from Huddersfield in Yorkshire. With pride in his voice, he declared, 'Yorkshire is the biggest county in England. Just like Texas is the biggest state in the U.S.A.'

'So you're the Yorkshire Cowboy, Bernie,' I said jokingly.

'Oh, I like that. The Yorkshire Cowboy, indeed I am.'

After completing his university degree, Bernie had traveled around the world for several years. He told me tales of long journeys and the lusty women he met along the way. He had only arrived back in England six months earlier, with a view to starting a career.

'You already look well settled in the job Bernie, as if you've been here for years.'

'Ah, that's the knack, Eamon. When you start a new job you've got to work bloody hard for three months. Have a success or two, and then you can relax and carry on as you like. It's all about attitude. You've got to act as if you're good at what you do. People will believe you if you have a positive attitude.'

It reminded me of the advice I'd received at Chelsea school. Although I'd better not punch anybody, I thought. I worked hard, as Bernie suggested. I settled down and went to bed early as Mum asked me to. Everything was going along okay. But I had a feeling of nausea every morning as I took the tube to work.

I had been so preoccupied with my own life that I had failed to notice what was going on with my family. My father's business was in difficulty. His brother urged him to buy a grocery store near Shepherd's Bush. To my amazement, he bought the shop and the family was arranging to move into the flat above it.

'Dad, what's happening to us?'

'Eamon, the economy is in bad shape. I'm in a tight spot here lad.'

'So you're going to buy a shop?'

'It's tough, my boy, when you have a family to feed. All these years I had to work all the time. I had to bring home the bacon. Bringing up seven children, please believe me, it motivates you. I had to make a certain amount of money each month come what may. God has been good to me, but every now and then he gives me a bit of a kick just to make me realize who's boss. I have few choices right now, so we have to get moving again.'

Dad was a couple of years older than Mum and nearly sixty. Yet he was starting a new career and all I could manage to do was take the tube to Soho each day. I sat at my desk and picked up the bloody phone. I felt I was just holding on, waiting.

Not long after the conversation with my father, Vincent and I helped our parents, the three girls, Charlie, the cats, and the accumulated possessions and memorabilia of our lives move to the new shop.

The two of us were to stay living in Royston Gardens until the flat could be sold. I never actually left home, home left me.

10

Gene picked me up in the MG, and we drove the short distance to Flood Street. Bart's folks were away, and he was throwing a New Year's Eve party. He had just returned from Munich where he had been to see his sister who was on an overseas study program. 'I travelled back to London by train with a girlfriend of my sister. She's soooo cool, a real California girl,' said Bart on the phone.

Gene and I weren't sure what to expect at this party. It might just be the two of us and Bart, California-style, with some freshly squeezed carrot juice. Gene and I thought we would go to another party we had been invited to in North London later on - a proper English one where everyone would get drunk and stand around in the kitchen. I was wearing my Prince Edward check jacket, black pegs, two-tone pointy shoes and a white shirt with silver cufflinks.

When we arrived, a group of Bart's friends were bantering about how much money their parents made as investment bankers. A French girl who Bart had met somewhere along the way was there, but the party was dull and didn't seem likely to improve.

'Gene, this party is boring, let's go to the pub on the corner.'

'Okay, but let me ask the French chick if she wants to come, too,' he said and he went to look for her.

Some people standing next to the sofa across the room from me moved aside for a moment and I noticed a girl sitting with her hands gently clasped in her lap. Her curly blonde hair rested on her shoulders, and she had a sweet smile. She looked relaxed and composed. A chiffon scarf was tightly wrapped around her neck with a flamboyant knot. She was wearing a short black fitted jacket, a blue-stripped skivvy, blue pegs and elegant black shoes. Her clothes were stylish, but she didn't look like a Londoner, and she certainly didn't look like the girls I had seen in California. No, she must be French or German, European in any case. Then I realized - she's the American girl Bart came back from Munich with. He was right - she looks cool. I walked over to her and said, 'Hi, I'm Eamon. My friend Gene and I are going to the pub on the corner. Do you want to come too?' She looked down at my shoes, tilted her head back up and smiled at me, 'Sure,' she said, in a sweet, happy voice.

Gene found the French girl and the four of us went to the Phoenix. It was full of Chelsea groovoids. '…oh ya, absolutely amaaazing ... oh you are a one…'

The fashion had evolved from the punk days. The guys had shaggy black hair sticking up in points. They wore sleek jackets, tight black trousers and short high-heeled boots with large silver buckles. The girls also had pointy hair but died blue, white or pink. They wore bright-colored tops and skirts with black or purple lipstick, dark eye makeup and white powder on their faces.

The four of us found a quiet corner and had a couple of drinks. Gene chatted to the French girl, and I talked to Lucy, the California girl.

'Where are you from?' I asked.

'I'm from a town near San Francisco,' she said her eyes cast downwards as if embarrassed.

'I was in California last year, which town are you from?'

'It's called Mountain View'

'That's the next stop on the train line from Palo Alto. It's in the heart of Silicon Valley.'

'Yeah, I suppose so.'

'You're studying in Germany now?'

'Yes, I'm studying French and German. My university in Oregon has an overseas study program. This year I'm in Munich, last year I was in France.

She seemed shy but lively with big blue eyes and dark mascared eyelashes.

At about eleven o'clock, Gene said, 'Let's go to that other party.' His car was parked right outside and we all jumped in. However, as the MG had only two bucket seats, Lucy and I had to squeeze into the tiny baggage space behind them and perch on the ledge underneath the soft top. It was cramped but intimate, and we had no choice but to put our arms around each other. I looked into Lucy's eyes, and she smiled at me. We kissed. Her smell was tantalizing, and her hair felt soft. The MG vroomed off into the city night.

Our route took us through the centre of the West End, and when we reached Trafalgar Square we got stuck among crowds of people walking, singing and dancing all over the road. Shirtless young men danced and hollered on top of the enormous bronze lions. Gene drove slowly through the throng, and we eventually emerged on Charing Cross Road. Vroom, we were on our way again and soon arrived at the party. Lucy and I danced together and kissed as midnight struck.

'HAPPY NEW YEAR, HAPPY 1980' everyone cheered.

Later I called a mini cab to take me and Lucy to Royston Gardens.

The next day we woke up late. 'Do you have to go right away?' I asked.

'No, I have no plans.'

'Would you like to have lunch?'

'Would you like me to?'

We went to the Chelsea Pot on the King's Road. Lucy ordered minestrone soup.

She had round rosy cheeks and a broad smile, but not a toothy American smile. She titled her head slightly to one side and her eyes shone. Her whole ambience was serene and peaceful. She was an attentive listener and didn't mumble 'uh huh' or 'I know'. Her voice was soft and slightly high pitched with a lovely round Californian accent. Although I could tell she was American, I suspected that many English people would be confused and not know where she was from. We were the same age - she had just turned twenty one.

Lucy was staying with friends of her parents in Wimbledon. After lunch, I took her to the bus stop on Fulham road opposite the ABC Cinema.

'Lucy I'd like to see you again, can I have your phone number?'

She hesitated. 'It might be better if I call you, what's your number?'

The bus came and off she went on the red double-decker. I gave her my number of course, but didn't think she would call me. I felt a pang in my heart as I watched the bus bounce slowly down the road in the grey winter light.

Back at home I walked into the kitchen, and Vincent was sitting at the table ashen faced. He looked as if he had been on the road to Damascus. I said, 'What's up?'

'I just had an idea. I'm going to Vietnam.'

'You're crazy.'

I shook my head and went to my bedroom.

Later in the evening Vincent explained, 'I was looking at travel guides in the Penguin Bookshop on Fulham Road, wondering where to get some winter sun. I opened the All Asia Guide and was holding it in one hand when it flipped open it from the back. The last country listed in the book is Vietnam, and it struck me. I have to go there.'

The next morning Lucy called, 'Lucy, you called me!'

'I said I would call, didn't I?'

Sometime later the doorbell rang, and there she was. She noticed that I was glancing at the back pack she was carrying in one hand.

'I'm going back to Germany tomorrow. I didn't want to tell my parents' friends that I met a guy, so I just pretended I was leaving today,' she said sheepishly.

Later that afternoon, as we lay dreamily in my bed with the soft light creeping down the inner courtyard and in through the window, I asked her, 'Do you really have to go so soon?'

'Well, my ticket's for tomorrow.'

'Can we change it?'

'Do you want me to?'

'Yeah, why don't you stay for a while?

'If you want me to stay I can.'

We sat in the kitchen looking out at Blakes Hotel wrapped in blankets. She called British Rail and moved her ticket to a week later.

I was supposed to go back to work on the Thursday after New Year, but it never even crossed my mind to do so. Instead, I took Lucy to Westminster Abbey, to see the Stone of Scone, or Stone of Destiny, upon which the High Kings of Tara were crowned. We sat in front of Rodin's sculpture *The Burghers of Calais,* in the shadow of the Houses of Parliament, and to the Tate Gallery where we sat by the Henry Moore sculpture looking at the grey water of the Thames.

'Do you like art galleries?' I asked her as we stood in front of the Turner paintings.

'I love art galleries. I could spend all day looking at paintings and dreaming.'

'Why did you decide to study languages?'

'I did well at languages right from the beginning in Junior High School,' she said in her soft and delicate voice. Although she was from the same district as Bart, she didn't speak in the Bear-ea dialect. We talked and had tea in the gallery café. She smiled and looked away shyly when I asked too many questions.

We walked from the Tate down the embankment all the way to Albert Bridge and home. So soon after mid-winter's day, the sun went down before four o'clock. The short, misty sunset over Father Thames threw up a blazing display of magenta and grey in a wash of color and muted tones that more than resembled the Turner paintings in the Tate.

Each day we went on a different excursion. We walked to St Paul's Cathedral, up to the Whispering Gallery and climbed the metal staircase to peer out at London from under the cross on the top. We wandered through the square mile of the City to the Tower of London and from Sloane Square all the way down the King's Road to Putney.

'I love to walk around cities, Paris, Munich, San Francisco,' said Lucy.

'Today I'll take you to the ICA. I used to work there.'

The ICA was showing an exhibition of video art. We tiptoed into a darkened gallery with a large video screen at one end. We could see a few people standing in the gloom waiting for something to happen. The video was of six people sitting on chairs in a white room staring blankly with no sound. After a few minutes, one of the sitters stood up, screamed at the top of her lungs and sat back down again. Lucy turned towards me and clutched my arm. 'Let's go before she screams again,' I whispered in her ear.

We carried on around the corner to Trafalgar Square and the National Gallery to look at the Da Vinci drawing. We walked down Whitehall and stood outside 10 Downing Street, then back through Horse Guards Parade, and up into Soho to have lunch at Pollo on Old Compton Street. Sitting in the cozy booth with red checked table cloth Lucy had minestrone soup again, and I ordered Stracheatella alla Romana.

'Lucy, it's fun having someone to show around.'

'You're a good tour guide, you seem to know the city like the back of your hand.'

'The sign of a miss-spent youth. I've been walking all over central London for years.'

'It's your home town I guess.'

'My home town? Funny, I never think of it in that way, but maybe it is.'

Back at the flat Lucy made tea. I gazed at her back with her hair dancing over her shoulders as she washed cups and boiled the kettle. I caught a glimpse of her eyelashes flashing and her red but unrouged lips.

I touched her hand, and she let go of the tea cup. She turned her head just enough for me to kiss her.

In what seemed like an instant our week together was over, and Lucy had to go back to Munich. We took a black London taxi to Victoria Station.

'Will I see you again?'

'I, I don't know… when we can… I have to go back to America in a few months. But if you want to see me, maybe.'

Lucy looked at me with her soft, round eyes, searching my face as if to see if I wanted her to say something more. With tears in our eyes, we said goodbye and I watched as she walked down the platform and climbed aboard the train.

'Ding dong - the train on platform 12 is the Dover Express'

I walked home, alone again in dreary old London in mid winter. Since the family had left us Vincent and I had grown used to our newfound independence. It was so peaceful at the flat now. But I felt vacant, abandoned. Who should I call? Gene, Bart? I didn't feel like talking to anyone. I *should* go to work, but my mind was filled with Lucy.

The following day I forced myself to get out of bed and take the tube to work. As the train chugged along to Piccadilly Circus, I wondered what I was going to say to my boss. I could say I was sick. 'Why didn't you call?' he would ask me. I decided to act naturally and pretend that this was the first day back at work after Christmas and New Year, as if I had been on school holidays.

I strode over to my desk purposefully. I had quickly learned not to meander around an office - you will look like you're slacking, which no doubt you are. It's better if you pick up a sheaf of papers, and walk quickly with an intense look in your eye then you can stride out of the building and have a swift half pint of Burton's Ale in the pub, and no one will think anything of it. I sat down at my desk and picked up the telephone trying desperately to remember what I was supposed to be doing. My boss came and stood beside me. 'Can I have a word in your shell like ear, Eamon?'

We went into a meeting room and sat down. 'Eamon, we were expecting you to come back to work last week. We were worried about you, what happened?'

'I had problems at home, and I was sick. It was my mother you see. Anyway I thought we had last week off, Christmas holidays and all, like at school. I met a girl and in any case I am so enthusiastic about working here. I have lots of sales in the pipeline and I'm confident that I'll reach my targets ...' I blabbered.

'All right mate, get down to work, will you? We have a deadline coming up,' he said in a friendly tone and left the room. Phew, I still have a job, cool.

Christmas time was always an extended family holiday. Mum cooked voluminous amounts of food and the whole family would be together right through until after New Year. But this year I had neglected them. We had Christmas dinner together, but that was the only time I had seen them. I hadn't even telephoned Mum on New Year's Eve.

So, after work, I took the tube straight over to the shop. Dad took me to the pub next door. He said, 'What are you doing?'

'What do you mean?'

'With your life, what are you doing with your life? We need you here.'

I had helped at the shop now and then since the move, but I realized that I had let them down - again.

'Who are you? We don't know you anymore. You used to be reliable and caring.'

'Maybe I've just grown up. I'm trying to find my own life.'

'What do you think you want out of life?'

'Freedom, that's all I want.'

'Freedom from what, responsibility?'

'I've got a job, I'm being responsible, sort of, aren't I?'

'You let us down. You're just acting like a playboy, drinking and carousing all the time.'

'I just don't want to be told what to do.'

'Well do what you like then, but don't go too far down the wrong track. It can be awfully difficult to come back out again.'

'I'm just looking for something, that's all.'

'What are you looking for?'

'I don't know yet.'

I walked home distressed. I don't know who I bloody well am. Was I actually looking for something?

I called Bart. 'Bart man, what's up?'

'What happened to Lucy?' he asked in a subdued voice.

'Lucy? We had a thing, you know, after your party. How did your party end up, by the way?'

'What happened to the French girl?' he growled in a menacing tone.

'The French girl? She was with Gene, why?'

'Well it's just that the last thing I saw - of *any* of you - were your backs as you walked out the front door, early, from my New Year's Eve party. The French chick was *mine*, and I really *liked* Lucy, *man*. That's what the fuck is up!'

'Ah, er, well I guess I'll call Gene and ask him about the French chick… call ya later.' Click.

Oh dear, I guessed I should have called him earlier. I phoned Gene right away.

'Blue Gene baby, where's the French chick?'

'The French chick dumped me,' he said. 'After you left with California girl, she asked me to take her back to Bart's place. She went in and got her bag, and then slept on my sofa and left the next day. She said, "You are not right for me," in a French accent.'

'Oh shit, I wonder what happened to her.'

'She said she had a train ticket to go back to Paris. I took her to the station.'

'Oh… You up for anything?'

'No man, leave it a while will ya?' and he hung up.

I called Bart and let him know that the French girl had gone home to Paris. He was most annoyed and said I should give him a call, s*ometime*.

Vincent walked in the door and said, 'I really am going to Vietnam.'

'I thought you were joking about that?'

'No, not at all, I'm going in April. I'll be travelling with a tour group of former Vietnam War correspondents. We'll be the first tourists allowed into the country since the end of the war in 1975. Why don't you come with me?'

'No, I don't think so. I couldn't handle a war zone.'

'You'll regret it. Imagine what a left turn your life will take if you come to Vietnam with me? Who knows what doors it will open?'

I had enough to think about, and I just laughed and walked away. Vincent had graduated from university sometime ago and had a well paid job, although he'd stayed on living at home. But now the flat was up for sale, and we both knew that the end was nigh. Over the coming weeks, Vincent made his preparations for the trip. He would make a good journalist, I thought.

January was cold and miserable. In the evenings, I turned on the TV news only to be confronted by Thatcher, moaning on. I walked to Gloucester Road station to catch the tube to work each day. The Farsi writing was still there but 'Down with the Shah' had been replaced by a new set of squiggly lines. Now the Shah was gone, I wondered what they were demanding. It was only five stops to Piccadilly Circus, but it was a tortuous experience. The passengers were damp, pasty faced and glum, with eyes glued to the tabloid newspapers. According to *The Sun*, the Soviets were about to invade.

SHOCK HORROR SOVIETS

Never mind the bollocks! I couldn't concentrate at work. I tried, but my thoughts, feelings, visions turned to Lucy.

A postcard arrived from Lucy written in neat and delicate handwriting. She said Fasching, the Bavarian carnival was taking place during February and asked if I wanted to come over for a visit. She was staying in student accommodation on the university campus and had written the number of the communal telephone on the card. I called her right away.

'Servus,' a German voice said.

'Can I speak to Lucy please?'

Moments later there she was, giggling. I asked her, 'Should I come over for a few days during Fasching?'

'Oh, I guess, if you like, I suppose…'

'It's just that you suggested it in your postcard.'

'Did I? Well, sure come over I guess.'

'It's okay. I just thought… well you mentioned it in your…'

'Yes, yes, come over it'll be nice to see you.'

Nice to see me, bugger! Nice, the most horrible word a bloke ever heard a girl say. I thought I was nasty, but no, she thought I was nice. Lucy did make it clear that she might be *busy*, but 'yeah, why not come over for a few days'. This time, I asked for some time off work and took the train over to Munich for a long weekend in late February.

Munich's Fasching, or Carnival, is a month long series of parties, street parades and costume balls leading up to Ash Wednesday. It's a Catholic celebration, or at least, it's in Catholic regions that they celebrate carnival. In protestant England, there is only Pancake Tuesday.

Lucy lived in Studentenstadt, a purpose-built suburb for students, comprising numerous two story buildings dotted in between tower blocks up to twenty stories tall. Lucy's room was in one of the two story buildings. It had been snowing and between the buildings were fields of white crisscrossed by walkways cleared of snow. The weak sun twinkled off icicles on leafless trees, and the pale blue sky looked cold. Lucy took me to a Fasching Fest with people in masks and strange ghoulish costumes. Children danced in the streets dressed as witches - die Hexen.

A German student, Waltar, who lived in Lucy's building, explained to me, 'Bavarians are normally staid and undemonstrative. However, during Fasching they let their hair down and go wild. Ja, stimmt, it is a requirement to party wildly, get drunk and have numerous liaisons during Fasching. Infidelity during Fasching cannot be used as grounds for divorce, nein, ha ha ha! When Fasching is over, everyone just goes back to their boring, normal faces, all grey and German - no questions are ever asked.'

Lucy took me to a disco in the basement of one of the buildings, appropriately named, Das Underground. She seemed to know everyone and had clearly made lots of friends in Munich. I watched from a distance as she chatted to classmates from her university.

A French guy stared knowingly into her eyes and smiled at her as if sharing a secret and a German guy just grabbed her, 'Luzee mein Liebling.'

She flew around the dance floor to *Le Freak* by Chic, her blonde hair changing color to red and green in the disco ball lights. She looked like the queen of the dance floor.

I had not expected this at all. I was being ridiculous, I told myself. What right did I have to be jealous? After three days and nights, I had to leave her world and return to London. I feared that she would never come back into mine.

Lucy took me to the Hauptbahnhof. We ate semmel mit wurst und senf, and I drank a Paulaner Weissbier.

'Lucy, I… like you, I mean…'

'Oh you're so sweet Eamon.'

Oh no, sweet, the only thing a girl can say that's worse than nice. She thought I was nice and sweet, it was hopeless.

Forlorn, I waved at her from the step of the train. She turned her back and, just like Sally Bowles in the movie Cabaret, raised her hand and waved goodbye without turning around to look at me.

'Bing bang bong - This train goes to Frankfurt, stopping at Wurzburg...'

Chug, the train lurched and left Munich right on time. As the train sped through the German countryside, my mind was in turmoil. In London, we seemed so similar and close to each other. She liked my ways, and we were at ease in each other's company. In Munich, it was as if we were strangers. It dawned on me that I had never even asked her if she had a boyfriend.

Perhaps I was just one guy she met along the way. My seat faced backwards, and I peered through the window as Lucy disappeared further and further into the distance. I moved to a seat that faced forwards, but it did nothing to alter my feeling of loss.

Back in London none of my friends were enthusiastic about going out or seeing me. I just trudged to work in the mornings and back home again in the evenings through the miserable, cold London weather.

About two weeks after getting back I took the bus to the shop. 'Eamon, you should help us more here. We need you,' Mum implored.

'Okay, I'll try and help, more but once the flat is sold, I don't know what I'll be doing, I don't know where I'll end up.'

'Vincent says he's found a place in Belgravia.'

'Yes, he's going to move into a room in a big house, but he's going to Vietnam first.'

'Eamon, can we rely on you? There is so much work to do I don't know if we can cope.'

'Sure, of course, I won't let you down.'

I called Lucy but got a recorded message, 'Kein Anschlus unter diese Nummer' - no connection on this number. I called her again numerous times. Sometimes the phone was answered, 'Nein, sie ist nicht zu Hause….'

On one occasion, someone else answered, 'Servus.' said the voice.

'Can I speak to Lucy bitte,'

'Ich verstehe nicht,' and click, they hung up. Bugger!

Gwyneth came around to see me one night. She was her usual matronly self. She wanted to know all about what I had been doing and who I was seeing. 'I'm not seeing anyone Gwyneth.'

'Don't tell me that you're still pining for Amanda?'

Amanda! The name made my heart pound. I had finally, after more that a year, stopped thinking about Amanda every waking moment of the day. Now, all the ecstatic and painful memories came flooding back like a wave of water and swamped my consciousness.

'Why did you mention her? I haven't seen her for ages. I had just about put her behind me Gwyneth!'

'I knew you were still in love with her!' she said, her eyes flashing in triumph.

'I'm not, I swear.'

'Oh well, never mind. I had a drink with Amanda the other night. She's unattached at the moment you know.'

'Did she mention me?'

'No of course not, you silly boy,' she laughed.

'I did meet a girl, but she's in Germany, and she'll be going home to America soon.'

'Ah, long distance love. A feint heart never won a fair maiden.'

That night I lay in bed tormented by dreams of my two lost lovers.

On Friday, my boss pulled me aside again. We sat in the meeting room, and he asked me, 'So Eamon, how are you enjoying the job?'

'It's terrific, and I'm enjoying immensely. I'm learning all the time. Actually, I think the most important aspect of all is that I'm continuing to learn and improve,' I lied.

'We think you have a talent and could do well here, if you applied yourself.'

Crikey, I thought. This is just what they were always telling me at school, and at Putney College, 'Eamon could do better if only he would apply himself more, C minus.'

'Oh, em, thanks, I'll try harder, sure,' I stuttered.

'Look, it's a way in, Eamon. This might not be what you want to do forever, but it's a foot in the door of publishing. Nothing comes easily, you have to work at it. You have to plan and decide what you want to do with your life and decide if you want to be in publishing…' and on he went. Will people ever stop telling me what I have to do?

I was at home alone watching TV one Sunday when Vincent arrived back from his trip to Vietnam. He walked in with two fingers held up in a v-sign, although I wasn't sure if he meant peace or victory. His curly hair had grown and poked out from under a headband, and his face was deeply tanned. He was wearing a khaki safari jacket and trousers, a floral shirt open nearly to the waist, and a leather string around his neck with numerous medallions and charms hanging from it, like a mojo. He said, 'Vietnam, Vietnam, Vietnam, we've all been there,' then walked straight into his room and slammed the door. I didn't see him again for two days.

Without hope of success, I dialed Lucy's number again. Beeeep...beeep, click, a girl said, 'Hallo.'

'Lucy, is that you?'

'Yes, is that Eamon?" she giggled.

'Yeah, it is. It's so nice to hear your voice. How are you?'

'I'm fine, how about you?'

We chatted for a while, she seemed pleased that I'd called.

'Lucy, I'd really like to see you ... before you go back to America. Can I come over to Munich?'

'No, no, I don't want you to come here again. There's too much other stuff going on here, it'll be too weird.'

'Why don't you come to London?'

'No, it's too far, I don't have much time. Easter break is coming up though, so we could meet somewhere I guess.'

'How about Amsterdam?' I suggested. ' It's kind of half way between us. What do you think?'

I asked my boss for two weeks holiday. He said, 'Alright Eamon. I hope you know what you're doing.'

The only thing I knew was that I had to go and see Lucy. She said she could only stay in Amsterdam for ten days. This was her final year at university and would finish in June when she was due to go home to California.

My train arrived in Amsterdam in the morning, and we planned to meet at the station when she arrived later in the afternoon. I had managed to save up about £500 and had brought it all with me. The first thing I needed to do was find us a place to stay.

I headed out of the train station and down the big street in front to the famous hippie hang out, Dam Square, which is dominated by a tall phallic looking statue. The obelisk was circled by shallow, wide steps with groups of long-haired people playing guitars sitting and standing around it.

I walked past the King's Palace on the other side of the Square and came to Singelgracht, a canal crossed by small humpback bridges. I crossed the first bridge, and continued on to Herengracht, an elm tree lined canal, with tall brick houses with long, elegant windows on either side. I noticed that, unlike in London, the windows didn't have lace curtains, and I could see people moving around in their houses. It was like a living movie with me peering through the projection box window. Hundreds of bicycles sang out, ring ring, as they passed by and many tourist barges drifted along the canal with guides talking through loudspeakers in Swedish or Japanese.

I continued up to Haarlemmerstraat were I found a backpacker hotel, one of a few along the street, with a bar and a pool table on the ground floor. The owner took me up a winding staircase to the fifth floor and showed me into a small room with a window that looked out across the picturesque roofs and tree tops. Church bells chimed, and the echo of bicycles bells drifted up pleasantly from the street below.

Lucy was due to arrive just after five in the afternoon. I had a few hours to spare, so I walked around the centre of Amsterdam. As the afternoon progressed, towering clouds formed, and distant thunder mingled with the sounds of the city. Just before five I set off from the hotel for the train station.

KRAAK

An enormous thunderclap rattled the windows, and rain poured down in sheets. I dashed along the flooded streets and ran into the station as the rain made a machine gun noise on the roof.

'Bing bang bong - Damen und Herren, Mesdames et Messieurs, Ladies and Gentlemen the 5:15 from Frankfurt is delayed by approximately one hour - bing bang bong'

I found a bar to wait in and drank several tiny glasses of beer. After about an hour, I ran back through the still pouring rain to the platform, but a train was already there - empty.

'Is this the delayed train from Frankfurt?' I asked a porter.

'Yes, it arrived about 20 minutes ago.'

I looked all over the station but couldn't see Lucy. Eventually I ran outside in the street, crowded with masses of umbrellas under the hard driving rain.

I walked towards Dam Square, unsure what else to do. Lucy didn't know where we were going to be staying and we had no way of contacting each other. By the time I reached the obelisk, my clothes were drenched. I circled around peering in all directions. Then, walking towards the square from the station, bedraggled, carrying two small bags and wearing a little back pack, her beautiful blonde hair all matted and wet, I saw Lucy.

As I ran towards her, a little green Volkswagen taxi stopped at a traffic light. I clambered in and told the taxi driver to keep going straight. As we pulled up to Lucy, I opened the door and leapt out. She was crying, tears of frustration and relief. I peered into her blue eyes crying in the rain. Our hands clasped, and I said, 'Jump in!'

We kissed as the taxi, its windscreen wipers swaying back and forth, edged towards Haarlemmerstraat. My heart was pounding. What a way to meet.

… ding dong, ding dong, ding... ding... ding…

Church bells tinkled in sweet rising and falling feminine tones unlike the macho dong of Big Ben. We opened our eyes at the same time, and Lucy smiled. Our little room was so cozy with a double bed, one chair, a sink with a mirror above it and a Van Gogh print on the wall. It was only slightly bigger than the bed with barely enough space to stand at the sink. The single window gave just enough light in the daytime and the naked bulb above the bed lit up the night. We wrapped our arms and legs together, and I kissed Lucy's cheek. Perhaps we could stay in bed all day today I thought, but Lucy said, 'I want a coffee.'

We had been in Amsterdam for over a week and had walked all over the city, visited the Stedelijk and Van Gogh museums and ridden around the Vondelpark on bicycles.

We dressed and clunked down the five flights of stairs to the bar on the ground floor and out into the street, and turned onto Herengracht, one of four main canal streets that wrap around the centre of Amsterdam in a crescent. Crossing the little humpback footbridge we avoided the many bicycles ring ringing past us and followed the canal all the way around to the other side of town to what had become our favorite place, the Literary Café. The entrance was up a stoop about six feet above street level and a full length bay window with a table in it overlooked the canal. This was our regular spot and we sat there watching the world pass by.

The spring weather was pleasant and warm, and the laid back atmosphere of Amsterdam was a complete contrast to the hustle and bustle of London. Lucy and I were natural together. We could sit and say nothing to each other, and there would be no tension. But we did talk, lots, and we seemed to be interested in the same things.

We both liked to walk around for hours finding things to look at. We liked to visit art galleries and bookshops and sit in cafés. Lucy liked movies and seemed to have seen most of my favorite ones. She didn't drink much and wasn't interested in fancy restaurants but preferred picnics on a park bench or beside a canal. I realized that I liked eating alfresco too.

'The best things in life are cheap, eh Lucy?'

'I don't need diamond rings or fancy pearls,' she said with her head cocked to one side.

I finished my coffee and asked, 'What shall we do this afternoon?'

'Let's go look at some of the private galleries.'

We had noticed several small art galleries around town, and went to see what they had on display. As we wandered through one of them looking at strange new Dutch art, Lucy said in a subdued tone.

'I have to go tomorrow, Eamon.'

'Can I come with you?'

'No,' she said with an air of resignation.

'Can I come and see you when you've finished your course?'

'No, then I have to go back to America.'

'Can I come and visit you in the Bay Area?'

'No.'

'Why not?'

Hesitatingly she whispered, 'Eamon, I'm… expected…'

'Expected, by who?'

'My family, of course.'

'Anyone else?'

'There is someone… at home.'

My heart dropped. I didn't know what to say. I walked quickly out of the gallery but was relieved to see Lucy running after me as I rounded the corner into the next street. I sat down heavily on a bench overlooking the canal and curled myself into a knot as a Japanese tour boat slunk by. Lucy caught up to me and slumped slowly down on the other end of the bench. We sat in silence until eventually I said, 'I guess I don't really know you, and you don't know me.'

'We just met,' said Lucy. 'We just met... by accident.'

'Who are you?' I asked.

'I'm just a blue Kentucky girl,' she sighed and flashed her eyelashes at me before looking down at her lap.

'Well, we still have tonight to get to know each other, don't we?'

We walked slowly around the city for the rest of the afternoon. I asked her about her family and chit chat questions, the ones you never think to ask your lover.

When we were in each other's arms, I didn't want to hear about her father. Then, it was as if no world existed outside of our embrace - living in the moment. Perhaps that was my mistake, I should have shown more interest in her background, who she was. I watched her animated face as she told me about her life. The life she had before she knew me and the one she was going back to.

Lucy was born in Mountain View. Her mother was from Illinois, and her father was born in Indiana. Her father's family came from across the Indiana border in Kentucky and had fought on both sides of the American Civil War. Her mother's family were mostly Norwegian by heritage and her Father's family mostly English. However, her folks had been in America since way before the revolutionary war and Lucy was as American as blueberry pie.

Her father had been a bomber pilot stationed in England during World War II. After the war, he married her mom and they moved to California with an aching in their hearts. Lucy was born and raised in what was now known as Silicon Valley, the heart of the computer industry, but until the mid 1960s, it had been mostly peach, apricot and walnut orchards.

'Lucy, that all sounds so exotic to someone from London, you have no idea.'

'Yeah well, America is weird. I guess that's why I wanted to study in Europe.'

'Weird, how so?'

'Everything's made up, ersatz, a pastiche. Everyone's pretending they're somebody from somewhere.'

That evening as we strolled home to our love nest for the last time, I couldn't stop myself from asking, 'Lucy, this someone, who's expecting you. What's he like?'

'He's a poet.'

'A poet, like T.S. Eliot?'

'Kind of, well anyway, he's studying poetry at my university.'

'Does he write poetry about you?'

'Some…he mostly writes about other stuff.'

'Is he handsome?'

She gave me a sour look. 'Don't you worry about him,' she snapped and rushed ahead of me, hurt by my indiscretion.

I felt so stupid - a poet, how could a klutz like me compete? We clambered up the stairs to our room, brushed our teeth, and climbed into bed like an old, married couple. Lucy said goodnight, and we lay back to back and fell asleep.

…ding dong, ding dong, ding... ding... ding…

We awoke wrapped around each other, but Lucy had to go, and we spent a subdued hour together as she packed. I walked behind her to the station carrying her backpack in my hand. The train came in the station. She stood on the platform with her bags wearing a black T-shirt and German army trousers. I kissed the tears from her cheeks and looked her in the eye. She stood on the step of the train for a photograph - click - and clambered inside. I stood on the platform and watched the last carriage disappear out from underneath the high station roof and into the distance. It had two lights on behind.

11

I had never felt so desolate and alone. It was Wednesday, but I wasn't due back at work until Monday. I returned to the hotel and slept. Eventually I woke up and in the afternoon I wandered aimlessly around the city. As dusk was falling I turned left into a side a street. Lights blinked on in the windows of shop fronts. I walked past a curtain that was draped across the full length of a single tall window when, swish, it opened with a flourish. A woman was standing there with the curtain edge in her hand. She had deep red shoulder length hair, scarlet lipstick and was in her underwear. I stopped with a shock until I realized what I was seeing, lowered my eyes to the pavement and continued on down the street.

I turned left into a small side street and again, a curtain was drawn to reveal a woman standing next to a bed covered in fluffy white pillows wearing red lingerie. The tall glass window was only inches from my face. It was as like staring at an exotic fish in an aquarium. The fish smiled at me. She looked mischievous, but I walked on. I hurried past shop front after shop front, and they all had women in them. Some of them waved at me, one girl lay on her bed, crooked her finger and pouted her lips inciting me to come in. Some looked African others Chinese. Enormous blonde Valkyrie types contrasted with dark-haired petite ones.

I was sweating nervously as I turned yet another corner into Oude Hoogstraat and found a bar with a skull in its darkened window. Several small, white plastic coffins were placed decoratively as a display and the name of the bar was painted in large white gothic script on the window glass

Café De Dood (Café of the Dead)

It also had a Heineken sign. I have to get off the street, I thought, what the hell, and went inside.

The bar was decorated with pentangles, ouija boards and tarot card images. A large black and white photograph of the English occultist Aleister Crowley glared at me with intense eyes. People sat in dark alcoves drinking out of beer mugs shaped like gargoyles and skulls. Plastic bats hung from the ceiling. Lights hung down with plastic skulls for lamp shades. On a large mirror behind a coffin shaped bar, the names of drinks on offer had been printed in black - Black Death, Dracula's Blood followed by a long list of other ghoulish names. The bartender, dressed in black, came over and placed his hands on the bar in front of me with his fingers lightly clenched. He had tattoos on his knuckles that read 'DEAD' on his left hand and 'EVIL' on his right hand. He shook his head back and stared at me from under his black-painted eyelids as if challenging me to order a drink.

'I'll have a Heineken please mate,' I said nonchalantly. He didn't know it, but I had been to bars in the Polk district of San Francisco. This place seemed fairly staid compared to some of them.

A tall, blond guy standing next to me burst out laughing. 'Ha ha ha, you don't scare so easily do you, my friend?'

He introduced himself. His name was Olaf, and he was from Copenhagen. 'What are you doing in Amsterdam?' I asked.

'Maybe I'm here on holiday, like you,' he said.

'How do you know I'm on holiday?'

'What, are you on some important mission? Ha ha ha. Here, let me buy you a beer.'

Olaf was strikingly handsome. He looked like a Viking chieftain with a strong jaw and chin, straight, elegant nose, blue eyes and long, silky, blond hair. He was over six feet tall, muscular but slim. He spoke confidently with a round, deep voice, and his Danish accent made the words sound attractive and musical.

He was a bookbinder by trade, or at least he had completed an apprenticeship in bookbinding. 'I am a member of the Book Binders Union. Of course, there are no bookbinding jobs in Denmark anymore, but because I am in the union I get 75% of the bookbinder's salary paid to me for two years. Then it decreases to 50%. Ha ha, yea, Denmark has a great social security system. Skol,' and we downed another frothy Heineken in one gulp.

Olaf's real calling was playing bass guitar. 'I'm good, you know, Eamon. Yea! One day I will be famous.'

He made enough money from not being employed as a bookbinder, to spend his time playing in bands and travelling around Europe.

'So Eamon, what is your mission, your adventure?'

'Oh, I don't know,' I sighed. 'I was just chasing a girl. That's what brought me to Amsterdam.'

'Just chasing a girl? There is, of course, nothing better to chase than a girl. But you lost your quarry?'

'Yes, she's gone. I don't know what I'm going to do now.'

'What do you do in London?'

'Nothing, I mean, I have a job, but I don't know what I'm doing.'

'So you have no direction home?'

'I don't have a home any more. My parents left me, my girl left me. I have no idea where to go from here. I don't really want to go back to London.'

'You need to figure out who you are. Me, I'm a bass player, yea, so I know what I need to do because I know who I am. I need to play bass.'

'I don't know who I am. I've never known who I am. I'm…just a foreigner, a visitor.'

'That is good, Eamon. You are nobody, so you can become anybody. You are a free man and you can do whatever you desire.'

'Perhaps, but I don't know what I desire.'

'You desire that girl, don't you? A faint heart never won a fair maiden, ha ha ha. Barman, two more beers!'

'So, tell me, in truth, why you are in Amsterdam, Olaf?'

'Ah Eamon, somehow I knew I would meet you here at The Festival of Fools.'

'What do you mean?'

'You know that for the next two weeks there will be a carnival with clowns, minstrels, puppeteers, street musicians and fools from all over Europe taking place in Amsterdam?'

'No actually, I didn't know about that at all.'

'Well my young traveller, the official reason I am here is to play on Saturday night with my band, The Sandflies, at the Melkweg as part of the festival. Oh yeah, you must come and see us. I will put your name on the door for sure. Come backstage and find me.'

'But what do you mean you knew you would meet me here?'

'Well, I had to meet you somewhere didn't I? I think the last time we met was in a Viking ship a long time ago, ha ha ha. Don't worry Eamon, I'm only joking my friend. Skol!'

Several hours later I stumbled off drunk, into the cold wind that was now blowing off the North Sea and along the canals. I turned my jacket collar up and found my way back to Haarlemmerstraat.

...ding dong, ding dong, ding... ding... ding…

I awoke alone in the double bed. The room no longer looked romantic. For the first time, I noticed that the wallpaper was hanging off all around the edges, and the ceiling had a bulge in the middle. It looked as if it would drop onto the bed any second. I heard footsteps on the stairs and noticed that the walls were paper thin. The room stank of stale beer and worse. Our love nest, I now saw, was just a doss house. Well, as mother always said, home is where the heart is. Lucy and I had been happy here, and that was all that mattered, except that Lucy was gone, and I was now just a tourist.

Without Lucy, Amsterdam took on a different atmosphere. I tried many bars and coffee shops, and in all of them someone tried to sell me some exotic herbs. On Saturday afternoon, I was in a coffee shop on a houseboat moored on the river Amstel. It had a poster advertising the Sandflies gig at the Melkweg pinned on the wall. I was staring at the poster thinking that I should go along to see Olaf when a bearded man sat next to me, too close I thought. He nudged me with his elbow and said, 'You will need these for the Festival.'

'I will?'

'Oh yes, are you not a fool?'

He gave me, or I should say, sold me, six little mushrooms. 'Will they be good with french fries and mayonnaise?' I asked, referring to an Amsterdam fast-food specialty.

'Sure, but try peanut butter with your fries,' he advised, sage-like, nodding his head and squinting his eyes.

The Melkweg, was on Lijnbaansgracht, the fifth crescent-shaped canal that wraps around Amsterdam. The venue was famous for its hippy happenings, music, arts and subculture. As I entered the warehouse-sized doors, the mushrooms were starting to affect me. 'I am with the Sandflies,' I told the ticket seller.

'Oh yea? Wat is uw naam?'

'Eamon'

She pointed her finger at a door. I pushed it open and walked down a long a passageway until I came to another door with the word, Artists, printed on it. I turned the handle and entered the room.

'Eamon! I knew you would come. Are you ready?'

'Ready for what?' I said as Olaf's face danced in multicolored circles.

'Sit down and have a beer. We aren't on stage for another hour.' The band members lounged around cracking jokes in Danish and fiddled with their guitars. I sat in the corner confused and unable to say anything at all. When it was time for them to go on I left and found my way to the auditorium.

I stood ten feet from the stage surrounded by long haired girls and bearded men, but no one dressed in punk-style gear. Many people in the audience had bare feet and wore swirling Indian scarves, Peruvian woolen hats, jeans and tie-die shirts. Coming from new wave London, visiting the Melkweg was like entering a time warp going back ten years.

I stood transfixed by the flickering stage lights and the people dancing and twisting around me. Time slowed almost to a standstill. Sound flowed out from the guitars, and Olaf stood before me on the stage with a golden light streaking out from behind him and a white spotlight illuminating his face. With twisted mouth and intense eyes, his long mane-like hair slashed from side to side. My mind danced circles to the crooked beat of his bass guitar.

... dum dum dum dum-m-m, di dum di dum ...

The next morning I awoke alone once more in Haarlemmerstraat. The bells chimed, and I cracked open my eyes to see the sink and mirror above, and smell the stench of stale beer. I didn't remember coming back to the hotel or going to bed. I clunked down the cramped stairwell to the bar on the ground floor. Two odious looking characters were playing pool, Linda Ronstadt's cover of *The Tracks of My Tears* was on the jukebox, and I ordered a beer.

I sat at the bar looking at the passers by huddled up against the chill north wind, swigged the beer and reflected on my situation. Lucy had done the right thing in leaving me, for sure. She had to go home to America. But going back to my job and London just seemed impossible.

My life there seemed like another world that had been left behind. The person I was in London seemed a stranger to me, and I decided not to go back, not yet anyway. Mum's words rang in my ears, 'you won't let us down will you?' Of course not, I've just got to figure out what to do next.

I finished my drink, packed my things and paid the bill for the room. I said goodbye to the hotel clerk and the two freaks playing pool and meandered down to Dam Square.

The previous night seemed like a familiar presence, something I had always known but never acknowledged. I had a warm feeling of being home, somewhere more comfortable than the day before, transformed, subtly, perhaps immeasurably. I still felt like myself, but more integrated, determined. My father had warned be about going down the wrong track, but I had to go somewhere.

Who was Olaf? Was he real of was he just part of last night's dream? I remembered the Jean Cocteau film *Orpheus,* where the characters entered the underworld and came back again through mirrors that quivered like mercury. I wondered which side of the glass am I on right now?

I walked along Paleisstraat, and as I entered the southern end of Dam Square, the sound of bugles and trumpets jarred me back to the present tense. The square was filled with people and on large a stage at one end was a band of twenty or so musicians all playing wind instruments. They were dressed as clowns and were leaping around the stage ferociously blowing their horns.

Intermingled with the big crowd of onlookers were fire eaters, jugglers, sword swallowers, unicyclists and all manner of circus performers. I made my way through the throng jostling with happy carnival goers eating french fries and drinking beer from bottles. 'Ho ho ho, ha ha ha,' they chirruped.

A clown with a white face, red painted lips and Mickey Mouse ears stuck his tongue out at me. A middle-aged Dutch couple standing nearby thought this was hilarious. 'He he he,' they giggled, their rosy cheeks jumping up and down.

I made my way through the square to Damrak and the spot where I had intercepted Lucy in what seemed an age gone by. Involuntarily, I continued up the road to the train station and sat on a bench by the platforms. Above, a mechanical board displayed the train schedules. Every few seconds, the names of destinations rotated and were updated as trains arrived and departed. Clack clack clack, Frankfurt, Paris, Antwerpen, Genève, clack clack clack. I remembered that Tim and his girlfriend now lived in Geneva. I had also met a girl in London through Gwynneth called Gabrielle who lived in Bern, the capital of Switzerland. I thought I might visit her, as well.

Olaf walked by me with his guitar case and a backpack. 'Olaf!'

'Eamon, so you are off on your adventure. Where are you going first?'

'I have some friends in Geneva, so I think I'll drop in on them. Where are you going?'

'Tonight we are playing in Hamburg.'

'Like the Beatles?'

'Stimmt, we are playing on the Reeperbahn alright. Here, I want you to take this.'

He held out his hand, and in his open palm, was a medallion. I picked it up, and held it up close to see the engraving on it. It had an image of a robed woman on one side and two hearts with a letter 'M' and a cross on the other side. 'Olaf, thank you, I don't know what to say except I hope to see you again someday.'

'Okay, brother, you must come to Copenhagen. Be careful on your journey, stick to the path.' We shook hands and he left to find his train.

I bought a one way ticket to Geneva. The train was scheduled to depart in an hour. It was Sunday, and I was due at work on Monday morning. Humm, If I don't tell my boss where I am, he'll get worried and start calling the flat. Vincent will answer and …

I found the Western Union kiosk in the station and sent a telegram to my boss.

Eamon Curran Resigns Post
Gone to Tahiti
Urgent affairs to attend to.

12

'Passporte,' the uniformed man in a kepi demanded. He had a large black handlebar moustache, the buttons of his tunic were done up tightly, and he stood as if he had an ironing board stuck up his back. I handed him my passport, and after looking me up and down, he asked in a stiff French accent, 'How long do you intend to rest in Switzerland?'

'Oh, I don't know actually. I hadn't thought about it. How long can I stay?'

'What is the purpose of your visit?'

'Tourism, just passing through.'

He impatiently stamped my passport and tossed it back to me with a contemptuous glare, and I crossed the frontier into the Confédération Suisse.

Tim had sent me his address in a letter and added that his apartment was close to the train station. I located it on a city map displayed in the entrance hall and saw that it was close indeed. As I walked out of the station, I caught a glimpse of the Jet d'Eau spraying water high into the air.

I turned into Rue de Lausanne and found his building, marked 37 bis on a small blue plaque above an arched doorway leading into a gloomy little courtyard. Inside, I started up the spiral staircase to the first landing, the second, and then the third. Eventually, out of breath, I arrived on the top landing and a door with 6 written on it. I leant on the door and knocked, still panting.

'Eamon! What the fuck are you doing here?'

'Can I come in?' I gasped. Brushing past Tim into a living room with a kitchen at one end, I collapsed on the sofa. 'You - don't have a - telephone, I'm just - passing through - how are you?' His girlfriend, Louise, came through a door, which I presumed to be the bedroom, we all hugged and smiled at each other.

Their flat had two rooms and a toilet outside the front door, no shower. It was in the attic of the building and the ceiling sloped down on the side facing out.

Toot toot, chug chug hissssssssss, I looked out the open window and six floors below was Geneva Railway station and the multiple railway lines leading into it. A lone engine car, not pulling any carriages, ran along the tracks away from the station. It was painted red with a small white cross on it and looked like a Swiss Army Knife scooting along the rails.

'What an incredible view,' I said. 'It's every schoolboy's dream - your own full size train set.'

'Ya, it's great, I must admit. A bit noisy, though,' Tim mused rubbing his pointy beard.

They had been living here for several months. Tim was working as an homme déménageur, a removal man, and Louise had a job in a restaurant.

His father was Swiss, therefore, so was Tim. He boasted, 'My dad is from Obwald which is in the centre of Switzerland. It's one of the original three cantons that formed the Confédération Suisse. I have the right to vote in my canton by holding up my sword to be counted in the town square. I'm more Swiss than William Tell.'

I looked at a Swiss five frank coin that I had in my pocket. On one side was an image of William Tell. His face, shown in profile with a determined jaw and long, straight, thin nose, bore a remarkable resemblance to Tim all right. It was funny to think of Tim, with his posh English public school accent, as Swiss, although he had the air of a mountain man.

I recounted how I had met Lucy, and that she had left me. 'What about the other girl, the girl Amanda?' asked Tim. 'I thought you loved her. So who do you love?'

I realized that the one thing I had not said to Lucy was that I loved her. Although I could see her in my mind's eye, smiling and twisting her curls in her fingers. 'It doesn't matter, does it, Tim? They don't love me.'

'There are plenty of fish in the sea, old chap. If you don't have a girl you just go get one.'

'I guess it's easy for you.'

'It's never easy. You have to apply yourself, obviously. Anyway, you're not exactly an ugly mug yourself. A bit pasty faced though. You need some sun. But now I'm hungry. Let's go the pub and have un sandwich jambon.'

We trundled down the six flights of stairs. 'Keeps us fit,' yelled Tim up the stairwell to me. 'It also keeps strangers away. No one's game to climb these stairs on spec.'

Tap tap tap went our feet on the concrete steps. We emerged out onto Rue de Lausanne, and Tim strode off in the direction of Mr. Pickwick, his favorite pub, with Louise wrapped around him.

'Hmmm, Feldschlossen beer, sandwich jambon….' It was never advisable to interrupt Tim while he was imbibing. He wouldn't hear what you had to say anyway. Finally he finished and said, 'So, what are you going to do Eamon?'

'I guess I'll just travel around until I run out of money. While I'm in Switzerland, I think I'll go to Bern and visit Gabrielle.'

'Who's she?'

'A girl I met in London. I hardly know her but, she gave me her telephone number. What are you going to do Tim?'

'Hang out with La Louise, my bird.'

'Do you have any longer term plans?'

'Sure, going back to India … and other places.'

The last time I'd seen Tim, we both seemed much younger. Neither of us had any plans. Olaf was right, I had no direction. But Tim hadn't changed. He lived day by day - from one sandwich jambon to the next beer. Now I was doing the same as him, drifting along.

Tim's family were wealthy, although I never knew exactly how wealthy. He never accepted any money or any help from his mother, 'She drives me bonkers!' he said. However, I could tell that he loved her. I always suspected that he was going to come into an inheritance someday - if he lasted that long. When he was at public school, he ruptured a blood vessel in his stomach and nearly died, and I wondered how that affected his outlook on life. 'One day you're here and the next - puff, bag of shit!'

He acted as if he didn't have a care in the world, and I wanted to be like him. But, I could see now that like everyone else, he really was just acting. He did care about his fate - about how his life would turn out before he went 'puff'. But he shrugged off his cares and instead lived for the moment - the sandwich he was enjoying or the girl he was with. He tried to put off any long term ideas. At least until he had finished his beer.

Louise worked day shifts in a restaurant nearby, but Tim's job was only casual and he had no work on while I was there. When Louise was at work Tim and I walked around Geneva and drank beer in his favorite pubs. The two of us could stand together propping up the bar, and drink all afternoon. With Tim time passed lazily. Sometimes neither of us would utter a word for half an hour, both lost in our reveries. He was easy for me to be with.

'What time does Louise get off work today?'

'Humm, around seven I think. Let's go home and wait for her'

We walked from the Café du Centre on Place du Lac where we had been perched through the afternoon into the Jardin Anglais. We stood on the shore of Lac Leman and looked at the Jet d'Eau gushing water 450 feet into the air. In the other direction, we could see the Pont du Mont Blanc where Lac Leman empties into the Rhône. Across the bridge was the Beau Rivage, Les Bergues and several other expensive 19th century hotels with elaborate facades.

'Let's take a longer walk home,' suggested Tim. We walked along the bank of the Rhône as it rushed along, deep emerald green, like an enormous sheet of molten glass. We wound our way past the grand French style buildings to Rue de Lausanne.

Louise cooked us dinner as dusk descended and in the greyness, I sat observing the station below. Trains from the Deutsche Bundesbahn, French SNCF, and the Swiss Army knife FCC rumbled in, their brakes squealing as they pulled into the station. The PA called out the arrivals and departures in four languages, French, German, Italian and English.

I had been in Geneva a week, and I said, 'Tim, in the morning I think I'll go to Bern.'

'Hey man, follow your bliss. See you on the King's Road.'

Tim had a two-man tent that he didn't need. I bought it off him for £5. I thought it could save me spending money on hotels.

The next morning I said goodbye and walked to the station. I was getting fond of train travel. It felt as if I had found sanctuary, a peaceful place where I knew no one and no one knew me, yet the world continued on while I observed. Towns, fields, factories, mountains, rivers all flashed by me in my pod, my cocoon. Albert Einstein developed his theories of special and general relativity in Bern. He traveled to work on the tram looking backwards as it moved away from the town clock. It was on the tram one day that he realized the possibility of time travel, or so the story goes. On trains, I felt like a time traveler, and I was on my way to Bern.

I asked at the tourist office in Bern railway station where I could put up a tent. I was directed to a campground at Eichholz on the banks of the River Aare that runs through the middle of the city. Like the Rhône, the river was fast flowing, deep emerald green but translucent.

The campground was empty. The wide grassy banks of the river were marked out into campsites, and I picked a spot and put my tent up. The Zoo was across the river on a tree covered hill, and behind the campground a dense copse extended back up a hill. Although it was in the middle of the city, the location was picturesque with no buildings in sight.

I looked around for a telephone box and called Gabrielle. She hardly remembered who I was but was welcoming. She was staying at her family home, but her parents were away, and she invited me over for dinner. I took the tram past the town's famous medieval clock the Zytglogge and found my way to her house.

Gabrielle was a few years older than me. She had dark nearly black hair, pale green eyes and was tall and slim. Her English was flawless, as she had been to a Swiss finishing school. She was attractive, more so than I remembered. I had met her in London at one of Gwynneth's parties after I had broken up with Amanda. We got on well together, and when I told her that I had friends in Geneva, she gave me her phone number in case I ever made it to Switzerland.

She opened the front door with a smile and said, 'Come I'll cook din din for us.'

Din din, that sounds promising, and I felt my pulse increase. We drank red wine and together we chopped vegetables. I turned to pour another glass and glimpsed her from behind her as her hair danced around her bare shoulders. She turned her head slightly towards me, and her dark eyelashes and red lips moved close to my face. I was suddenly struck by a memory of Lucy in London and turned away quickly.

After did din we sat on a big sofa, sipped wine and she dimmed the lights. 'Eamon, where are you going after Bern?'

'I don't know. Maybe I'll go to Italy.'

'You can stay here for a while if you like. We have the house to ourselves.'

The night was young, she was beautiful, I was alone and so was she. My mind and body were in a terrible conflict. I felt a hot rush in my face and my head started pounding.

'Ahhhhh, I don't feel well…'

I woke up before dawn. Where am I? Oh yes, humm. I could have, maybe, but, yes, I'm in my tent. What a pillock I am!

I was disgusted with myself. Maybe I was nice and sweet, or gay or something. What was I thinking of? All I could remember was the taxi door slamming and me waving goodbye. Gabrielle looking puzzled as the car sped away leaving her on the doorstep with the porch light shining on her face - two objects moving in opposite directions at the speed of light.

I was wide awake, and I crawled out of the tent. It was a clear night and a half moon was shining, poking out just below the level of the trees on the hill. The river gurgled by with moonlight bouncing on wavelets and making soft shadows through the trees and on the grassy banks. The delicate scent of pine trees mingled with forest undergrowth and wildflowers filled the air. Insects and bats flittered around, and an owl hooted in the distance. I walked to the river bank and dipped my hand in the water - it was freezing but deliciously fresh. I sipped the liquid off my hand and sat down on the damp grass, which felt as soft as a down pillow.

Sitting still taking in the primordial atmosphere, I felt as if I were in pre-Christian times deep in the alpine forests of ancient Europe. I noticed movement on the bank of the river not far away from me and saw a shape move in the moonlight. What was that? My eyes took a few seconds to focus in the dark, but yes, it was a woman with long hair. She was sitting on the grass like me, staring at the moon, and she turned and looked at me. I could just discern a smile and a little wave of her hand. Oh, she'll think I am some kind of stalker if I just sit there in the dark. So I stood up to retreat to my tent, but she beckoned me to come to her.

I walked slowly towards her, and she laughed, a soft, delicate tinkle. She stood up and danced further away from me, turned around and giggled, 'You're so sweet, you silly boy, can't you see?'

The moon was obscured by a wisp of cloud, and I could no longer make her out in the darkness. I sat back down and stared at the flowing river as the dawn broke. Little by little the green color of the water emerged from the darkness. Mist wafted up the valley, and the moon sank behind the hill. Birds started to sing, chirrup and tweet. First one, then more, until a cacophony of sound erupted. I returned to my tent and slept.

13

The small suitcase I had brought from London was proving cumbersome, so on the way to the station in Bern I bought a backpack and threw the case away. Once again I felt out of place in my London clothes, but I spotted an army surplus store in the main street and bought a blue air force shirt and a pair of German army trousers. Stowing my pointy two tone shoes in my backpack, I tried on a pair of army desert boots. I shaved in the station toilets and, noticing in the mirror that my hair was getting long, combed it back over my ears. The train was due to leave in 90 minutes and would arrive in Munich that evening.

The train zipped through the Bernese Alps to Zurich, past Lake Constance and arrived at Münchener Hauptbahnhof. During my brief stay in February, Lucy and I had walked all over the centre of the city and it felt familiar to me. We had passed by some cheap looking hotels on the other side of Marienplatz so I headed over that way. At least now I had direction, although I didn't yet know what my next move would be.

Marienplatz is in the heart of Munich where the Rathaus or Town Hall and the Mariensäule column are located. The tower of the Rathaus has a famous Glockenspiel with mechanical, performing figurines that emerge from it on a circular track. The instrument chimes as the twirling figurines parade out and in again, much to the amusement of tourists.

It was dusk as I entered the square and, judging by the crowd dispersing from underneath the Glockenspiel, I had just missed a performance. I walked past a busker who was playing an electric guitar with a little amp and speaker on the ground. His clipped German voice and clanging guitar caught my attention as he played an old Beatles song.

'… All of my l-i-i-ife
Ich been suchen for a gir-r-r-r-r-l, to love me
Like I-i love you-u-u-u
But every girl I've ever had
Brecht meinen heart und leave me-e zad.
Vat am I, vat am I, suppo-o-o-osed to dooooo?

Ha-a-na
Komm closer und ask me, girl
To zets you frei girl
Du say he loves du more than ich
So I will zets you frei
Go mit him, go mit him ...'

That's about right, go mit him - if he loves you more than me, that is. As I passed, I threw a Swiss 10c coin, in his open guitar case.

After checking into a backpacker hostel, I went for a drink at the Hofbräuhaus. It was a noisy cheery place with groups of people sitting at long wooden tables. A buxom Biermädchen in a dirndl took my order of Würst mit Kartoffelnsalat und Sauerkraut und ein Weissbeer. The people next to me were merry and were singing.

'Ein Prosit, ein Prosit der Gemütlichkeit
...uins zwoi drei gusuffa!'

The next day I walked down Leopoldstrasse to Ludwig Maximilian University. The campus stretches across the wide avenue with many buildings on either side and a large, round fountain at the main entrance. I sat on the ledge with the water spurting into the air behind me and watched the thousands of students come and go.

They looked so earnest and young. Bavarian girls with long blond hair wearing tracht - traditional Bavarian clothes - chatted with more modern looking girls in jeans, Afghan coats and Indian scarves. Men in lederhosen strode by, their jaws jutting out as if they were about to climb a mountain followed by Africans, Chinese, Iranians and people from all over the world. My eyes darted and focused on every blond curly-haired girl that passed, but no, I didn't spot her. I didn't even know which building her classes were in.

It was early May, and the trees were covered in fresh, new leaves, flowers were blooming, the warm sun was shining, and the atmosphere of the city was different to cold, stark February. The sound of the splashing water reminded me of sitting by the fountain in St James's Park with Lucy. It was winter then, but her sunny smile was etched on my mind.

How long could I wait, hoping that she would stroll by? Maybe I should just call her. Eventually I walked to Universität U-Bahn station.

'Bing bong - Zurückbleiben bitte, der nächste halt ist Studentenstadt,' sounded the prerecorded announcement on the U-Bahn train.

It was just six stops to Studentenstadt, and the student accommodation was a short walk from the station on Grassmeierstrasse. Lucy's room was in one of the two story blocks, but I was unsure which one as it all looked so different now without snow and leaves on the trees.

The corner of my eye caught a glimpse of a scarf, waving in the wind and instantly I knew it was Lucy. She was walking away from the Brotladen with a girl chatting and smiling, looking happy and at ease. They stopped on the path and continued talking to each other. They kissed each other on the cheek, and Lucy, preoccupied with a laughing smile on her face, walked into her building.

I thought I might as well just go knock on her door. It'll be natural enough. I could just say, hey Lucy, I just happened to be in the neighborhood ...

Oh good grief. What was I going to say to her anyway? This is crazy, vat am I going to doooo! I plucked up my courage, took a few deep breaths, marched up to her room and tap tapped on the door. Lucy opened it as if she were expecting someone else.

'Ahhh!'

She threw her arms around me, and we kissed in the doorway. It was as if we had been separated for an age. She stroked my hair and held my face between her hands and looked into my eyes as if to make sure it really was me. It was as if I had been in exile - forced to walk a foreign land until permitted to return home.

Some time later we were lying quietly in bed. Lucy asked me, 'Eamon, why did you come here?'

'Because…because, I love you.' There I said it. If she rejected me, so be it.

'Why didn't you tell me before, in Amsterdam?'

'I think - I was afraid - afraid of being hurt, of losing you.'

'You silly thing, can't you see?'

'See what?'

'I love you too.'

The next morning Lucy had a tutorial at the university. I took the U-Bahn with her and waited in the university library. It was only a few more weeks until she finished, she didn't have to take any exams, just complete her last two course units, and she would be free. After an hour or so, she came in with a smile and put her books on the table.

'So Eamon, what are you going to do now?'

'Now I've got you back?'

She smiled hesitantly and looked down at her books.

'What's the matter?'

'Nothing...'

'Do you still want to go back to him?'

'I don't know. I'm confused. I do have to go back to America no matter what.'

'When do you have to go back, by the way?

'Well, I have a one year open return ticket. I arrived in Munich at the end of September, so I have to book a flight for sometime in September.

'That's not so bad, I didn't realize. I thought you had to go home as soon as your course was over.'

'My folks are expecting me to go home in a few weeks.'

'Why don't you tell them that you've decided to spend the summer in Europe travelling around?'

'Then what?'

'We can spend the summer travelling around Europe!'

I hadn't spent much money since leaving Amsterdam. Nevertheless, cash was flowing out of my pockets as quickly as the Weissbier was going down my gullet and was fast running out.

Lucy had an English friend called Richard, who lived in a high-rise student building above Das Underground nightclub. He gave me the address of an employment agency that specialized in temporary laboring and cleaning work for non-German speakers. I got a job filling in for someone on holiday who looked after the swimming pool at the Munich Hilton hotel. The pay was 12 Deutsch marks per hour, cash in hand, but it was only three weeks work. To keep hold of Lucy until September, I would have to take her somewhere cheap.

'Lucy… do you have any money?'

'For what?'

'Travel, food, tickets.'

'I have some but not a lot.'

'Lucy… let's go to Greece!'

'You don't want to go to Italy, France?'

'No no no, they're really boring. In Greece, we can live in a cave.'

'Live in a cave? You must be kidding!'

'It's all right, friends have told me all about Greece. We can find a secluded beach and live on it. We don't have to sleep in a cave, I have a tent.'

'How big a tent?'

'It'll be great you'll see. We can go to Athens and drink ouzo and everything.'

The next day I went to the supermarket. Lucy was hanging up the phone when I returned. She looked away from me furtively. I put my things in the fridge, and she walked out. I followed her into her room, and she sat on the bed her eyes downcast.

Sitting beside her, I asked, 'Who were you talking to?'

'No one…'

'You look sad.'

'No, I'm fine.'

I stood up and went to the window and looked out at the peaceful scene. The trees were leafy, and the lawns were freshly cut. Students walked lazily along the path, and puffy white clouds drifted by, but I sensed an uncomfortable atmosphere between us that I hadn't experienced before.

'Should I go?' I said not looking away from the window.

'I had to call home.'

I turned slightly and looked at her out of the corner of my eye. She sighed, and her shoulders slumped. I felt a cold sweat and a hollow feeling in my stomach.

'I told them that I was staying for a while.'

'Great, that's great. Were they okay about it?'

'Yea fine,' she said unconcerned what her parents thought.

'I called him.'

'How was he?'

'I don't want to talk about it.'

She rushed out of the room and slammed the door.

14

Lucy finished university without fanfare. We went to a few parties with her fellow American students. Some of them were going home, but many of them, like her, were intending to remain in Europe for the summer. Richard was enrolled for the following academic year and was planning to spend the summer in Munich. The lease on Lucy's room was up, and she had to clear out. We put her books, clothes, personal things and my London clothes into boxes. Richard agreed to look after them until we returned at the end of August.

Richard reckoned he would be able to find a room for us to stay in when we got back as, during the summer break, many German students went home until the next semester began in late September and rented out their empty rooms.

'Lucy let's hitchhike to Greece, it'll be fun. It's only twelve hundred miles.'

'Only - are you kidding? Why do you want to hitchhike at all?'

'Because of the adventure, you know I hitched in California.'

'Yeah, that was a crazy thing to do.'

'It's the best way to see the country and meet people. Don't worry, it'll be great.'

'Well, all right, then. If you say so,' she said looking at me with a frown.

It was a warm, bright Saturday when we set off. I was wearing my German army trousers and desert boots, Lucy was in jeans and sneakers, and we both had backpacks. We took the U-Bahn to Karl Preis Platz and walked about a mile to the on-ramp of the Autobahn.

Our route would take us southeast to Salzburg just over the border in Austria, then across Austria and into Yugoslavia, passing through the cities of Ljubljana, Zagreb, Belgrade and finally into Greece to arrive at Thessalonica.

It seemed straightforward enough. We would just stand with our thumbs out and say 'Griechenland'. Everyone knew the way, I presumed.

We waited on the side of the hot, dusty road for about three hours. It was not the same hitching with a girl. On my own, I could convince myself that it was not so bad standing there, vulnerable and alone. At the end of the day I was sure to have somewhere to sleep, a full belly and beer to drink. With Lucy as my travelling companion, I was the leader of an expedition, responsible for her well being, safety and contentment as well as my own. After all, she was supposed to be back in America with her poet, not lost on some highway with me.

I imagined him standing in his underwear, notebook in hand, while Lucy lay naked on the bed looking up in admiration as he read his latest masterpiece aloud.

But soft, strange loneliness of daffodils
The burning deck bemoans
Outrageous times changing
The turning point of the still, still world…

Yes, that's how long we were on the side of the road. My mind was drifting.

'Eamon, EAMON! I'm hungry, tired, hot, bored…' Lucy slumped down on the hard shoulder of the Autobahn. Then I heard the first thunderclap.

KRAAAAAAK

Moments later driving rain lashed and whipped us. We were drenched with nowhere to run to, nowhere to hide.

A little BMW came coughing its way up the on-ramp, windshield wipers flailing at full speed but making little impression against the torrent of water. It was obvious that the driver could hardly see anything as he chugged forward, moving at a snail's pace. I stepped into his path, held up both my arms and waved them frantically. He stopped the car and wound his window down a few inches to see what the matter was. Before he had time to reconsider I opened the rear door, pushed Lucy in and followed her in a tumble. The young driver turned his head and glared at us as we streamed water onto his upholstery.

'Danke, vielen Dank, Salzberg bitte,' I tried my best to pull a friendly smile.

'Scheisse was macht ihr? Raus!' he protested, but after a few seconds he reluctantly put the car in gear, and we were on our way.

Lucy looked miserable, and the driver looked angry. I could see his eyes and eyebrows glaring at us in the rear view mirror. After a while the rain stopped, but grey looming clouds filled the horizon. As we approached the off ramp for Rosenheim, the driver pulled over to the side of the road and said, 'Raus, ich drehe von der Autobahn ab.'

We were back on the roadside again. Lucy looked pale and desperate. Almost immediately a truck stopped, and the driver shouted down from his cab to us, but I couldn't understand him. Lucy translated and said that he would take her but not me. I shook my fist at him, and he drove off. I turned away and shook my head in shame. This was turning into a fiasco. What were we going to do? Then the soft toot toot of a car horn made me turn my head around to see Lucy beckoning me towards a large Peugeot that had stopped for us. We clambered in, and vroom, we were off to Salzburg.

Our driver was from Salzburg, the birthplace of Mozart, and he was on his way home. Mozart was playing on the car stereo, the car was plush and air-conditioned, and I sighed in relief. Lucy fell asleep her head on my shoulder. Soon, we crossed the border into Austria.

It rained on and off the whole way, and we could see only dark clouds. As we entered the city, it looked grey, and wet. Lucy asked the driver if he knew what the weather was going to be like the next day. He turned on the radio, and we caught the weather forecast. Just about the only word I could understand was regen, rain, which was used several times. Deciding we had better take the train through Austria, we asked him to drop us at the Hauptbahnhof. We could try hitching again at the border into Yugoslavia.

He left us at the main entrance to the station and sped away in his Peugeot. Our troubles temporarily over, we checked the schedule and found the train from Munich to Villach on the Yugoslav border was due in ten minutes. 'Good timing,' I smiled at Lucy. She rolled her eyes and shook her head.

The train had several carriages, which were separated by glass doors, so we could look from one end of the train right down to the other. We parked ourselves in an empty carriage. The route crossed Austria at its narrowest point to Villach, only 200km away.

As twilight descended the sun shone underneath the dark clouds and bathed the sides of the valleys in a golden glow. Water sparkled on the buildings and trees as we passed fairy tale villages and castles. The train ducked in and out of tunnels as we crossed two mountain ranges.

For a time, the train followed the banks of a fast-flowing river crowded with flocks of geese, then made its way up another ridge and down into another hidden valley. Lucy and I waltzed in the aisle, humming *The Blue Danube* to ourselves. We spun around and could see the astonished, disapproving faces of our fellow travellers in the adjoining carriages.

The streetlights were just blinking on as we entered Villach.

'I feel happier now Eamon,' Lucy said as we disembarked the train.

'Hopefully we've left the troubles of today behind us in Germany,' I said with my fingers crossed. On our way out of the station, the ticket office closed with a clunk and the station master put up a red sign

GESCHLOSSEN (closed)

The area around the station was totally dark, and the streets were empty of traffic. 'We had better go and find somewhere to stay the night,' I said. We were not fifty yards from the station when rain started pouring forcing us to run back to the cover of the closed station.

After a while, the rain eased a bit and I said, 'I'll go find a hotel. You stay here with the bags and I'll come back for you.' I left Lucy huddled under the awning by a vending machine and ventured out to see what I could find.

Some time later I returned, having found no hotels, shops, bars or anything open. We had nowhere to sleep, nothing to eat, and I had no beer to drink. I had changed some money before we left Munich and I pushed coins into the vending machine hoping to get a bar of chocolate. But no chocolate came out, and the machine kept the money. Fortunately the toilets were still open, and we filled up a water bottle so at least we didn't die of thirst in the pouring rain.

We lay down on the concrete floor, and Lucy wrapped her spare clothes around herself and fell asleep. It rained and thundered until the early hours of the morning, and I sat up fitfully all night unable to sleep. As the dawn finally broke Lucy rubbed her eyes, and a beam of sunlight streaked on the hillside, mist was rising from the wet hills, but directly above us the sky was blue.

'Are you okay Lucy?' I put my arms around her damp shoulders.

'No, I'm exhausted, hungry and wet.'

The stationmaster arrived and opened up. Lucy asked him in German for directions to the Yugoslavian border. He waved his finger across the tracks and pointed to a footbridge. We walked across and from up on the bridge we saw that the town was actually on the other side. The previous night I had walked in the opposite direction where there were only factories and warehouses. We soon came to a busy road with several cheap hotels. I said, 'Local knowledge, very important to have local knowledge.' This time Lucy didn't just roll her eyes, she punched me in the arm.

We had coffee and a bun for breakfast in a Konditorei. Then we found a supermarket and bought some cheese, bread and other basic food. I bought a half bottle of brandy. 'Live and learn hey Lucy? We should never travel without food and water.'

'Eamon, I think you should just shut up - don't say anything okay?'

We found the highway to Ljubljana and after a short while a Yugoslavian registered truck stopped and we clambered up into the cab. The driver, who spoke German, was going to Zagreb. It didn't take long to reach the border, where we joined a queue of trucks waiting to enter Yugoslavia. As we left Austria, the customs official waved us through into the area in between the two border posts. Two Yugoslavian soldiers approached our truck, one holding out his hand for the driver's documents. When he saw us in the cab, he opened the cab door and yelled at us 'Runter runter, raus raus.' (get down, get out).

We were hustled into the guard house and told to sit down. Ten minutes later two border guards, one enormous and fat the other short and skinny, called us over to a bench grabbed our bags and emptied them out demanding our passports. When they saw that Lucy was American, their ambience changed, from gruff to nasty and menacing.

The fat guard grimaced slapping his palm on the table as if he had made some incredible discovery. The small guard goaded Lucy, 'Zo, Yankee? Vat do you vant in Yugoslavia, eh, vhy do you come here?'

I said 'We're ...'

'Shut up you! I asked the American. So, San Francisco nights eh? You think we are going to let a Yankee in?'

The short guard gave me my passport and waved, 'You, go through.'

'Not without her.'

'Vhat? Go, go.'

'No sir, I will wait for my friend. We are travelling together, sir.'

He ignored me and started on Lucy again. 'Zo, Miss Yankee, vhat do you vant?'

'We are just passing through Yugoslavia on our way to Greece,' said Lucy calmly.

A few minutes later they stamped Lucy's passport and let us through. We found our truck driver in the parking lot, but as we approached he shook his head. He told Lucy that they had given him a hard time for bringing hitch hikers into the country, and he couldn't take us any further.

There were more than a dozen trucks in the parking lot. The soldiers were looking the other way towards Austria and, now that we were across the border, no one paid us any mind. We stood at the exit to the parking lot where it rejoined the highway, and soon we were back on the road in another truck.

Hitching in Yugoslavia proved to be easy. Our lift took us to a truck stop just out side of Ljubljana. Within minutes, we had another ride in a private car and were dropped at a truck stop just outside Zagreb and, again, after a few minutes we had another ride, this time in the slowest truck in the world.

The driver was friendly but spoke no English or German. We never found out what his cargo was, but it was obviously extremely heavy. We plodded through the central plains of Serbia between 20 and 40km per hour. The driver kept going right through Belgrade until we stopped for a meal at a road house. He insisted on paying for us, and then we continued on until late evening when he ran out of diesel.

As the three of us got out of the cab, he shooed us away from the truck. Through sign language, he made it clear that eventually the police or soldiers would spot him and give him more fuel, but if they found us, it would mean trouble for all of us. He crossed his hands and clenched his fists to indicate hand cuffs. It dawned on us that hitch hiking was actively discouraged or illegal in Yugoslavia. Perhaps we never had to wait long for a ride because the drivers knew we were in danger. He indicated that we should get off the road and go to sleep in a field. It was not safe to be on the road at night.

Not waiting to be told twice, we scooted down the road until the truck was well out of sight. We were now in the heart of the countryside. There were no lights, houses or traffic on the highway. Beside the road, down a steep, ten foot slope lay a field of ripening corn. We ran down the embankment and pulled out the tent but didn't want to put it up for fear of being seen by the police. We climbed inside the unerected tent and tried to sleep in the humid heat with mosquitoes whining around us all night.

At first light, we clambered back up to the road. We obviously had to keep hitching but, unsure of the consequences, we were afraid that a cop might drive by and apprehend us. A few seconds later, a station wagon came speeding towards us. It screeched to a halt, and a young German guy leaned out the window smiled and said, 'Steigt ihr ein, get in, get in.'

Still rubbing the sleep out of our eyes, we climbed on top of a double mattress in the back of the wagon. A black dog wagged his tail and a bearded guy in the passenger seat outstretched his hand for me to shake and said, 'Ve are going to Thessalonica.' Vroom, we were on our way again.

'You are hitching in Yugoslavia! Schwer, das ist not zo kool you know. You ver glucky ve found you. You haben kein drugs oder? You get thirty years for bringing drogen in Griechenland, ja, super schwer.'

By that evening, we were in a camping ground in Thessalonica. Twelve hundred miles south of Munich, the weather was hot and sunny, everyone was wearing much lighter summer clothes. We felt overdressed, and our backpacks seemed heavier.

We walked the short distance from the campground into the city to change money, and found a bank with high a ceiling and several fans whirring overhead. Greek drachma in hand, we bought a bag of sweet, juicy peaches from a street stall.

We bought a road map, unfolded it on a park bench, and crouching over it considered for the first time where we would go in Greece.

'Look Lucy, we are here,' I said pointing at Thessalonica at the northern end of the Aegean Sea.

'What about these islands here? They look as if they are the closest ones to where we are now,' said Lucy.

She put her finger on a group of islands about half way to Athens jutting out into the middle of the Aegean Sea. 'Move your finger so I can read the name. Ah, the Sporades.'

'Do you know anything about them Eamon?'

'Nothing at all, but maybe that's a good thing. They look perfect don't they?'

Dotted lines indicated ferry routes to the islands from the town of Volos. We found the bus station and were soon on our way.

As the Greek countryside slid past us, I relaxed.

'Happy, Lucy?'

'I'm okay now.'

'We survived. It wasn't that terrible.'

'It wasn't that much fun either. I don't know why I let you bring me here.'

'Lucy, we came so that we could find somewhere beautiful to spend the summer - sunny, peaceful, with nice water to swim in.'

I had been longing to swim in a warm sea ever since arriving in England from India. But more importantly, I wanted to be somewhere alone with Lucy, so we could try and make our romance last. She had to go home in less than three months, and I didn't want to waste any precious time.

We arrived in Volos in the mid afternoon and bought tickets for the evening ferry to the Sporades. It was a fairly large ship that could take up to two hundred passengers or so, but only a handful of people were on board that day. The ferry vibrated and swished its way out into a large gulf. We found seats at the bow outside the main cabin and peered up at rocky hills on three sides.

As it was a pleasant evening we decided to stay out in the fresh air, and watched the setting sun make a blaze of red in the western sky as it dipped below the horizon. With the last rays of light, we turned into a narrow channel and approached a large, circular eddy ahead in the water until the boat made a sharp turn away as if to avoid it. 'It looks like a whirlpool,' said Lucy. The boat seemed to veer straight towards the jagged cliffs, looming above us, but suddenly turned again and we slid out to sea.

The ferry stopped at all the inhabited islands in the Sporades archipelago. We hadn't decided exactly where we were going to get off, but thought we would simply wait until we arrived somewhere that seemed right.

After an hour or so, an island loomed large in the darkness. We rounded a harbour wall and saw a town cascading down a hillside to the ferry quay. It was the port of Skiathos. The foreshore was festooned with multicolored lights, and as we approached the dock we heard pulsating Euro-pop music.

… Yes Sir, I can boogie, boogie woogie, all night long …

Lucy looked horrified. 'Look!' she said and pointed at figures dancing on the promenade and sandy beach below it. The boat stopped at the jetty, and some passengers got off. We hadn't noticed them before, but they seemed to be delighted to have arrived at this particular spot.

On the beach, hundreds of young men and women wearing satin shorts and sleeveless T-shirts were laughing drunkenly and guffawing at each other, in a chaotic melee.

An especially loud group of half-naked drunken people dancing in front of the ferry noticed that we were staring at them. One of them, a fat, stubby English bloke with no shirt and wearing pink satin shorts, shouted at us, 'Ey, ey, come yao. Ouu d'ya tink yer oggolin, eh?' He moved forward from the crowd, pulled a hideous face and yelled at us. 'Wheahahahaha - hurrreeegh!'

Then he poured a bottle of beer over his hairy, sunburnt stomach. His companions burst out laughing and swore at us in Yorkshire accents. 'Fook-off, yau b'stards, fook-ya.' The fat guy in the pink shorts shouted at me, 'Come on yao wog Gearman b-stard, come dawn and fight, yau foreign poofter!'

Lucy and I repelled by the hideous scene stepped back to escape but were stopped by the metal door of the cabin. Then the ghoul turned around, pulled his shorts down and waggled his hairy, pimpled bottom at us.

'Good Lord above,' cried Lucy and buried her face in my chest. Thankfully, the ferry gave a toot and pulled away from the jetty. Soon we were back out in the harbour with no sound but the chug of the ship's engines and the smell of diesel as the lights of the town receded into the distance.

We sat down on our seats. I felt sick in my stomach. 'Ewooo, that was disgusting,' said Lucy. 'What was that place and who were those people? I didn't know such people existed.'

'Humm, well I'm not sure, perhaps the next island will be more, peaceful.' We sat in stunned silence as the ferry churned away through the night. Lucy fell asleep, her head on my shoulder, and I had some time for reflection.

Lucy wanted to go to France and Italy, the pinnacles of European culture, and I dragged her here to barbaria because it's cheap. Why did I want to go to Greece in the first place? I remembered Tim telling me how fantastic it was. 'Oh ya, absolutely am-aaaaa-zing, Greece is boss! So cheap, oh ya what. You can live in caves on secluded beaches. Gorgeous chicks, sun, sand, warm sea. Oh ya, you absoluuutly must go…' Oh absoluuutly, thanks mate!

An hour passed, and we approached the island of Skopelos. The boat slowed down as we passed the entrance to the harbour. The small town cascaded down the hills to the sea. There were lights, but they were all white. We heard music, it sounded sweet, lovely, in fact, and as we approached I felt enchanted by the picturesque scene and lilting sounds.

As we came closer, I recognized that the song was, *The Girl from Ipanema*, being sung in French.

… la fille d'Ipanema s'en va, marchant, et quand elle passe
Quand elle passe, tout le monde fait Ahhh! ...

The boat stopped at the jetty, and we stood up nervously to look at the scene. The waterfront was filled with charming looking restaurants. Couples and small groups of smiling people sat at tables eating delicious looking fish and salads. They chatted and waved their arms descriptively, laughing happily. The beautiful music echoed off the buildings, and the smell of Gitanes smoke wafted aromatically on the air. Lucy looked at the scene with interest. I noticed a girl, a beautiful girl, and she seemed to be gazing back at me.

She was sitting at a table nearby with five other women but no men, wearing a white short pleated skirt and white blouse with its buttons opened revealingly, smiling sweetly at me. Her lips pouted, and I was sure I saw her blow me a kiss. Her attractive companions also appeared to be staring at me. I glanced over my shoulder - surely they must be looking at someone behind me. I smiled and gave them a little wave. I saw Lucy grimace at me out of the corner of my eye.

The girls seemed so lovely, beautiful, immaculately dressed as if they were in a Fellini movie. I must be crazy, but they genuinely do seem to be staring at me I thought. Some were blonde, others were dark, but all seemed to have the same deep, round eyes and rich pouting lips. They weren't that close, but I was sure I could see their décolletage and imagined what must lie beneath their tantalizing white skirts.

'Hey, Lucy, this place looks perfect. Let's get off here.' I grabbed my bag and started to rush for the gangway.

'No, this place is no good I'm not getting off here. It's weird, everyone looks phony!'

'Lucy, what do you mean? Look at the nice restaurants, the handsome men. It all looks so cool and groovy.'

'Handsome, men? The last thing I need is another handsome man. I came here to be with you. I can see you eyeing up those girls!'

'Don't be silly. I really want to stay here, at least for a while. It doesn't have to be forever...'

I thought you wanted to live in a cave? You said you wanted to take me somewhere secluded and beautiful, so we could be in love with each other.'

'Lucy, you know I love you, but…but…but…'

Toot, toot, the ferry's engines kicked into action and once again we were churning the water and heading off into the night.

Tall and tan and young and lovely, sigh. I couldn't get those girls out of my mind. This time it was me who fell asleep on Lucy's shoulder.

Toot toot, chug chug. 'Eamon, wake up, this is the last stop.'

Once again the ferry turned around a harbour wall and slowed. There were a few lights on the waterfront and one or two street lamps on the steep stepped streets of the village. We heard a soft tingling of a bazouki and the murmur of Greek voices.

We had arrived on Alonissos, the last harbour the ferry was calling at. Whether we liked it or not we had to get off here. It was around ten in the evening, and as we walked down the gangway an old man with a white moustache greeted us.

'Efharisto,' he said. He took Lucy's backpack and held her hand in his. He smiled and nodded, 'This way, my friends.' He kept hold of Lucy's hand and led us up into the village behind the harbour. We climbed up the steep street a short way to a whitewashed terraced building.

We creaked up one flight of stairs to a small white room with a double bed covered in aqua blue sheets. I opened the double wooden shutters and let the sumptuous sea breeze blow in. We fell asleep in each other's arms naked, warm and exhausted.

Tweet tweet, tweet tweet, si-cou si-cou si-cou, twerp!

I opened my eyes, and a little blue bird was sitting on our windowsill. He burst away into the brilliant blue morning sky. I propped myself up on my elbows and could glimpse the aquamarine water of the harbour. It was a perfectly sunny day. A fresh zephyr blew in carrying the smell of strong coffee. Lucy stirred and turned over, the blue sheet fell from her breasts. She rubbed her eyes, opened them and smiled at me.

Some time later, we found our way downstairs wearing our long army trousers and T-shirts. We walked outside into the street. Steps ran down both sides of the narrow, cobbled pathway, lined with two-story, whitewashed buildings. I noticed that there were no cars to be seen. We went to the waterfront and sat down at a little café looking out into the harbour. A lady greeted us, spoke several words and smiled, waiting for a reply.

Lucy said, 'Café, parakalo' Oh, so Lucy knows some Greek as well, I thought.

'How do you say eggs in Greek, Lucy?'

'No idea. I just know the word for please.'

We ate our breakfast of dark black coffee served in small glasses, eggs fried in olive oil, doorstops of white bread and something we didn't order but seemed to be part of the breakfast service, rich yoghurt in a bowl with a blob of honey in the middle.

'That was the nicest breakfast I have ever had,' I exclaimed. Lucy picked up her coffee cup with a smile and tilted her head back to glug down the last bit and suddenly coughed and spat. 'Ewe, it's all the dregs!' I saw that the bottom of my coffee glass was also filled with coffee grounds.

The harbour and foreshore below the town were apparently free of beasts, ghouls and beauteous maidens. There were only the inhabitants of the village. We had found our Greek island, but no secluded beach as yet.

After breakfast, we made a few enquiries and, using mostly German and English, were able to communicate without too much difficulty. We asked about beaches, and the locals nodded their heads upwards, pointing with their chins, to indicate further east along the coast. They answered questions about the best way to get there by nodding downwards, pointing to the harbour.

At the jetty, a small boat with an outboard motor pulled up to us.

'Efharisto,' the boatman said. 'Tak-si, tak-si?'

Taxi boats sounded like a good idea. 'How much to go to a beach,' we asked, 'Wieviel Geld, combien ça coûte?'

'Cento, hunderdt, cent, one hundred drachma parakalo,' the water cabbie rattled off. Remembering our hitchhiking experiences, decided to go shopping before venturing out.

'I saw a covered market in the village, let's go and buy some vegetables.' Lucy looked happy as she wandered through isles of market stalls selling tomatoes, lettuce, cucumbers, feta cheese and fish. She spent what seemed an inordinately long time selecting every item, picking up each one and examining it closely, rejecting most of them.

'Lucy, I'm bored with this. I'll see you back outside.' I sat on the waterfront with the fishermen watching boats come and go. One of them asked me, 'Friend, are you German?'

'No, I'm from Ireland.'

'Ah good, Rotterdam, great city.'

Eventually Lucy struggled out of the market carrying numerous plastic bags of food. I remembered the final, all important ingredient and bought a bottle of Metaxa - Greek brandy. All set, we went back to the jetty and boarded our tak-si.

The little boat headed out of the harbour with its two stroke engine purring away. Along the coastline, craggy orange colored headlands alternated with beaches nestled in bays. We came to a beach with several small huts and numerous naked people frolicking around. 'Keep going, please, go on,' we waved to the boatman.

On the next beach were only two or three huts and a handful of naked people. I tried to see if the women looked like the mysterious beauties I had seen the night before, but we were too far away. We passed several more headlands and bays until - finally, the boatman turned in towards the shore. He indicated that this was the easternmost point of the Island, and we could go no further. The beach was deserted. We jumped into the knee deep water, took our bags and said goodbye to him. As he turned around and left us, quite alone, I wondered how we were going to get back to town. After all, there were no phones, so we couldn't call a taxi. 'What ever we don't have, we don't need, right?' I said to Lucy.

We surveyed our secluded beach. It was about four hundred yards long with craggy headlands at each end. The sand was golden blonde. We found a flat, open space among some pine trees behind the beach to put up our tent. It was mid morning by now and becoming very hot. Neither of us had shorts or swimming suits - but what did we need them for anyway? We threw off our clothes and ran into the calm turquoise water. It felt soothing and warm on our skin. After a while, we lay on the sand like shipwrecked lovers, alone and left to fend for ourselves.

When we became hungry in the afternoon, Lucy rummaged through the shopping bags and pulled out food for our lunch. We ate out of one bowl, sitting on one towel, naked, staring out to sea.

Our life fell into a delightful routine. When it grew dark, I made a little fire, more for entertainment than for warmth. We only needed a sheet in our tent at night. We woke with the dawn bird song and lazed in the warm water during the day. In the late afternoons when the harshness of the sun subsided we lay in each others arms.

One morning I asked, 'Lucy, what day is it, do you think?'

'We left Munich on Sunday, so I think today must be Saturday.'

'So we've only been here on the beach for four days?' I marvelled. Already our life here seemed perfectly natural. We were getting suntanned. I liked to look at Lucy as she lay on our towel in the shade of the pine trees. 'Don't look at me so much.'

'Why not, you're beautiful.'

'Well any way, I feel so healthy, we're getting so much sleep and eating so well, but we're running out of food.'

'So soon? I guess I'll have to catch a fish. You're not getting bored here, are you Lucy?'

'No, no at all. Am I boring you?'

'No, I feel relaxed being with you. I don't think I could ever be bored when I'm with you.'

'Oh, that's sweet.'

'Sweet eh?'

I grabbed her arm. She threw sand at me and ran off. I chased after her and caught her half way down the beach and we fell laughing into the calm sea.

Sitting in the shallow water I asked, 'Lucy have you been to Kentucky?'

'No, I haven't, but I've been to Indiana. My dad used to take us on road trips in the summer. He's a teacher, so he has long summer breaks. We drove all the way to Evansville one time.'

'How long did it take to get there?'

'Three days I think. We saw the Grand Canyon on the way. You would love the desert, there's much more texture to it than you might imagine. It's an unbelievable feeling to be under the big sky. The horizon seems so far away and makes a complete circle. I don't know why, but it puts my mind at ease.'

'I guess you're looking forward to seeing your family and getting back home?'

'Of course, but I'm not looking forward to being back in the U.S.A. though. Americans are so demanding - you have to conform, fit in and be popular. There's not much tolerance for people who are different.'

'I thought America was the land of the free? There certainly seemed to be a lot of weird people in Los Angeles and San Francisco when I was there.'

'Most Americans only ever see those people on TV. My folks never go into the city, they live in suburbia. America is a divided place. It's divided between the people living on the streets, illegal Spanish speaking immigrants, poor people, black people, anyone who doesn't conform, but Most of America is an enormous mass of normal people.'

'Living the American dream?'

'It's the American nightmare. Being American is supposed to be the pinnacle of human existence. All that matters is being American, what ever that is. It's drummed into you at school - the U.S.A. is the best of all possible worlds. Nobody wants to admit it, but it's obviously not true. It's like the emperor's new clothes. No one is prepared to tell the truth for fear of being called a traitor. You're supposed to be a good American and support the president, do your duty. I think that's why my dad is so disappointed.'

'He's disappointed with America?'

'He thinks that the people have let the country down. We all failed - Richard Nixon, the young generation, me. So many people haven't lived up to their responsibilities. I just feel more comfortable in Europe. It's a far less menacing place, and I don't mean the street weirdoes. I'm talking about the people you meet. They seem more down to earth, more genuine,' she said shaking her head.

'Do you like living in England, Eamon?'

'London is a harsh place. I don't know if I like it, but I do love London, and the King's Road. I love the kaleidoscope, the never ending variety of people that you meet. London feels like the centre of the world, and like a whirlpool, it sucks you in. It seems as if nowhere else could be as worthwhile or as valid.

I think of myself as a Londoner. I don't know about the rest of the country. The UK is divided too. Divided by its regions, London, the Home Counties, the north, Wales, Scotland. It's divided by class, by race, by accent, by the way you dress, north of the river, south of the river. It's an extremely tribal place. It takes up so much time just trying to fit in.'

'Is that why you had to leave, because you didn't fit in?'

'I thought I was leaving because I wanted to be with you, but maybe you're right. I've always felt like an outsider.'

'Well I guess we were made for each other - just a couple of kooks, misfits.'

I heard the chug chug of an engine and looked up. A taxi boat edged around the headland and came towards the beach. Just in time I thought, we need to get to the village somehow to buy more supplies.

The boat pulled up to the beach, and a young couple got out and splashed ashore next to us. It was only when we were standing in front of them and the boatman that I remembered we were naked. I felt like we were Adam and Eve before the fall.

'Grüss dich,' said the young man, they were Germans. Lucy conversed with them while I asked the boatman to wait a few minutes for us. The Germans headed off down the beach to find a spot to camp. Lucy and I ran up to our tent and put on some clothes. Soon we were past the headlands on the azure sea heading back to civilization.

We stocked up on food and took another taxi back to the beach. The German couple had set up their camp at the far end of the beach to us. Both naked, the girl was lying in the sun and the guy was striding around collecting firewood and doing other manly chores. In the mid afternoon, another boat arrived with about ten people on board.

They dropped an anchor into the shallow water, jumped ashore stripped off their clothes and frolicked on the beach. One Greek fellow, in his mid twenties, kept his striped T-shirt and shorts on and came over to us.

'Bonjour, gutten Tag.'

'Guten Tag. We are English speakers.'

'Ah excellent, I can speak English zer gut.'

He explained that he was a tour boat operator and took groups of tourists from the village to various beaches for day trips. In the evening, he brought them back to the village where they stayed in pensions. 'I am going to cook my customers a fish stew later on, please to join us.'

He was short but athletic looking with dark curly hair. We helped him dig a fire pit in the sand. Lucy and I put some clothes on for the task. The three of us collected firewood then he lit a fire and unloaded several cool boxes from his boat. We helped him chop up vegetables and fish and put them in a large pot on the fire.

As the twilight approached he beckoned his tourists to come and eat. Tired and relaxed, they lazily made their way over to the fire, and we all ate a delicious fish stew. He opened the cool boxes and passed bottles of Fix Beer and Orangina around to us all. Lucy and I were happy for the company and food. Everyone had a sunny glow as we watched the sun go down.

As abruptly as they had arrived, he signaled that they had to leave, and they all got back in the boat. 'Eamon and Lucy, I come to this beach every Saturday. If I leave this cool box behind, will you look after it? It will save me a lot of trouble.'

'Sure,' I said, 'But I can't promise I won't be tempted to drink a beer or two.'

'That is no problem, my friends, you can drink what you want. If you look after my box and help me build the fire next Saturday, is that a deal?'

We had a job and a cool box with six beers and six Oranginas in it. During the week, we prepared the cooking pit for him, so all he had to do was light it with a match. Then we cleaned up when his party left the beach to return to the village, and each week he left us more beer and soft drinks.

So our life continued. We rarely spoke to the couple at the other end of the beach. During the day, the German girl lazed around reading books while Mr. Industrious, as we named him, strode around cleaning, fixing, gathering with his manhood flapping from side to side.

It never rained and was sunny and hot every day. The beach was relatively small, and the hillsides behind us were rough and prickly, so our activities were limited. We hadn't brought anything to read with us. We swam, lolled around in the water, collected firewood, talked and kissed.

We spent many hours in the heat of the day sitting in the shade of an olive tree just behind the beach. We stared at the water, reluctant to venture out into the midday sun.

I remembered living on the beach at Juhu, Bombay. We had a chauffeur named Jagdish. He was a devotee of Hanuman, the monkey God. He became a friend to my mother and me, and he taught us the basic tenets of Hinduism.

He likened the Hindu pantheon to Christian saints. Like Christians, Hindus believe in only one God. But God has an infinite number of manifestations - after all, God is infinite. Like the Christian understanding of God, Hindus believe in the Trinity, Siva, Vishnu and Brahma. The other deities are but manifestations of Siva, the Father; Vishnu, the Son; or Brahama, the Holy Spirit. Jadgish taught us to meditate as we sat on Juhu Beach watching the orange sun merge into the infinite colors of the sea. I told Lucy how we used to meditate.

'Just close your eyes and listen to the waves.'

'There aren't any waves.'

'Well listen to the breeze then.'

So we sat cross legged and listened to the breeze. Then it happened, just like it did on Juhu more than ten years earlier. I was gone, as if someone had switched off the clock. Time had stopped. Until, in a flash of realization, I was back and the clock was ticking again. Where had I been? How long was I away? An ancient Irish poem my older sister used to recite came into my head.

> I am the wind that breathes upon the sea
> I am the wave of the ocean
> Who but I sets the cool head aflame?

I opened my eyes, but Lucy wasn't there. I looked down the beach, and she was nowhere to be seen. I jumped up with a start and looked all over for her. Then I saw her on the rocks beneath the headland. I splashed my feet in the water as I walked along the beach to where she was sitting.

Lucy had her chin on her knees, her long sunbleached hair flowing over her tanned shoulders. She looked up at me with her broad smile and soft eyes.

'Did you like your meditation?' I asked.

'Yes, I did. I think we've done it now. I mean, I think we can leave.'

***

The next day we packed our things, and sat on the beach until a boat glopped past the headland. We waved our arms outstretched high above our heads. The little boat saw us and turned toward the shore. The fisherman was on his way back to the village with his morning catch.

We climbed aboard and the boat turned back out to sea. Looking back as the golden red beach disappeared behind the headland, and the swell of the aqua blue Aegean arched out ahead of us, I said, 'So this is it Lucy. We're leaving our little paradise.'

'It's been lovely Eamon.' Lucy cried.

Our time on Alonissos seemed to last for an age, but now we were back on the road. I felt it was far too short, but it was late August and we had to get back to Munich.

Lucy hugged me and with her face buried in my chest she suggested, pleadingly, 'Rather than hitching, it might be best if we just take the train from Athens to Munich. What do you think?'

'Of course darling, if you want to take the train that's fine with me.' I rolled my eyes and shook my head. I had no desire to hitchhike back through Yugoslavia.

We caught the ferry to Volos and the bus to Athens. We spent the next few days visiting the Parthenon and the sights of Athens. Apparently we had missed the Moscow Olympics, which the USA and Western countries had boycotted because the USSR had invaded Afghanistan. 'Why would anybody with any brains invade *Afghanistan*, do they have loads of oil or something?' Lucy asked.

We bought train tickets and Lucy called the airline to book her flight home from Munich. She was due to fly to San Francisco and out of my life in just ten days. 'It's our last night in Greece, so why don't spend our remaining drachma on a big dinner?'

'Sure why not,' said Lucy.

We went to the Plaka district where the streets were lined with boisterous restaurants, and sat down at a table on the street surrounded by tourists from all over Europe. We ordered a feast of stuffed vine leaves, grilled sardines and Salada Greca.

A German guy sitting at the next table struck up a conversation with us. 'Oh yes, you must try retsina. I don't believe you are staying in Griechenland during two months and you are not trying retsina!'

'We only went to one beach, and kind of got lost there.'

'You didn't go to lots of vilde parties und many bars und discos?'

'No, we saw one town that had all of that type of thing but it didn't… seem right.'

'Vell, you must both try this drink. My name is Axel und das ist mein Freund Eddy, from Australia.'

He filled up our glasses, 'Prost, und in the hatch.'

Axel, Eddy and I poured the smooth retsina in our hatches. 'Wooaha, what is this stuff?' I gasped. It tasted like wine but had a strange under taste to it.

'It's vine but it is fortified with resin from pine trees.

'Noch ein mal?' said Axel, filling up our glasses again. When he came to Lucy's glass, he saw that she hadn't touched her drink. 'Vas? Drink up young lady.' Lucy just smiled, she didn't like to drink much.

As our food was served Axel threw a plate and smashed it on the floor. All the tourists cheered. There was a group of Danish people sitting at the table behind us, they all threw plates onto the tiled floor and laughed as they smashed to pieces. The waiters pulled half smiles as they cleared the shattered dishes glancing up nervously at the Danes while sweeping with dust pans and brushes and jabbering repeatedly, 'Das ist gut, das ist gut, ja, ha ha ha…'

I ordered another bottle of retsina. Eddy ordered another bottle. Axel ordered another bottle. Soon the three of us were gesticulating and shouting. Axel sang German songs and Eddy recited *The Man from Snowy River* by Banjo Patterson and the restaurant erupted in clapping and cheering. 'Ja, ja, gemütlichkeit!' everyone shouted.

Lucy looked bored, then annoyed. After a while, I didn't notice her any more.

'Axel, where are you guys going after Athens?'

'Ah, Eamon, you must come mit us too. You don't vant to go back to boring Deutschland.'

'I have to go back, I think. Lucy is going home to America soon.'

'Ja, exact! She is leaving so you should come mit us.'

'Where are you going?'

'Ah, Eddy, you tell him vhere ve are going.'

'Oh mate, Eamon, It'll be beaut I reckon. I've heard great things about the place.'

'Oh right. Where is it exactly?'

'Er, bugger, what's it called again, Axel?'

'Ah, er, ja, Eddy, you know. That place ve are going to! Ve have tickets don't ve? Vaiter more restina, bring zwei bottles bitte.'

My head was spinning. I looked around and couldn't see Lucy anywhere. 'Eamon, mate, where is it you're going again? I've forgotten what you said.'

'Me? Oh I'm going with Lucy to…to, er, what's it called? Axel you remember don't you?'

'Eamon, drink, drink, prost!'

We gulped another glass of retsina. Eddy and Axel were rubbing their chins. Axel sat back and rubbed his stomach and tried to speak. 'Ah! I remember, ve're going to… scheisse, lost it again.'

Eddy looked utterly confused, 'Bugger me! What's the bloody place called? It's on the tip o' me tongue. Oh Christ, It's somewhere in er, ah, um…'

Lucy reappeared from across the street. 'Lucy, where have you been?'

'I went for a walk. I couldn't sit with you drunks any more. Let's go. We have to catch a train in the morning.'

'We do? Where are we going? We only just got here... didn't we?'

She dragged me away from the table and pulled me down the street. I looked back at the restaurant. Axel and Eddy were clutching the sleeve of the waiter, and Eddy was sobbing uncontrollably. I heard Axel pleading, 'Please, please, tell me vhere ve are going I beg you!'

'Eamon, Eamon, EAMON! WAKE U-U-U-P!'

'Hey, Lucy, stop shouting at me, ouch. What's the matter? I think I'll just sleep for a bit longer.'

SPLASH

'Lucy, crikey! I'm all wet - what the hell are you doing?'

'GET UP! WE HAVE TO CATCH THE TRAIN!'

'All right, all right, stop shouting. Where are we going anyway?'

15

The first twelve hours of the train journey were the worst in my short life. 'I feel sick. What was that stuff I was drinking? My skin is all clammy, and I can hardly see, my head hurts, my bones ache...'

'Oh, stop moaning. It's your own fault. What do you expect when you drink twelve bottles of retsina?'

'Oh, retsina, that's what it was. I mean it this time, I'm never going to drink alcohol again, well, not retsina anyway.'

Forty-four hours after we left Athens the train pulled punctually into Münchener Hauptbahnhoff. Lucy telephoned Richard. 'He said there's a vacant room in his building where we can stay until Oktoborfest.'

'Terrific, how much is the rent?

'Nothing, it's rent free.'

'That's just as well, Lucy. I'm down to my last few marks.'

We took the U-Bahn to Studentenstadt, and Richard let us into his friend's room on the twelfth floor of his building.

The next day I woke up in our single bed. I lay with my arm under my head looking out the window at the sky. Further away from the equator in the middle of Europe, the light was softer with less yellow in it and the blue of the sky was pale, just like it was in London. The light in Greece was similar to Australia - at least, that was how I remembered it.

Even though, I was only back in Germany, I felt as though I had returned home after a big adventure. Now I was going to have to find some sort of normal life. Get a job, make a career. Oh my God! The horrible thought hit me like the previous day's hangover. What about Lucy? I love Lucy, and she's going to leave me. I'll have to take her to the airport and put her on the airplane with the whole Sally Bowles routine again. I lay motionless but inside I was like a can of writhing worms. No, no, I can't let her go. Does she want to leave me?

'Eamon, what'll you do now?' Lucy whispered in my ear.

Unaware that she was awake, I turned toward her worried face. Her suntan and bleached blonde hair looked out of place in the pallid light.

'I don't know, Lucy. I have no more money and no idea about what to do in the longer term, but today I thought I would go and see if I can get some temporary work.'

'I'll come with you,' she sighed.

We bought some bread and coffee at the Brötladen and after breakfast took the U-Bahn to the employment agency. They asked to see my passport to confirm that, as a citizen of the European Economic Community, I was permitted to work in Germany. I was offered a job in a warehouse and was to start the next day at 7am. The pay was 16 Deutsche Marks an hour, cash in hand, the equivalent of £160 per 40-hour week. The job I had abandoned in London paid £35 per week after tax. We didn't have to pay any rent and while, in general, Germany was expensive, beer was less than half the price it was in London. So my temporary financial worries were taken care of.

Lucy, even though she wasn't looking, was offered a job at an electronics factory making circuit boards for 12 marks an hour. Her study visa for Germany permitted her to do temporary work, and it didn't expire until the end of September. 'I'm not sure,' she told the woman at the agency. 'I'm going back to America in a week. I'll call you later if I want to take the job. Vielen Dank.'

We started to walk back to Studentenstadt through the Englischer Garten, a 10km long park that stretches from the centre of Munich to the outer suburbs of the city. Sitting on a bench looking out at the beautiful parklands, I asked Lucy, 'So, what are you going to do when you get home?'

'I don't know, Eamon. There doesn't seem to be anything for me to go back to. I mean, of course, there are my folks, but apart from that, nothing. I'll have no more university, no job… no you.' I was glad her poet didn't come into her thinking.

'Why don't you stay for a bit longer? We both have jobs if we want them. It may be short term, but the pay is fantastic.'

'What about my airplane ticket? It'll be wasted.'

'You could cancel it and get a refund.'

'Do you think I could?'

'We can try.'

'Why do you want me to stay?'

'Why? Because I love you of course!'

'Of course.'

'What, don't you believe me?'

'Oh sure, I guess so. Just because you love me, doesn't mean I can stay in Europe.'

'You just said you don't have anything to go back for, didn't you?'

'Yeah, but that would be true no matter where I was. If I had stayed at university in Portland, I would still be finished now and have to go back home.'

'If you'd stayed in Portland I'd be your American boyfriend wouldn't I? Would you throw me over just to go home to California?'

'I don't know. You'd probably be going home to New York or somewhere else. That's the way it is at university, people have romances, and then go home to start their lives.'

'Well I didn't go to university, and you're more than some casual fling to me' I turned away and looked across the gardens towards the twin towers of the Frauenkirche.

'Eamon, I don't think of you that way either, but I have to start my life sometime. I have to be good, get a job, buy a car, go to horrible shopping malls and do all the mundane things Americans think they're supposed to do.'

'You think you have to conform?'

'What's the alternative? Live on the lam, like a fugitive?'

'You don't have to conform. Stay with me. You prefer Europe to America, you said so. Maybe we can start something here, together.'

'What are you saying?'

'I'm saying I love you, don't leave me.'

'Nothing more?'

'I promise I won't let you down. I promise I won't stop loving you. I don't have anything more than that to offer.'

Lucy stood up and began walking. We meandered through the gardens in silence, Lucy staring at the ground. Eventually we came to the Studentenstadt gate and, as we were leaving the park, she turned to me and said, 'Well okay, let's just see if I can get that refund on the ticket.'

'Wow, Lucy, you're staying with me.'

'But I have to go back home sometime. I have to.'

The previous year, Lucy had studied at the university in Toulouse, and she pointed out that France was much cheaper than Germany. 'If we go to France they'll give you a new three month tourist visa at the border. Maybe we can find work there, too.'

'I won't have a work visa though,' said Lucy.

'Yeah, but I'll be allowed to work and maybe it won't be a problem there. The French are more easygoing than the Germans.'

We decided to work in Munich until Lucy's visa expired at the end of September. Then we would go to la belle France.

Summer was turning into autumn, and we wrapped up against the cold, crisp air and began our new routine. We awoke early and travelled to work on the U-Bahn. The journey was reminiscent of the London Underground. Although it wasn't as miserable, damp, pasty-faced or unpunctual. The passengers read *Stern* magazine instead of *The Sun,* but the headlines could almost have been directly translated from English into German. Instead of

SHOCK - HORROR - PROBE
they read
SCHOCK - HORROR - MIT SEX.

On Saturday nights, we went to Das Underground discothèque in the basement of our building and danced until the early hours. There, we met Irish students who had come to Munich looking for summer work. Like us, they were staying in vacant students' rooms and found temporary jobs.

Towards the end of September, we took on extra part time work putting up fly posters for one of the side shows at Oktoborfest called *Der Acapulco Todespringer* (The Acapulco Death Leaper). Like Dumbo, the act involved diving off a gantry into a tub of water. The posters depicted a man dressed in a leotard with a Salvador Dali-style upturned moustache about to leap fearlessly into the unknown - or in this case, a tub.

In the afternoons when our regular jobs had finished for the day we walked around the suburb of Schwabing sticking up the posters in shop windows. I covered one street while Lucy took the adjacent one. The pay was surprisingly generous, and it was a pleasant way to see the city with its delightful parks, wide avenues and fountains.

One evening we went to Oktoberfest with Richard. The fairground was covered with large tents filled with long tables where buxom

Biermädchen served litre mugs of beer, oom-pah bands played. Outside, a carnival took place among the tents with a Ferris wheel, shooting galleries, a ghost train ride and, of course, *Der Acapulco Todespringer.* He really did jump off a gantry in a leotard. The enthusiastic crowd ahead of us blocked our view so we couldn't see the tub he landed in, but we supposed he survived.

As the end of September approached, we prepared to head off to France. On our last Saturday night in Munich, we went to Das Underground for the final time. We'd arranged to get a lift with a friend of Richard's who happened to be driving to Strasbourg the following day. The new semester had already begun, and that night the disco was packed with students from all over the world. The DJ played recent disco hits such as *Ring My Bell* by Anita Ward.

As we walked into the disco we were surprised by a group of American sailors, all 'talkin' that bad lang'age...yo!... mutha fuk... right on bro'...yaw'll gotta' get up te get down...'

They were on shore leave and had taken the train from Bremen to Munich for Oktoberfest. 'Maaan, I can't be-lieve the size of those beer glasses mutha fuk...'

When the DJ played *Don't Stop 'till You Get Enough* by Michael Jackson they all jumped up and each one grabbed a girl around the waist. They swirled across the dance floor smiling, laughing and all the while looking their girl in the eye.

... Keep on, with the force don't stop
Don't stop 'til you get enough ...

Black sailors, white sailors, short and tall, and they all danced with grace and rhythm. The Germans, on the other hand, danced stiffly, bobbing up and down like jack-in-the-boxes. The Iranians danced in their own style which they called oriental, with their arms above their heads swirling their hips. The French danced like rag dolls, their limbs flopping in all directions with no obvious connection to the music. The Irish were enthusiastic and kicked their feet out unexpectedly while the English bobbed their heads and strained their necks with fists clenched.

The Americans were by far the best dancers. After all, it was *their* music, a mixture of African, Irish, Spanish and other European influences, cooking together as if in a big pot. This mélange of musical traditions exploded out of the Americas and reverberated around the world, its myriad forms were the soundtrack of our lives.

Remembering my conversation with Lucy on the beach at Alonissos, I was struck that Germany was a divided country, not just divided by class and race like most countries, but by a thousand mile long wall and machine guns. Ireland was divided by a deep psychological scar kept open by fear and loathing, barbed wire and watchtowers. The Iranians were exiles unable to return to their homeland because of the revolution and the Lebanese were escaping civil war. Despite all the divisions in the world, I had a deep sense of togetherness with the people in the crowded room that night. We forgot our differences, if any actually existed, got up on the floor and boogied. I felt as if the world had come together in the rhythm and music, united in one, ecstatic bliss experience.

As the last be-ba-be-lo-bep faded away the room fell around in a lather of perspiration and amity. The Germans cheered, 'Ja super schwer, sehr gemütlich'

The Americans laughed and hugged crying, 'Right on bro', Outta sight man!'

Out of breath, I felt I couldn't dance any more then a Kraftwerk-like, electronic staccato beat, and sharp, high hat sound began to pulsate

...duca-duca duca-duca duca-duca duca-duca duca-duca...
... Oooooohhh, it's so good, its so good, its so good,
Oooooohhh, I'm in love, I'm in love, I'm in love, I love oohh...
I feel lo-o-o-ve, I feel lo-o-o-o-ve, l-u-u-u-u-u--vvvvvvvv ...

The DJ purred in a fake American accent, 'Yes folks, *I Feel Love* by the grand dame of soul Donna Summer-r-r-r-r-r-r.'

The strobe lights caught our every second move and we appeared to be gyrating in slow motion, dancing like a tribe in a communal trance.

... Oooooh, fallin' free, fallin' free fallin' free, fallin' free
Oooh, we felt lu-u-u-u-u-u-ve!

BAM

The record scratched to a stop. The house lights flickered on.
'What the fek d'yus t'ink the fek'n fek fek fek, shite FEK!'

In the middle of the room, swinging his gigantic, outstretched arms around to push everyone back from him in a circle, stood a grotesque six-foot-six oaf with a huge protruding forehead, one eye closed and the other open as wide as a dinner plate. He swore and slobbered at all of us in an unmistakable, drunken, Dublin accent.

'You're all gob-shites! Fek the lot o' yus bastards I'll take yus all on I will. Fek, shite, drink!'

Two Germans guys tried to calm him down, 'Ha ha, Paddy it's all okay, stimmt, ha ha.'

He thrashed his arms around, and they withdrew to a safe distance. He turned in a circle and challenged anyone to take him on. The guy standing next to me, looked me in the eye and said, 'Those disgusting drunken Irish. We should throw them out of Deutschland.'

I felt a terrible shame that one of my own, on my side in this divided world, should destroy the perfect moment and behave like an uncultured barbarian. He looked like the giant from Irish legend, Balor, of the One Baleful Eye. I felt my face go red as the beast continued to rail against one and all.

My legs marched forward without my consent, and I stood before him, looking up at his baleful eye. He looked down, focused his eye on me and said,

'Wha the fek dy'a want ya little puke?'

'I'm Irish,' I said.

'Yer fekin' Irish are ya? You - worthless - English - gobshite!'

Involuntarily my left arm swung. I felt a crack on my knuckles and saw spit splash out of the side of his mouth. Time moved slowly, sounds distorted as the giant swayed like a tree cut at the base. He fell and landed with a tremendous crash on his back. I found myself straddling his immense bulk raising my fists to punch his face. He opened his eye in disbelief that someone had actually punched him and gnashed his teeth as if to bite my head off. Then, I felt two firm hands grab my shoulders.

Suddenly I was pulled away from the ogre, hurried through the kitchen of the club and hustled out the back door. I turned around as it slammed. Lucy was there with panic in her eyes and her chest heaving. A calm hand clasped shoulder and a soft American voice spoke to me. 'Boy, you sure are one crazy motherfucker. That was a close call. That guy's friends were just about to beat the shit out of you. There were six of them. I managed to pull you out before they could get you.' My rescuer was one of the American sailors.

The next day I glanced around to make sure that Balor wasn't out looking for me as we loaded our bags into the car, and we were soon safely on our way. Our driver dropped us in Strasbourg, and a few days later we took to the road to hitch hike to Toulouse.

'Are you sure we should try hitching again?' Lucy asked me doubtfully.

'France is a different country. We can give it a go. Maybe it'll be as easy as it was in Yugoslavia,' I said optimistically.

'We could have ended up in a Yugoslavian prison, that is a fantastic example, Eamon.' Lucy turned her back and bowed her head, her shoulders slumped.

'Don't worry baby, everything will turn out all right.'

Toulouse is within sight of the Pyrenees Mountains, which lie along France's southern border with Spain between the Mediterranean Sea and the Atlantic Ocean. After ten hours on the road, we arrived there.

In Athens, we had worked out the best way to find accommodation together. I sat in a bar with our bags, had a few drinks and relaxed while Lucy went off and comparison shopped for a room. This time she managed to find us a spot fairly easily. 'Okay,' she reported, 'there's a nice place around the corner for ten francs a night.' Ten francs equaled one pound, a fraction of the cost of hotels in Germany.

A few days later, Lucy found us a studio flat to rent for the longer term. It was an attic room with a small kitchen and bathroom a short bus ride from the centre of Toulouse. 'A perfect hideaway, Lucy, well done.'

Across the street from our flat was a boulangerie, a Monoprix supermarket, a horse butcher, and most importantly of all, a cave that dispensed wine from voluminous vats for six Francs a litre.

For a treat, we bought une baguette from the boulangerie, saucisson de Paris from Monoprix and wine from the cave. We lazed in the park on the banks of the Garonne sharing our picnic using my Swiss Army knife and the wrapping from the bread for a plate.

We calculated that we could eke out the money we had made working in Germany for several months, as long as we didn't take the bus, eat out or drink in bars.

I looked for work, but as I didn't speak French I couldn't even get an interview. In Munich, the factories were hungry for labourers and ready to hire guest workers from all over Europe. But no such labour market existed in Toulouse even though it was an industrial town with a munitions factory and a large aerospace industry.

I didn't find work, but we did find the munitions factory. It was about 100 metres from our studio flat. One morning, still lying in bed, we were woken by the sound of nearby machine guns.

tschoot – tschoot – tschoot – tschoot – tschoot – tschoot - tschoot

'That sounds like machine gun fire,' I said, startled.

'I guess it does, but how would you know?' Lucy asked.

'I used to be in the cadets.'

The largest bullet factory in Europe was across the street from us, and they tested their product regularly. They didn't want to be caught selling duds to their global customers.

By February 1981, we were nearly out of money. Lucy telephoned her folks, and they sent us a few hundred dollars. One morning the machine gun sound gently woke us up as usual. Lucy's visa had expired. We had no work and no money, our apartment was cozy, and Toulouse was beautiful, but we needed to move again.

'Lucy… shall we go to London? You can get a three month visa, I expect, and we should be able to find work there.'

'Maybe I should just go home,' she said.

'Do you want to go home?'

'No, I want to stay with you.'

'Really? Wow, it's still hard for me to believe … that you like me.'

'Of course I like you. Why do you think I'm here?'

'For the adventure, the travel and so you don't have to figure out what to do with your life.'

'Why are you here? Don't say it has nothing to do with the adventure and the travel. What do you want to do with your life?'

'I don't know Lucy. All I can do is move in a direction that seems right. I have no answers. I do know that I love you and I don't want our relationship to end.'

I called Gene and asked if we could stay at his place in Willesden for a while when we got to London. We took the train to Calais and the ferry across the English Channel.

An immigration official was on board sitting at a low table, and we stood in line, looking out the windows as the grey and white waves splashed the side of the ship to have our passports checked. The deep chug chug of the engine muffled the official's voice. The smell of diesel mixed with stale vomit pierced my nostrils. After ten months away he was my first glimpse of England.

He was disheveled, dressed in a grey, un-pressed, ill-fitting suit. His skin was pallid, and he had coaxed his thinning grey hair into a comb-over. The next in line presented his passport, and the official looked up at him furtively through close set eyes. He averted his gaze as soon as he confirmed that the face he was looking at resembled the one in the passport photograph. He seemed ashamed, apologetic and bitter. He reminded me of the science teacher at Chelsea school. He looked defeated.

'How long will you be staying Miss Morris?' He looked straight up at Lucy with menace in his eyes.

'How long can I stay?'

'Three months,' he grimaced, stamping her passport loudly and tossed it on the table for her to lean over and pick up.

He opened my passport. 'Humm, Irish eh, but not born in Ireland,' he said querulously. He looked me up and down as if he were trying to decide what to do with me. 'Why are you entering the United Kingdom?'

'Just visiting,' I replied.

16

The train arrived at Charing Cross Station, and we took the tube to Willesden Park, walked up Kilburn High Road to Glengalls Road. Gene opened the door. 'Come in, come in,' he said, and seemed pleased to see us.

Gene looked different. His black hair was much longer, not spiky, and his clothes were better quality - he looked almost, debonair. He took us into the kitchen, which hadn't changed since the last time I was there. The ceiling and walls, originally painted white, were stained yellow with cigarette smoke and grease from cooking. A single bare bulb covered in yellow grime and dust dangled from the ceiling, casting an odd yellow light. The room had one window that looked out into a small yard that backed onto another terraced house. It was bitterly cold outside and obviously just as cold in the kitchen as the inside of the window was covered in a layer of ice that made the view distorted and cloudy. The sky was grey, and the yellow light gave us a waxen, jaundiced look.

'It's great to be back in London,' I said. 'Your place is just the way I remember it, but you look different, Gene.'

'Yeah well, I have to look cooler at work nowadays, and Vincent is always on at me to smarten up.'

'Vincent?'

'Your brother, mate, we've been chasing girls together.'

I was astounded as I'd scarcely been aware that they knew each other. But apparently, after I had left London, they had been going to parties, gigs and night clubs together.

We talked for a while until Lucy complained, 'It's freezing in here.' Gene took us into the living room where his younger brother was lying on the floor in front of the little gas heater. This type of heater was common in London. It had been recessed into the opening for a fireplace. A small metal grate protected the gas flame, and it looked a bit like an old radio.

Underneath the grate, was a piece of orange plastic that was supposed to resemble a burning log. We sat on the floor and huddled as close to the flame as we could get. Our fronts cooked, but our backs stayed frozen, like camping in the woods. Yup, this was London all right. It was exactly the way it had been when I visited Albert when I was a teenager.

Willesden is just north of Kensington and Chelsea, only a mile or so from the Westway - a raised motorway that divides Kensington at Notting Hill from the suburbs to the north. Royston Gardens with its leafy elm trees and grand mansion blocks seemed a different city to me. Willeseden was like the Dickensian London of Oliver Twist updated to an Orwellian nightmare.

I wondered if I had made a terrible mistake. Gene said we could stay as long as we needed to, but we needed to find somewhere better than this to live. We would have to rent a flat on our own, but I didn't want to end up in some horrible suburb, miles from the centre of the city.

I had called my father from Paris, and he offered to lend me some money to tide me over, so the day after we arrived I took the tube to Shepherd's Bush to see him and the family at the shop. Many of the passengers were reading *The Sun* and their skin looked like melted grey candle wax. The family all seemed well, and Dad gave me some cash. 'What are you going to do now, Eamon?' he asked.

'Find some work and somewhere to live.' I neglected to mention that I had Lucy in tow.

We stayed with Gene for a couple of weeks while looking for work but had no immediate success. London was so cold, grey and miserable that already I longed to be back in elegant France. Gene's elder brother, Lachlan, owned a terraced house Notting Hill with an empty basement. 'It's pretty horrible, but you can probably rent it dirt cheap,' said Gene. 'Then Lucy and I had better go and have a look.' I said.

Notting Hill is in the north of The Royal Borough of Kensington and Chelsea, close to the north-western corner of Kensington Gardens and Kensington High Street. Ladbroke Grove straddles the hill from which Notting Hill takes its name starting at Holland Park, rising up over the top and following it down to Ladbroke Grove underground station beneath the Westway.

Lucy and I walked from the station up Ladbroke Grove to Blenheim Crescent and found number 17 near the corner of Portobello Road. The house was four stories high and the basement could be seen from street level down a short flight of steps fronted by a large bay window, with a separate entrance to one side tucked under the steps with the main entrance of the house above. I rang the door bell and soon heard a voice calling us. We looked up to see a man leaning out of the first floor window. 'Come on in, the door's not locked.'

As we entered, Lachlan rushed down the stairs into the front hall to meet us. With a smile, he led us down the back stairs to the basement. The paint and plaster were hanging off the walls of the hallway and, the damp smell was almost overwhelming. Lachlan opened a side door onto a large, empty room. Legs swished and clicked by the curtain-less bay window at street level. The only object in the room was an ancient looking gas cooker and just above it was a coin meter to pay for the gas.

'The rent is £25 a week, you can stay as long as you like,' said Lachlan.

'Perfect, we'll take it. When can we move in?'

'If you've got 25 quid you can move in now.'

I gave Lachlan the money. He gave us a key and left us to our dirty, filthy basement. Lucy and I hugged each other. It truly was perfect. After two weeks in Willesden, I realised that the only important consideration when looking for accommodation in London is location. We were back in the Royal Borough and as far as I was concerned that was the only place to live. It's true that the borough of Westminster includes Belgravia, Mayfair and Soho. But to me, Kensington and Chelsea felt like home.

Later that day Gene drove us back over to our new flat in the MG with our bags. Lachlan lent us a mattress and Gene bedclothes. The ancient cooker was labeled *The London.* It looked so old that I didn't think it could possibly work. I put 10p in the meter, and the money dropped out onto the floor as the collection box had been removed. I lit the burner, and it was warmer than the heater in Gene's place. We were all set, back in civilization.

The next day was Friday, market day. Portobello Market is one of London's most famous, known for its antique stalls, shops and arcades, second-hand clothing and fruit and vegetables. We walked up Portobello Road and rummaged around in the second hand furniture shops and bought a table, chairs, lamps and bookshelves. I ferried the bits and pieces back down 'Port-a-bella', as the locals pronounced it. Over the next couple of weeks, we purchased a rug, cooking utensils, a base for the bed and just about everything we needed to set up home.

I located the best place to buy beer on the day that we moved in. 'Thank you, thank you, thank you very nice,' said the check-out clerk at the supermarket around the corner that was run by a family of Pakistanis. There were so many corner shops like this in London that no matter who owned them, they were commonly known as 'paki shops'.

I waited in the queue clutching my six pack of Greenstein Bier cans. 'Thank you very nice,' he said to every customer in his grey shop keeper's coat and sporting a decidedly obvious toupee. In front of me was a guy, singing under his breath looking distracted, staring at his shoes and waving his head as he sang softly. After A few seconds, I realized that he was he was Joe Strummer from the band The Clash. They had just released a new album called *Sandinista* and the next day I went and bought a copy of it.

Lachlan was a journalist working for the Observer newspaper. He lived in the upper two floors of the house with his wife and two kids. He seemed wilder than Gene. Despite the crazy times we had spent together, I still thought of Gene as the stable, methodical technician who had been my boss at the ICA. Lachlan, however, was always laughing out loud or under his breath with a maniacal look in his eye. A journalist of some standing and seniority, he didn't have to go to the office often, and most days he worked at home, researching or writing.

We always knew when he did have to go to work as we would hear thumps, crashes, feet running up and down stairs until eventually, Lachlan emerged from the front door of the house. I had set up a breakfast table in our bay window, and we could see him leave wearing a suit and tie with his hair neatly combed, the maniacal grin gone from his face and looking stern.

When he returned in the evening his tie was crooked and his hair dishevelled. I assumed that he had stopped in for a few pints at the Mucky Duck or some other Fleet Street pub on his way home.

Portobello Road runs from Pembridge Villas near Notting Hill Gate tube station, down the hill towards the Westway in the North. The antique shops are located along the section closest to Pembridge Villas, with several antique arcades housed in a cavernous building filled with many small stalls. Portobello Road is lined with antique stalls on Saturdays. Moving down the hill you come to the fruit and vegetable section of the market and, continuing along the road, you reach the Westway. Underneath the raised motorway were second hand clothes, household goods and bric-a-brac stalls with second hand furniture and junk stalls up the hill past the Westway.

During the week, the street was empty of stalls and most of the used goods shops were closed. Several shops selling scarves and hippie style clothes from India, Afghanistan and Pakistan, such as Hindu Bazaar, did stay open, but the atmosphere mid-week was quite different to market days when the whole area came to life. The pubs were open every day, of course, including our local, The Duke of Wellington, on the corner of Portobello and Elgin Crescent.

Most of the fruit and veg sellers were white and a tribe in their own right, belonging to families that had been selling produce on Portobello Road for generations. There were also a few West Indian stall holders that sold yams, sweet potatoes, gourds, squashes, plantains and other Caribbean produce the white locals referred to as 'that food'.

We arrived in winter when large piles of Brussels sprouts, turnips, apples and citrus fruit on sale and at the end of the day bargains could be found. The sellers shouted out their prices, 'Here y'ar, sprouts 10p a pound, 10p a pound sprouts.'

When the spring and summer came, a far wider variety of produce was available.

'Five-for-fifty peaches! Peaches five for 50p.'

Next door to the supermarket was The Electric, a repertory cinema similar to the Paris Pullman or ICA. 'Look, Lucy! They're showing *Pink Flamingos* next week. I have to take you to see that one.'

'I hope it's better that the last movie you took me to see.'

'What, *Sebastiane* ? That's an excellent movie,' I protested. Soon, Lucy and I felt as if we had found a new home 'down the Bella'.

Notting Hill had a large, Afro-Caribbean population, and West Indian youths roamed the streets, bouncing up and down Ladbroke Grove wearing their abundant hair under large, colourful hats. Near the tube station where the Westway crosses Ladbroke Grove, several West Indian music shops were tucked in under the concrete supports. One had a sign

DUB VENDOR

Dub is a variation of Reggae music made by taking an existing track and pushing up the strength of the bass and drums and over dubbing it, adding echo, reverb and distortion. Live DJs mixed and intertwined different records so that every time you heard a dub it was different. Dub was everywhere, heavy and dark, it was not about sweet love, but resistance, standing up for your rights.

The Dub Vendor had large speakers facing out onto the street. Walking past the shop my body vibrated as the loud, heavy bass and drum sound waves struck me. I could feel the sound before I heard it. The vibration grew stronger, and the sound got louder and louder until in front of the speakers, I was nearly blown off my feet.

… **DUM dum dum dum, dum dum dum DUM!**
MURDAH !!!! DAH – DAH - DAH – DAH - DAH - DAH - DAH …

Lucy found a job working in the Hindu Bazaar on Portobello where the owner was actually Turkish. She was paid in cash, no questions asked, which was just as well because she only had a tourist visa and was not supposed to work. Her visa was due to expire at the end of May, and we didn't know whether she would be able to get an extension or not. The money Lucy brought home was enough to pay the rent and buy vegetables for us and beer for me.

'How was work today Lucy?'

'I just mind the shop all day, and occasionally someone comes in. But most of the time, after looking at something they say, 'I think I'll just leave it,' and walk out.'

I was unable to find any work at all. Since Margaret Thatcher and the Conservative Party had come into government the economy had collapsed, and unemployment was rapidly increasing. When Thatcher became Prime Minister in mid 1979, 1 million people were unemployed in Britain. By early 1981, the number had passed 2.5 million. Factories, shipyards, entire industries had closed down, and the country was desperate.

I asked my Mum how business at was at the shop. She said, 'Business is growing all the time. I think, because no one can afford to eat out or go drinking much anymore, they need to buy more basic food to eat at home. Baked beans and all the cheap foods are selling well.'

'Lucy, do you mind that you're the only one working?'

'No, but I worry about you just hanging around all day. I think you have to find something to do.'

Meandering through the market underneath the Westway, I asked a stallholder who was selling bric-a-brac, 'Where do you get your goods from, if you don't mind my asking?'

'Look in the *Evening Standard*. They have classified ads for wholesale auctions of household items and bric-a-brac,' she said.

I asked the man who collected the stall rental money how much the fee was. 'It costs five pounds on Friday and seven pounds fifty on Saturday. You have to be here at 7am, and you can have any one of the empty stalls that aren't taken by regulars, all right mate?'

I had to find some form of employment, so I decided to set up a market stall of my own. On a Wednesday morning I went along to an auction in Lots Road Chelsea, just off the King's Road a few doors away from the Country Cousins. Lot number 29 had silver plate, ceramics and other assorted bits and pieces that I thought I could sell.

The auctioneer shouted, 'Lot 29, assorted bric-a-brac. You have all had a chance to look through it. Will someone give me an opening bid of twenty pounds? No, how about ten pounds? Five pounds anybody?' Someone waved their finger and the auction was on.

At the end of the day, I was the proud owner of four boxes of junk for which I had paid £20. I had to take a taxi back to Blenheim Crescent, as I didn't have a car, costing me another £3.50. Back home I sorted through my acquisitions. I had purchased a set of silver plate spoons from the 1930s, various tea cups and saucers, other strange items from someone's house and a box of early 20th century postcards.

On Friday morning, I carried my goods down to the Westway and grabbed a folded up trestle table from a stack. The stall sites were marked out and numbered on the asphalt with white paint and measured about 10ft by 6 ft. Numerous, regular stall holders occupying multiple sites were already in the process of erecting their table, racks and other display materials. I planted my self in an empty site and looked around, but no one seemed to mind the place that I had chosen. After setting up my table and laying out my wares, I was in business. On the first Friday, I grossed £8.50, which covered the taxi fare and stall rental. However, I was happy that I had sold something, and I still had most of my stock, so I hadn't lost anything.

On Saturday, the market was filled with regular stall holders, and I was unable to get a site. A stall holder suggested I try the market at Swiss Cottage. 'There's a market at Camden on Sundays as well,' he advised me. Soon I had a routine of buying goods at auctions during the week and setting up stalls at Portobello on Friday, Swiss Cottage on Saturday and Camden Lock on Sunday.

Our basement was becoming quite comfortable, and now that it was occupied and heated the damp smell began to fade. However, it soon filled up with boxes of junk that I hoped to sell at the market. 'What's this?' Lucy asked as she held up a silver-coloured metal cylinder. 'It's a spittoon darling.' Actually, I had no idea what it was.

I bought a long bar and two bar stools that we positioned by the stove, effectively dividing the room into a kitchen and a bedroom area. The bar had shelves at the back on the kitchen side and was faced with bamboo at the front. I would sit on a barstool on the bamboo side while Lucy cooked dinner at the stove. I put posters on the walls, and we had our books, photographs and a coffee table. I bought a TV and had a telephone line installed. In one of the auction lots I even found a long string of multi-coloured fairy lights and hung them around the bay window, making it look like Christmas. I bought a cheap stereo system in Tottenham Court Road, and we listened to *Sandinista* every evening.

We also tuned into a weekly radio show called *City Beats*. The DJ Charlie Gillett played music from all over the world especially African music from Zaire, Tanzania and Zimbabwe.

The neighbourhood was lively and friendly, but we soon noticed a menacing presence. Numbers of police frequently gathered on the streets, often in groups of six or more and never standing still but marching around quickly, eyes darting left and right, their fingers twitching on their radios. The Thatcher government had encouraged the police to use a nineteenth century vagrancy law, known as 'sus', to stop and search people based only on a 'reasonable suspicion' that an offence had been or *might be* committed.

As I was leaving the basement one day Lachlan was going in the front door just as a troop of police marched past the house. 'Why do you think there are so many cops around here Lachlan?' I asked.

'They're the SPG, Special Patrol Group. They send them to trouble spots.'

'Is this a trouble spot?'

'No it isn't Eamon, but they think it must be because of all the West Indians around here.'

Sitting on the edge of my market table, I read in *The Times* that the Metropolitan Police had just begun Operation Swamp 81, a London-wide campaign of street searches. The following week I read that in Brixton, across the Thames on the south side, the police had searched 943 people and arrested 118 West Indian youths over the previous six days.

The SPG searched dozens of West Indians in Notting Hill as well. As I walked around the neighbourhood, I came across groups of policemen holding young blacks guys spread eagled against walls, searching them roughly.

That night I cautioned, 'Lucy be careful outside, there are loads of cops around.'

'I don't think we need to worry. I never see them stopping any white people,' she said.

I felt trepidatious as I bought the newspaper the next morning. What horror will I read about next I wondered. The headline read

BOBBY SANDS ELECTED TO PARLIAMENT

In Northern Ireland, another part of the United Kingdom, inmates of the Maze prison had been on hunger strike. On 9th April one of them, Bobby Sands, who claimed to be a political prisoner, was elected to sit in the British Parliament as the member for the constituency of South Tyrone.

Lucy and I tried to ignore the turmoil, but it soon became impossible to escape the growing sense of unease in the country. The atmosphere on the streets was electric, as if revolution was in the air.

On the evening of 10 April, a black youth, who had been stabbed on Atlantic Road in Brixton, was surrounded by police. Reports said that a crowd gathered, and as the police didn't appear to be calling for medical help for the victim, the crowd intervened. A struggle with the police erupted, more police poured in and a riot ensued.

On Saturday 11 April, 279 policemen and 45 other people were injured. Over 100 cars, including 56 police vehicles, were set on fire. Hundreds of buildings were damaged and many burned. The BBC news said that that up to 5,000 people were involved in the riot.

I spent the day working at Swiss Cottage market, and Lucy was at work in the shop on Portobello. We knew nothing about the riots until Gene called in the evening. 'Have you seen the news?' he asked. 'Switch the TV on. Maybe you should stay indoors tonight.'

The next day we poked our noses out onto the street. It seemed calm enough. On Sundays, Lucy worked with me at Camden market, and we took the number 31 bus together carrying two suitcases and a couple of boxes of goods to sell. As we walked to the bus stop, shop owners with sheets of plywood emerged to nail over their windows. 'Why are you boarding up the shop?' I asked.

'The riots are going to spread all over London, mate.' He shook his head and continued banging in nails.

Over the next few weeks, an uneasy calm prevailed. Some shops boarded up completely for a few days and then reopened, while others boarded over their windows but kept the front door open to continue trading. Many businesses just stayed open as usual, but the staff were on edge and seemed to be nervously watching everyone who passed by.

Lachlan lamented to me one day, his mischievous smile turned to a frown, 'The police are trying their hardest to provoke trouble. This neighbourhood has always been cool, no problems. Now these bastards are storming around trying to conjure up a riot. Instead of walking on their backs, the police should leave them alone, or they'll get a war alright.'

One day I was flicking through the stacks of records in the Dub Vendor. The Rasta who ran the shop was sitting on a stool behind a high counter top with his arms folded in front of him. He wore a large pair of dark sunglasses and a floppy woollen hat with yellow, green and red stripes, his dreadlocks stuffed inside. I tipped my head back to look up at him, and asked, 'What do you think of all these police and thieves in the streets?'

'Man, y'ave to treat us right. I an' I are here to *stay* inna Inglan.'

He put on a record, called *All Wi Doin is Defendin'*. It wailed about an impending war in London caused by police oppression

… All oppression can do is bring
Passion to the heights of eruption
Sounds of fire will sing
You did sound the siren of war
WAR, WAR, WAR!
Special Patrol Group fall …
… all wi doin is defendin' ...

'WOW, who is that?' I asked.

'Ea-mon, that was Linton Kwesi Johnson,' the Dub Vendor nodded his head knowingly. He put the record on again, and I listened in silence.

In early may, again sitting on the edge of my market table, I read that Bobby Sands had died of starvation in prison.

Buried on page 20 of the newspaper I came across a small paragraph at the bottom of the page. 'Sus' had been the subject of a Royal Commission which concluded that it was

... applied disproportionately against West Indians, and caused widespread resentment ...

Actually, the majority of the young black men the police targeted were not from the West Indies but were born in England, their parents having emigrated in the '50s and '60s.

In the evenings, Lucy and I wandered around the neighbourhood and dropped in for a drink at a few of the many local pubs. The Elgin was on the corner of Westbourne Park Road and Ladbroke Grove. It was usually full of shaggy hippies and assorted freaks, but just four blocks away in All Saints Road, the heart of the Afro-Caribbean community, the scene was totally different.

All Saints was always a bit intimidating, and few white people dared to walk down it. Restaurants specialising in fry fish and akee lined the short street and the paki shop sold Red Stripe beer, the West Indian's favored beverage. Outside, the Apollo pub on the corner of Tavistock Road, several tough looking guys were usually hanging around. But no one ever bothered Lucy and me as we walked past.

Nevertheless, the young West Indians there did look hard, or tough. They reminded me of the kids at Chelsea School, and I met two old school mates there, Eric and Derek, who were identical twins. They were both well over six feet tall and hard as nails, but Derek had always been friendly to me. When he saw me, his steely stare was gone in an instant and his face lit up with a big smile 'Ea-mon man what ya doin' in All Saints Road? Come, ya' hav' a hav' a drink in the Apollo.' He shouted at the barman, 'Two Red Stripes man!'

For all the toughness and cold, hard stares, the looks and behaviour of the West Indians were mostly just fashion and posturing. The young guys wanted to look cool, unruffled and in control. They looked mysterious in dark glasses, so they wore them. They looked happy and friendly when they smiled, so they didn't smile - that didn't look cool. They tried to look nonchalant with the corners of their mouths drooping like toughened fighters, but most of them weren't.

Not surprisingly many white people felt threatened by this macho aesthetic - it was different and unfathomable to them. Most people seemed to be afraid of punks and West Indians, and hippies were scared of everyone - hippies were not tough. The various tribes mixed at the edges intermingling in some ways but remaining separate in others. The Apollo was for West Indians, the Elgin for hippies, the Duke of Wellington for assorted locals and the Sun in Splendour at the Notting Hill Gate end of Portobello was for the gentle folk of Kensington.

Lucy and I carried on in our own little reverie although we didn't have enough money. After a few weeks, I began to make a small profit at the markets, but I soon realized that I lacked the essential ingredients needed for success down Port-a-bella. I didn't have any business sense or even a vague idea what people actually wanted to buy.

Mondays and Tuesdays were our days off, and we usually woke up late. One grey day I suggested, 'Lucy, let's go to Maison Bouquillon for breakfast.'

Maison Bouquillon was a French café in Bayswater, the next suburb on the way into the West End. We walked the short distance past Powis Square, up Westbourne Grove and into Moscow Road to the café and ordered, 'Deux expresses et deux croissants.'

Gazing out the windows at the passers by as romantic French music played in the background we pretended to read Le Monde and sipped our coffees. 'On continue?' Lucy suggested and we left our little bit of France to head back out into London.

At the top of Queensway, we crossed Bayswater Road into Kensington Gardens and wandered arm in arm along the shore of the Round Pond. Enthusiasts sent their radio controlled sailboats skimming across the water. Some of the boats were quite large, and the owners talked for ages about what they were made of and which class of boat they were. We pulled ourselves away and strolled through the gardens of Kensington Palace past the statue of William of Orange.

I enjoyed being Lucy's tour guide. It was as if she had parachuted into London. I could tell her anything, and she would say, 'How interesting.' In return, Lucy liked to tell me about living in the U.S.A. and its culture.

'On the last Thursday in November we have a celebration meal called Thanksgiving. We cook a turkey and pumpkin pie.'

'How do you make pumpkin pie?'

'It's an open custard pie with mashed pumpkins, milk, eggs, brown sugar and lots of ginger, cinnamon, nutmeg and cloves.'

'Hmmm, that sounds delicious. Maybe we should have a Thanksgiving dinner.'

Our walk continued through Kensington Gardens past the Peter Pan Statue and along the bank of the lake to the Serpentine Gallery where we held hands and cocked our heads at the strange modernist paintings and sculptures. 'Do you like this one Lucy?'

'Yes, it reminds me of a Kandinsky painting.'

From the gallery, we carried on past the Bowling Greens to the Albert Memorial and sat on Queen Victoria's monument to her beloved Prince.

'Let's have lunch at the Chelsea Pot,' I suggested. Our route took us past the museums, down Old Brompton Road and Royston Gardens to the King's Road and the Chelsea Pot where we had enjoyed our first meal together. Then we caught the number 31 bus at World's End, looking down on the streets as the red double-decker made its way slowly along until we jumped off at Notting Hill Gate and walked home down Portobello.

From our bed as we dozed in each other's arms, we watched the legs of passers by as the grey afternoon turned into darkness. After Lucy had cooked our evening meal we went to the Prince of Wales at the top of Ladbroke Grove, and I drank soapy Young's Special bitter. Just before 11pm the barman shouted at everyone, 'Finish your drinks. It's closing time now - go home!'

So, another perfect day ended down Portobello, with Lucy, my Kentucky Rose.

One day, I called Gwyneth, and we arranged to meet for a drink at the Magpie and Stump on the King's Road at World's End.

'Gwyneth, how are you?'

'I'm fine. How's married life treating you, Eamon?'

'Er, we're not married, just living together.'

'Oh well, you're sensible, I suppose. You never know how long relationships are going to last.'

'Good point I guess, although I'm not thinking of it like that.'

'Have you heard about Amanda?'

A feeling of dread overcame me and I could only mutter the words, 'Amanda, what about her?'

'She's in Munich.'

'You're kidding?

'She got a job working in a theatre there.'

'Are you in contact with her?'

'Yes, I spoke to her on the phone last night.'

A desire to talk to Amanda welled up in me. I had managed to put her out of my mind since the last time I had seen Gwyneth, and now, once again, the sensual feeling of being close to Amanda enveloped me like a fog.

'Can you give me her telephone number?'

'She doesn't want to talk to you Eamon.'

'Why not, and how do you know she doesn't want to talk to me anyway?'

'You were always so selfish Eamon. It was never about her, always about you - what you wanted. That's why you lost her. You need to grow up Eamon. You're such a silly boy.'

I was shocked by the way Gwyneth spoke to me. Was I genuinely that selfish with Amanda? I had thought that she was the one who was mean to me. I had spent the last two years reassuring myself that it wasn't my fault, that I was the victim, the one with reason to feel abused. Now Gwyneth was saying it was all down to me? Perhaps for the first time in my life I felt a terrible pang of guilt and disgust at myself.

Gwyneth changed the subject back to Lucy and asked, 'Do you feel committed to Lucy? I mean, do you think you'll get married?'

'I love her, that's all I know. Maybe the time will seem right someday. I don't want to be rushed or forced into a thing like that.'

'What does Lucy think about the idea of marriage?'

'I haven't asked her.'

'What about your parents?'

'My father said he realised that I was 'shacked up' with someone. All Lucy and I know is that we're in love and want to stay together - full stop. That is all there is to it. Our parents are from a different generation, from a different world. In their world people married and then hopefully fell in love. We're content simply to be together - at least I am. I guess I should ask Lucy what she thinks ...'

'I'm sorry Eamon, but it sounds like a bit of a cop out, oh we're from a different world...'

'Yeah, perhaps you're right, but I can't stand the hypocrisy, the false morality of old ideas about marriage. All I can do is follow my heart.'

'Perhaps you are no less a hypocrite, following false moralities too?'

'Without a doubt I am - mea maxima culpa.'

'Ah, religion, you were brought up a Catholic weren't you?'

'Yes, I think I still am one.'

'Don't you have to adhere to certain precepts, such as marriage?'

'Humm, it just seems to me that the essential thing is to try and follow your own conscience and do what you believe to be right.'

'Good luck trying Eamon. Are you going to call Amanda?'

'I thought you said she didn't want to speak to me?'

'You never know. She's still unattached.'

'So, are you going to give her number to me?'

Gwyneth put on her thoughtful, motherly, quizzical look, 'No, I had better not. We'll see when she gets back to London.'

I took the bus home to Notting Hill agitated. I wished Gwyneth hadn't introduced the tantalizing prospect of meeting Amanda again to me. When I walked into the basement, Lucy cocked her head and gave me her broad, knowing smile. But, now, I felt different inside as if I had a guilty secret to conceal.

17

Gene called one evening not long after Lucy and I moved into our basement, 'Eamon, I'm going over to Vincent's place tonight. We're going to have a few drinks there and then go out to a nightclub. Why don't you guys come along? I'll drive.'

I felt as if Vincent and I had become strangers, and I was looking forward to seeing my elder brother again. As I'd left for Amsterdam soon after he returned from Vietnam with his mojo, I hadn't seen him for nearly a year. While Lucy and I were in Greece the Royston Gardens flat was finally sold, and he had moved into a rented room in a large house on a square in Belgravia.

While we waited for Gene I thought back to the way Vincent was when he finished school and left the Oratory. After the summer holidays, he started university where he studied law. It was a difficult course and perhaps that was why during those years he was so intense and serious. He always seemed to have his head down reading or writing copious pages of tight, neat script. He studied all the time, apart from an hour or two in the evenings when he let his hair down and played guitar.

As he progressed through university I started spending less and less time at home and more time with my friends and then with Amanda. Vincent and I drifted apart, and as we didn't move in the same circles we rarely even talked to each other. When he finally got his degree the relief showed on his face, his shoulders relaxed, and he seemed to look around and see the world as if he had been away for a long time.

After graduating he made no attempt to start a career in law. Instead, he got a corporate job in Victoria, and before we knew it, he was in business - a man about town. He strode into the flat wearing perfectly pressed suits, expensive shirts with French cuffs and elaborate neckties.

Mother did his laundry and always seemed to be ironing his shirts with their long double cuffs. 'Ma I need a blue shirt for tomorrow because I wore a white one today,' he commanded as he passed the kitchen and slammed the door of his room shut. The Hiwatt Amp clicked on and he started singing.

'... Mary's dress waves, like a vision she dances
across the floor as the radio plays
Roy Orbison singin' for the lonely …'

Lucy and I pottered around in the basement until we heard the unmistakable exhaust note of the MG gurgling up Blenheim Crescent and the masculine beep of the horn. The two of us rushed up the stairs, squeezed into the front seat of the MG and vroom, we were off.

Gene parked across the street from Vincent's house, led the way up to the front door and rang the bell. An attractive young woman opened the door. 'Oh Gene, how wonderful to see you. We're all in Vincent's room, do come in.' We followed her up a large staircase.

'Nice house,' I said.

'Oh ya, it's on four levels. This is my room,' the girl said pointing to a door on the first floor as we clambered up the stairs.

'Are there many people living here?'

'I think there are ten rooms, and they're all occupied. You can ask Adrian, he owns the house and he's with Vincent.'

As we reached the top floor the girl flung open the door of a room where Vincent was standing with a chap who had a moustache twirled into points at each end and a pointy beard.

'Vinnie!'

'Eamon, you look so well and so does...'

'Lucy, yes, you did meet her at the old flat.'

'This is my landlord.' Vincent indicated the mustached fellow beside him.

'Hello, delighted to meet you,' he grinned with a knowing twinkle in his eye and the points of his 'tache sprang upwards.

POP

'Champagne, everyone fill your glasses!' said Vincent opening a chilled bottle of Moët.

POP POP POP

'Champagne!' we all cheered.

The door to Vincent's room was left open, and young women drawn by the sound of popping corks came running down the hallway and up the stairs. We all jostled elbow to elbow slurping champagne and Vincent put some music on. Junior Walker screeched out

... I said, SHOTGU-U-U-N shoot em for he runs now
Do the jerk baby, do the jerk now, HEY!...

Vincent jumped on the double bed and started dancing. Several of the girls and Gene joined him. His landlord stood laughing at them with a bottle of champagne in one hand and a glass in the other. He waved his arms in the air and with his big grin and pointy moustache he looked like the ring master in a circus. More people poured into the room, and everyone danced. When Junior Walker finished Adrian put on James Brown

... Say it loud, I'm-black-an-I'm-proud ...

Lucy and I were nudged into the corner of the room from where we watched the mad scene. Vincent, Gene and several girls were bouncing up and down on the bed their heads nearly touching the ceiling while a dozen more people danced around them.

POP POP POP

After a while Vincent shouted above the din, 'Come on everyone, let's go to the Alibi!'

'Yeah!' everyone shouted and we all ran down the stairs. Outside on the street, Adrian hailed a taxi then another and another.

Soon we were in a convoy of taxis chooglin' through Belgravia. 'Where are we going, Gene?' I asked.

'We're going to the Alibi. It's a club on the King's Road near Sloane Square.'

The taxis pulled up outside, and our troupe breezed up the steps to the club with Vincent and Adrian in the lead. Vincent said to the door clerk, 'All these people are with me,' and waved his hand backwards at the long train of people on the stairway. 'Let them all in.'

We crowded into the small club, lined with floor to ceiling mirrors. Multicolored lights flashed from under the dancer's feet, and a large mirrored disco ball hung from the ceiling sparkling light in all directions. Vincent ordered drinks from the bar, 'Champagne for everyone.'

POP POP POP

Champagne flowed, and the young women skittered around the dance floor as Vincent and Gene danced first with one girl, then with a flourish changed to a different girl. They looked like debonair rock stars surrounded by their adoring entourage. Yes, the Debonairs, that's who they are I thought.

After a couple of hours, Vincent emerged from the dance floor and said, 'We're going over to a friend's house in Chelsea, come along.'

Leaving most of the group we had arrived with behind, Gene, Vincent, two girls, Lucy and I walked a short distance down the King's Road. We turned into a narrow side street and, a few doors along Vincent stopped and knocked on the door of a mews house. His friend Tim, a photographer he had met on his trip to Vietnam, ushered us in. After more popping of champagne corks Vincent announced, 'He is one of the most famous Vietnam War photographers - he was mentioned in dispatches.'

Lucy found the kitchen and went to make herself a cup of tea. Tim spoke excitedly to Vincent. '...Oh, you know what I mean? I mean those guys, like wow, what were they on eh? Too bloody amazing pictures all over everywhere. Kaboom crash, know what I mean? I said hey, when are you going to, you know, it's just too much, is it? To ask I mean, up the gonzers eh what? You should see those guys.... Hey wait a minute, something's cooking,' and he rushed off into the kitchen.

'What the hell was he talking about? I asked.

'Never mind, he always psycho-babbles like that,' said Vincent.

We heard a screech coming from the kitchen and rushed in to see that Lucy, not realizing that the kettle was electric, had put it on a gas burner on the stove. Its plastic base now covered the stove top like molten lava.

The party continued on, and before long everyone was psycho-babbling. 'I'm tired, let's go,' pleaded Lucy. We snuck out the front door unnoticed while the others were talking in tongues, and caught a taxi home.

The next day we awoke late. Boy, those guys have so much energy they're like whirlwinds I thought. I could see why Gene liked hanging around with my brother. He was far more likely to meet girls with Vincent than he ever was with me. Now Vinnie and I were back in the same circle after diverging for a few years. It was as if, thanks to Gene, I had just made a new friend and he was my brother, Vinnie.

At least the two of us were in one of the circles that were spinning around me. In another circle were my parents and little sisters. Dad invited me out for a drink one evening. We met at a pub near the shop and sat at a table with pints of beer while a small Irish band played in the corner. The singer was a tenor crooning popular show band tunes.

'... I'm off to Lisdoonvarna at the end of the year
I'm up for a bit of craic, the women and the beer!
I'm awful frisky for a man of fifty,
Catch me if you can, me name is Dan, sure I'm yer man!'

When the band finished their set Dad asked me, 'So what are you going to do now Eamon?'

'I don't know. Why does everyone ask me that? Do I always have to have a plan?'

'Life is a dynamic place Eamon, you can't just sit still. You're young and you can't just let life pass you by. You do have to do something.'

'All right, I guess so. I'm trying to make a go of the markets.'

'That's good, I suppose. I could give you a job at the shop if you like. It would be a big help to the family you know.'

'Dad, I realize that I've been remiss, absent, neglectful.'

'That's okay. I've always let you have your head, and I've never told you what to do. Except go to Mass, of course. You do go to Mass, don't you?'

'I go now and then. I like to, I just don't have the time.'

'You should always make time. After all, it's just one hour a week. Just do it, don't think about it, just always go to Mass on Sunday. You'll see in the long run it'll bear fruit for you.'

'Yeah well, I don't think I'm a Catholic any more.'

'Don't say such a thing! Always remember that your ancestors paid for their faith in blood. In blood, do you understand? Don't fritter your faith away. That would be a terrible thing.'

'What am I supposed to do, pretend I believe in something?'

'Not at all, but you do believe Eamon, don't you? It's easy to be swayed off course. Please believe me, it's easy for a man to go down the wrong path in this life. You must be true to your beliefs and your heritage. Each and every one of us have been saved. That's right, all our descendants until the end of time, Jesus promised us that. Don't turn your back on what you know to be true.'

'To be a Catholic don't I have to be good? I mean, I'm living with someone.'

'Sure everyone makes mistakes. That's why it's important to go to mass so that you're at least acknowledging that you are on the wrong track and trying to put things right. Of course, you can't go to communion because you're not in a state of grace.'

'I'm in love. It feels graceful.'

'Well perhaps you just feel lust. If you loved her I guess you'd have thought of marriage by now.'

'Marriage? Not now… I don't feel ready.'

'You may never feel ready, but that doesn't mean that you aren't.'

'I don't feel secure or sure of anything. All my life our family has been on the move. We've never settled anywhere. Besides, I only just left home. I have no real job or prospects. I can't think about marriage, settling down and getting stuck in one place. I don't feel that I'm home yet.'

'You know, Eamon, that's the whole point of marriage, to create a home. It's not about the house you live in. You're a young man, so you need to think about your future. You've always had a good head. I'm sure that you'll do the right thing.'

'I'm just not ready to be told what to believe or do.'

'Well, I'm a believer - I believe. God is good, and if you ask he will help you. So pray to him and ask for help. Jesus said, "Ask and it will be given to you, seek and you will find, knock and it shall be opened unto you."'

'Well anyway, I think I'm more of a Hindu.'

'Don't be crazy, you were brought up a Christian. All your ancestors were Christians.'

'All religions are the same,' I said as a challenge.

'No, they're not!' Dad said, rolling his eyes upwards.

'I mean that they're all trying to achieve the same thing - union with God.'

'Well yes, but you can't achieve union with God. Only God can grant you that blessing, you can't achieve it.'

'Buddhists think you can achieve it. That's the whole point, to achieve Godhead in this life... or the next one or something.'

'Just follow your own path and not someone else's. Pray and go to Mass then you won't go far wrong.'

'You're right. I need to follow my own path. If only I could find it.'

'Seek and you will find.'

As I walked back up to Shepherd's Bush, I was in turmoil. What the bloody hell am I seeking? I didn't know, but I was sure that I hadn't found it yet.

I felt as if I had grown up and changed a lot since I'd met Lucy. If I had gone to university everyone would have left me alone. I would have only recently graduated, and no one would be expecting me to have done anything remarkable as yet. But as I didn't, it seemed that I had been out in the 'real world' for a long time and that by now I should have 'settled down'.

I thought, I don't know if I ever want to settle down, to be finished, like a portrait '... that's Eamon, let's put him up there over the mantle. Now he's finished we can forget about him, thank God.'

I remembered the beautiful woman by the river in Bern, and Olaf in Amsterdam. I didn't know exactly where, but I felt I was getting somewhere with my life.

Time slipped by until late May when Lucy's visa was about to expire. 'Lucy you better apply to get your visa extended.'

She called the Home Office and asked if she could renew her visa. They said it was possible for her to get a six month extension, and posted her an application form. The main requirement was that she should provide evidence of enough funds to support herself for the duration of her visit. However, after nine months as a tourist, it was clear that a further extension would become more difficult. After all, how many pubs and B&Bs could someone endure?

'Eamon, I don't have enough money to show that I can live without needing to work here.'

'We could get married. I mean, then you can get a residents visa.'

'Oh, just like that, how romantic Eamon. Thanks for the offer but no.'

'No? Why not, don't you love me?'

'Yes I love you, but we never said this was going to be forever did we?'

'I never thought to ask what you about marriage, but I didn't think that meant we would ever split up.'

'Eamon I don't want to get married anyway.'

'Never?'

'I don't know. We don't seem settled together. It's like we're on holiday all the time. I feel as if you could pack up and leave any day.'

'I make you feel that insecure?'

'I feel as though I'm a passenger. You're driving, but you don't know where you're going.'

'I guess you're right, I don't know where I'm going, but that's life isn't it? Who can say where they're heading? It's only a guess, or a desire. No one actually knows where they're going to end up.'

'No, things always turn out different to the way people expect. But it's disconcerting not even having a plan.'

'We have a plan, to stick together and see what we can do together.'

'That's not enough any more. I'm going to have to leave London. They're going to throw me out.'

'We could hit the road again.'

Lucy sighed and shook her head. 'I'm tired of travelling now. I want to be somewhere.'

'The marriage idea would work you know.'

'Eamon, I'm not just going to get married for an idea that will fool the authorities. I don't mind. I never wanted a conventional life. I don't want anyone else's name. I want to be me, Lucy, but at the moment I feel as lost as you do. If you wanted to marry me you wouldn't suggest it as a workable idea. Who do you think I am? You're supposed to win me over, carry me away in your arms.'

'Why can't we just be together and live wherever we want to? I can live in Europe, but not America and you can live in America, but not Europe - to hell with these stupid immigration rules,' I exclaimed.

We borrowed money from our parents, Bernie and Gene. We put the money in Lucy's bank account and asked for a printed statement for the immigration department, then paid everyone back.

Lucy took the train to the Home Office immigration centre at Lunar House in Croydon. She queued for hours and got her visa extended until early December.

18

Flicking through the classified section of the *Evening Standard* one evening I saw an ad for part time carpet cleaners. I wasn't making anywhere near enough money from the markets so I called the company, and they suggested I try it for a few days. No interview was necessary. My workmate was an Australian freelance photographer called Brendan. Like me he needed to supplement his income and worked part time cleaning carpets. It was hard work and I only managed three days before quitting, but Brendan and I became friends.

Brendan was a few years older than me in his mid twenties, tall and slender with short dark hair and piercing blue eyes. He lived with his Australian girlfriend in King's Cross, not far from Fleet Street where the newspapers were based. He was making a career as a news photographer, selling his pictures directly to the newspapers and to syndication agencies. He had recently returned from the Thailand-Cambodia border where he had photographed the conflict after the invading Vietnamese army had driven the Khmer Rouge to the Thai border.

He said, 'It was the most exciting thing I have ever experienced. You don't know how good it feels to have your face stuck in the mud until you hear the whip crack of bullets over your head. Your body just does things without asking you. One minute you're standing there and the next thing you know you're desperately trying to climb into the ground.' As he spoke his blue eyes twinkled in nostalgia at the happy memory. Brendan had a gentle Australian accent and he spoke in soft tones, which seemed at odds with his longing to be in the thick of the action, camera clicking.

He dressed in denim from head to toe and had rolls of film stuffed into the pockets of his tight fitting jacket. He usually carried three cameras around with a variety of lenses, and was hoping for a big story to photograph that he could sell to *The Sun*, front page, a big shock-horror picture that would be syndicated around the world. Then his reputation would be made, and his career assured. So when the riots started, Brendan became a civil war photographer.

After the Brixton riots in April an uneasy calm prevailed. Unemployment kept rising and the police forces around England kept harassing West Indians and arresting them on 'sus' charges. On 3 July police in the Toxteth district of Liverpool were searching people on the street. They arrested a boy, an angry crowd gathered, and a riot erupted.

As soon as he heard the news of the Toxteth riot, Brendan jumped on his motorcycle and rode up to Liverpool. 'Eamon, I can't make it for a drink tonight, I'm going up to Liverpool,' he said on the phone.

'Be careful mate,' I said in my best Aussie accent, 'they're a weird mob up there.' He didn't think I was Australian. I had been away from Sydney for twelve years and as far as he could tell I had a London accent.

The Toxteth Riots started on a Friday, and the next morning as I carted my goods to the bus stop to go to Swiss Cottage the shops on Portobello were boarding up. In the weeks after the events in Brixton the shopkeepers had taken their boarding down one by one but now were all rushing to put it back up again.

The Swiss Cottage market was almost deserted with few sellers and even fewer customers. I packed up at lunchtime, there's no point hanging around I thought. Portobello was chugging along as usual, and although by now, most of the shops had boarded up, they remained open. In the antique section the arcades were also open, but few stalls had been set up on the street. Scarves and Indian skirts had been pinned onto the boarding outside Hindu Bazaar, and the other shops had pushed their clothes racks out onto the pavement. The fruit sellers were shouting, 'Five for fifty, peaches' and 'Here y'ar, Kent cherries,' while music pounded out into the street from the Dub Vendor's shop.

As I walked in the door to the flat, the phone rang. 'What's happening down there?' Brendan asked.

'All quiet so far. What's going on up there?'

'A bloody riot mate, it's great! Look, I gotta go - they just set a police car on fire. I just don't want to miss anything in Notting Hill. It's bound to blow up, isn't it?' he asked.

'Crikey, I hope not. Are you trying to scare me?'

He said he would keep calling to check what was happening, and was prepared jump on his motor bike at a moment's notice to be back in London in a few hours. He was pretty sure that one of his photos would make the front page of the *News of the World.*

I called the shop to see how my folks were. 'Mum any sign of riots, have you boarded up the shop?'

'No, nothing is happening! Board up the shop, do you think we should?'

I could feel the tension rising in her voice. 'No, no, it's alright,' I said. 'It's just that the shops around here are boarding up again. I'm sure they're overreacting, but I'll pop around to see you this afternoon.'

'Okay, see you later.'

I imagined my mother nervously lighting a cigarette. I thought I would walk by Hindu Bazaar then go over to the shop and see how things were.

'Av'oes, ten for a paund, ten for a paund av'oes.' Portobello seemed its usual cheery self in the grey summer afternoon. People were stuffing over ripe avocados into their mouths, and a group of West Indian teenagers bounced past me laughing and beaming smiles.

'Lucy what's happening?'

'Happening?' said Lucy warily her eyebrows furrowed.

'I knocked off early and just came by to say hello. I'm going over to my folks shop now, so I'll see you tonight.' Lucy smiled her warm California smile and cocked her head to one side as she always did. We kissed, and I walked to Ladbroke Grove tube station past the Dub Vendor who waved and smiled at me, 'Wha's 'ap-nin' Ea-mon?'

I took the train four stops to Goldhawk Road Station. As I ran up the exit steps, I heard hammering and saws scraping. On the street, shop owners were busily putting up boarding. I hurried down to the junction with Ashley Road. The family's shop was in a double fronted, two-storey building with large, full length, glass windows on either side of the entrance. It was too big to be a corner store and was actually a small supermarket with four aisles. I shuddered as I looked at the vast area of glass without shutters or bars or any protection, just glass. The shop stood on a prominent corner visible from three directions, normally an excellent location, but now it looked so open and vulnerable.

'Hi Mum, where's Dad?'

'Out the back, Eamon.'

I smiled and rushed past her. 'Hi Dad, how are you? Are you worried about there riots? Can I help you board up the shop?'

'Not at all, I'm not going to board the place up - no one is going to loot us! Besides, I don't want to spend money on plywood and nails, and if our customers see the shop covered with boards they'll think we're closed, and that won't be good for business.'

'But, the whole country is about to erupt.'

'Look Eamon, we're made of sterner stuff than that. This place is too visible. If we board up, it will be like an invitation to rioters. They'll think we have something that's worth looting. I don't think anyone's going to be that interested in stealing eggs and ham. We have to make a statement that we don't believe that there will be any trouble around here. Why should there be?'

I was impressed by how cool-headed Dad was. Fear had gripped the nation, and the crisis was real. Millions of people were unemployed and desperate. Yet here was my father, cool as a cucumber with a smile on his face, an island of tranquility.

I stayed for dinner. My sisters were growing up, and they didn't run around squealing any more. Instead they lounged on the sofa looking self-absorbed and barely raised an eyebrow to say hello to me. When my mother asked my sister Katie to set the table she sighed, 'Do I have to?' and rolled her eyes. Even my youngest sister was now fourteen. I supposed it was only natural for them to act like sullen teenagers.

We switched on the TV and watched the news. The riot at Toxteth looked horrible. Police charged crowds of black youths, cars were burning, and bottles were hurled at the police. Thatcher intoned her admonitions and I felt sick. 'Turn that crap off', I snapped.

After dinner I took the bus back to Notting Hill Gate. From the front seat of the top deck I looked down on the streets. It was mid-summer and sunlight was glowing softly on the houses and leafy plane trees. There were still people on ladders hammering away at sheets of plywood and men with saws cutting wood to fit windows and doors. The atmosphere on the bus was tense as passengers watched the city prepare for battle. 'It's like the blitz,' remarked one old woman to her middle aged daughter. 'Then we'll all 'ave to pull together, won't we, Mum.'

I walked down Portobello Road and pushed the plywood-clad door of the Duke of Wellington open to peek inside. The usual crowd was drinking away as if oblivious to the impending doom. I closed the door of the pub again and from outside, it was perfectly dark. The street lights had not come on yet, and the setting sun made a blaze of colour in the sky. People brushed past me on their way home. Cars parked and the drivers hurried up their front steps slamming doors behind them. Everyone on the street seemed to be rushing to get securely home before the danger and darkness of night enveloped the city. Would the enemy strike tonight, and whose house would be rubble in the morning? I thought this probably is what it was like during the blitz.

It was then I realized something that I hadn't noticed earlier in the day. Where were the police? Normally you couldn't get away from them as they marched around in groups, but today I hadn't seen any cops at all. Did they truly want war on the Grove? Maybe, realizing what they were on the brink of they had decided to take a step back from the abyss.

I walked past Blenheim Crescent up to All Saints Road. I thought I should have a quick look as Brendan would call tonight and want a full report. The Apollo was not boarded up however, and was crowded with happier than usual West Indians. No one even looked at me as I glanced inside. The sky turned grenadine red, and the long summer twilight gave a beautiful glow to the neighborhood. Everything was peaceful, and I strolled home to Lucy.

Early the next morning we were getting ready to go to Camden Lock market when Brendan called, 'No, nothing's happening.'

He said that his picture had only made page four of *the News of the World*, but he was hopeful that several of his other photos would be syndicated widely. He sounded happy. 'No more carpet cleaning, mate!'

Over the next week a series of pitched battles took place between police and youths at Toxteth. Petrol bombs and paving stones were thrown and the police used CS gas for the first time in the UK outside of Northern Ireland. One person died after being hit by a police car, hundreds of police were injured, masses of people were arrested, and dozens of buildings were set ablaze.

During July riots broke out in 12 cities and towns around the county. But by the end of July the wave of disturbances had petered out. However, nothing at all had happened down Portobello.

On 29 July Charles Prince of Wales, and Lady Diana Spencer were married in St Paul's Cathedral, and their wedding day was declared a national holiday. Crowds lined the streets to catch a glimpse of the couple as they made their way to and from the cathedral, and London erupted into a spontaneous street party.

'Lucy there is only one place we can go today,' I said, and at lunch time we walked over to the Prince of Wales pub a short distance from our house.

The pub had a beer garden, and by the time we arrived it was full of revelers. Lachlan was there sitting at a table with his family and some friends, so we joined them. I had never seen so many happy Londoners. After the fear of the riots that had gripped the city such a short time before, it was an incongruous sight. Normally grey Londoners had transformed into jolly, happy, laughing people, singing and hugging each other.

A group of people gave an impromptu performance of London's most famous songs including, *Knees Up Mother Brown*. We all jumped to our feet, stuck our knees up in the air, linked arms and danced around the garden, spilling beer. The party continued on into the night until Lucy, possibly the only sober adult in London, finally dragged me home.

After the royal wedding, it was as if the riots had never happened - or so it seemed if you read the newspapers or watched TV - and Notting Hill began to get ready for Carnival.

A few days later the phone rang, and Lucy answered it.

'Just wait a minute please.' She cupped her hand over the mouth piece, 'It's someone called Gwyneth for you.' She had never spoken to Gwyneth before and I had never mentioned her to Lucy.

'Hi Gwyneth.... oh yes wait a minute... okay, I have a pen now... got it. Why are you giving it to me now?... Oh... I see... Take care now, see you soon... uh uh, byeee.'

'Who was that?' asked Lucy.

'Just an old friend from college. She wanted to give me a classmate's phone number... er, Bill, yes Bill's number.'

19

During August walking past church halls and warehouses we could see floats under construction, dance troupes in their elaborate costumes, and hear the distinctive sound of steel pan music as various troupes and bands prepared their floats, and practiced furiously.

It was refreshingly light hearted after so much heavy, dub. The music echoed through the neighbourhood as drum sticks vibrated on the polished, carefully tuned oil barrels.

...dum, da da dum dum,
dum dum dum dum da-di-dum
da, da, di,di, di, di, deeeeeeeeeeeeeee...

A Caribbean carnival has been held in Notting Hill over the last weekend in August since the early 1960s. Traditionally, Carnival marks the beginning of Lent, and in the West Indies, Brazil, New Orleans, Germany and Venice, it takes place in February. However, while the Trinidadian and Tobagonian community in London was still young, it joined a pre-existing street fair that was held over the public holiday weekend at the end of August, and the Notting Hill Carnival was born.

Lucy and I walked through Powis Square as the Metronomes Mas Band were loading their instruments into a van. I asked one of the band members, 'How do you make these drums?'

'Alright man I'll tell you. Steel Pan music originated in Trinidad and Tobago. Look at this pan,' he said.

He picked up one and turned it around. 'Now, the pan is made from 55 gallon oil barrel cut to various depths. Some are made of the whole barrel with just the bottom cut off. Others range in size from half, to just the top portion of the barrel. We can get tones varying from deep bass and baritone to alto and soprano from the drum.'

'When will you be performing?'

'We'll be diving through the streets on a float playing every day of Carnival.'

As the end of August approached, sound systems began to appear on the streets. I was passing the Dub Vendor one day as he hauled a massive speaker off a truck and set it up out the front of his shop.

'Dub Vendor, wha's 'appenin man?'

He wasn't wearing his hat and his long dreadlocks flicked back as he lifted his head to see who was calling him. 'Ea-mon man, I'm setting up mi sys-tem, fa Carnival.'

'How many speakers are you going to have?'

He showed me inside the truck which was full of large square speakers and several amplifiers.

'Man, you're going to blow the Westway over!' I exclaimed.

He laughed and said, 'Ya right man, ya right.'

He was wearing a sleeveless T-shirt with the words Two Sevens Clash on it.

I pointed at his T-Shirt and asked, 'What does that mean?'

'That's the day of judgment Ea-mon, have dread man.'

'What does dread mean?'

'Fear of the Lord, have fear of the Lord.'

Brendan asked if he could use our basement as a base during Carnival - somewhere he could leave his extra cameras and film while he was on the streets looking for action. Most of our friends said that they were going to drop by at some time over the weekend.

On 27 August, the Thursday before Carnival, following the advice of the Royal Commission, the hated 'sus' law was repealed.

There was no market on Friday or Saturday, the official opening day of the carnival

On Friday sound systems began to spring up all over the area. One was put up on the corner of Blenheim Crescent just fifty yards from our front door. Food stalls and stages were erected in Powis Square and on Portobello Road underneath the Westway. Shop owners emerged with their plywood boards and banged them into place once again.

The streets were eerily quiet until, in the late afternoon, the police arrived. After the first day of the Toxteth riots, they had slowly re-emerged onto the streets but kept a low profile and refrained from searching people. Now, dozens of busses, trucks, vans, cars, and paddy wagons rolled up, and hundreds of police spewed out. Brendan was delighted and rushed outside to take pictures.

The police marshaled themselves into various units, formed columns and lined up like soldiers. Just as I had done in the cadets years before, they raised their arms first to the front and then to the side so as to space themselves exactly one arm's length from the next policeman. They stamped their feet and stood at attention. Officers with clipboards inspected the columns and counted the men to make sure they were all there and that no one had nipped off for a swift can of Red Stripe. Then the columns marched away in different directions. Several columns stomped straight up the middle of Ladbroke Grove, others up Westbourne Park Road and all over Notting Hill.

Barriers were unloaded from police trucks, and various streets were cordoned off. Blenheim Crescent was closed on the other side of Ladbroke Grove, and a large dark blue truck was parked there. It had a door at either end with steps and lots of aerials poking out of it. Policemen ran up the steps, disappeared inside while others emerged from the other door and hurried away.

More busses arrived, and large numbers of policemen streamed onto the streets. They were placed with their backs to the houses about fifty yards apart all the way up Ladbroke Grove and on the side streets as well. So many blue clad soldiers were deployed, and carnival had not even begun.

After an hour or two, the bustle stopped, and the streets calmed down. The policemen began to look bored and relaxed, and people engaged them in conversation. Periodically columns marched down our street, and we looked up through the basement window to see dozens of blue clad legs filing by. 'Let's go and have a wander around,' I suggested.

Night descended and as we walked up to All Saints Road a sound system in the middle of the road boomed.

…YA ya ya ya RIGHT!
OUTTA SIGHT sight sight sight sight …
PING... SPLASH…DUMMMMMMM, dum dum dum dum
DUMmmmmm...

A small crowd had gathered around, so we joined them, and had our innards massaged by the heavy bass sound. A ring of policemen stood behind us, passionless and blankly staring, but we ignored them and pinged and bopped away into the night. Brendan darted around in his denim jacket whipping out his camera from time to time to click-click until eventually we went home to bed.

The next morning was bright, sunny and peaceful until the mid morning when the sound systems started up. I had stocked up on cheap beer, so I grabbed a can and opened the door, 'Let's Carnivaaaal!' We didn't have to go to Carnival, we were already in it.

We walked all over Notting Hill stopping at the numerous sound systems grooving out for a while before moving on to the next one. When we got tired, we went back to the basement for a rest.

In the mid afternoon Lucy and I sallied forth again and walked around the corner to Powis Square where a float was being prepared. The float was a platform with framed sides and a canopy roof on wheels attached to a truck cab at the front with a big banner.

MANGROVE MAS BAND

The band was based in the Tabernacle, a Caribbean community centre in the church at the north end of Powis Square.

Several young West Indian men wearing white jump suits with long fringes on the sleeves laughed as they strode out of the Tabernacle. One by one they clambered on board the float and began to play. Soon over twenty musicians stood behind their drums facing out on either side. The music grew louder and louder, and a crowd gathered around and we all danced, bumping into each other in the tight space.

I asked a young woman dancing next to me where the band were from. 'They were mostly born in England, but really, they are from Trinidad and Tobago.'

'What is this music?'

'SOCA, from Trini-Bago,' she laughed back at me.

The steel pan sound was rich and harmonious, like bells. Drummers came in and out, and as they tired or took a drink from a can. Sometimes they stopped to talk to a friend, but there were always enough playing to keep the rhythm going. They smiled at each other and the crowd of dancers. The sound waxed, waned, built up into crescendos and faded back down again.

The dark atmosphere of fear and violence that was created by the massive police presence was dispelled. I glanced up and saw that we were still surrounded by dozens of police, but no one cared. The syncopated music made us move from side to side and back and forth in a shuffling two step. We all bounced left and right up and down and around in small circles. Lucy shuffled closer and beamed at me - she was so beautiful and seemed so happy. A man jumped on the back of the float picked up a microphone and sang.

'... Mirantie, hummm, Mirantie, hmmmm
Oh Mirantieeeee, everybody dancing so-ca ...'

The float bounced with the rhythm of the musicians and the crowd of dancers bumping into it.

'... she could she dance all night
Until broad daylight
I say time to go, Mirantie shout out NO!
Oh Mirantieeeeee everybody dancing so-ca ...'

Girls in shiny green, red and yellow body suits ran out of the Tabernacle and joined in the dancing. Some were covered in feathers, and they all had sequins while others wore wire frames draped in chiffon. Many had elaborate head dresses made from feathers and shiny cloth. They were all ages, from young girls to old ladies and were mostly West Indian, but white women and Indians too. Men and boys in costume danced out of the Tabernacle behind them.

Everyone danced, throwing their arms in the air and sang, 'Oh Mirantie! Everybody dancing so-ca...'

We made space for the costumed troupe at the back of the float and they lined up putting the youngest people at the front and the most elaborately costumed dancers in the middle including several voluptuous young women dancers in exotic and scanty costumes.

After a long while, the truck choked to life, and suddenly the whole parade was off. The float and costumed troupe, followed by the now large crowd of revelers, slowly danced around the corner into Colville Terrace and Elgin Crescent. We turned right into Ladbroke Grove where more and more people joined the parade many squeezing alongside the float. We came abreast of Blenheim Crescent as I was twirling around with Lucy in my arms, a green plastic feather between my teeth with my head thrown back, and streamers the musicians had thrown from the float stuck in our hair and clothes. Out of the corner of my eye I saw Gene and Brendan standing on the corner. The two of them joined the parade and bumped and twirled up the Grove with us.

'... No more punk and rock, no we done with that
Only soca dance, everyone romance...
Mirantieeeeeee...everybody dancing so-ca...'

A couple of hours later we were still only half way around the carnival route on Westbourne Park Road at the corner of All Saints Road. Gene gestured, and the four of us made a conga line into the Apollo. We stood in the doorway of the pub and watched the parade bounce along its route the sound slowly fading away into the twilight.

My body was still shuffling back and forth to the soca beat, I couldn't stop. Gene bought us beer and we went back out into All Saint's Road to the sound system. At about 10pm, the police began circling like vultures and the DJ spoke to the crowd.

'Na listen up mi friens. Da policeman say we hav'a go to sleep now, b-bye! Now, we don't want no war at this carni-val. So re-luc-tant-ly, we are stopping after this next one, and we will all come back tomorrow.'

The 'next one' went on for about an hour, and when the music stopped we danced home to our basement, tripping over empty beer cans. The police looked somber and determined, but there was no hint of trouble from anyone. The sound systems switched off, and people filed into their houses to continue the party inside. Gene and Brendan went home and Lucy and I fell into bed exhausted.

The next day was Sunday, but Monday, a national public holiday, was when the largest crowds were expected. Brendan was still half-hoping for some trouble, but even he was now in the carnival mood.

The next morning we were woken by the sound of the system on the corner.

... Dum, dum dum dum dum, dum dum dum
MURDAH! dah dah dah dah dah dah dah ...

Bernie and his girlfriend came over, so did Gene. We gave Brendan a key and he had been running in and out since before we had woken up.

'Brendan, are you getting any decent photographs?' I asked.

'Yea, lots of great ones. They aren't very saleable though if there's no trouble. If there isn't a riot the only pictures the newspapers want is of a policeman dancing with a black girl and she has to be wearing his helmet. They stage that one every year, so they don't need me to take it. Oh well, still two days to go. See you all later,' and he dashed out again.

The rest of us followed him out soon afterwards. It was more crowded than the day before, and we made our way down Portobello to the Westway. We bought fry fish and akee from a food stall. I smothered mine with Encona hot sauce. I bought a green coconut and drank the juice - laced with rum - through a straw. Now that we had breakfast we were all ready to go.

We joined in the dancing at various sound systems and in the afternoon steel bands bounced through crossroads going in different directions.

On Ladbroke Grove, the Metronomes made their way towards us. The sound grew louder, and when the float was passing we joined in and followed. It was as if we had been caught on the tail of a comet and swept along.

We danced and shuffled up the street until we ran into another float going in a different direction. We jumped ship and danced along with them for a while and so it went all day.

In the early evening, we came across The British Airways Steel Band that was parked in Elgin Crescent. Lachlan was there as his daughter Kia, was in the band. She was only nine years old but looked as if she had been playing her steel pan for years. By now we were drunk with rum and beer, and the beautiful atmosphere. Many hundreds of police still lined the streets, but the idea of a riot seemed a strange impossibility.

On the final day, the weather was sunny and warm, and the police took off their heavy blue jackets buttoned up to the neck - they looked much friendlier in shirtsleeves. Just as Brendan had described, the front page of *The Sun* had a picture of a policeman with a big smile hugging a West Indian girl wearing his helmet. Sadly for Brendan none of his pictures were included with the story.

In the late afternoon Lucy and I were on Talbot Road coming up to Powis Square when a rush of people came running toward us. I instinctively grabbed Lucy and moved to the side of the street where we were crushed up against a steel fence as the panicked crowd ran past us followed by a line of policeman brandishing truncheons.

The police came to a halt just in front of us, and the crowd stopped just beyond us. Lucy and I were hugging the steel railings with our feet off the ground in no man's land. The police shuffled together into a phalanx and waited. The crowd puffed and panted and just stood there. Should we make our way to the police line or join the scared crowd who thought that they were about to be charged by cops brandishing sticks, I wondered.

Lucy glared at me, and I said, quietly, 'Let go of the fence. Now, follow me slowly.'

We unclenched the fence and stood on the pavement. Slowly we tiptoed towards the crowd and kept on going into their ranks. The sound system in Powis Square, which had gone silent during the sudden confusion, gently started up again with the soothing tones of Sugar Minot singing *A Good Thing Going.*

The crowd relaxed and began to move around. Within a few seconds, the carnival atmosphere returned and everyone was smiling. The police line broke up, and they returned to their usual positions lining the road.

I asked a white guy standing beside me what happened, 'Dunno, do I, it was a pick pocket or something. Suddenly these three blokes rushed by knocking people over. They were followed by three other blokes and I reckon the police just joined in the chase.'

Later on as the sun was setting, Lucy, Gene, Brendan,Vincent and I were lounging on the corner of Ladbroke Grove drinking cans of beer and watching the parades go by. I looked up Ladbroke Grove, and the street was filled with thousands of people all the way to the top of the hill. The sun glistened through the trees as distant sounds of soca and dub reverberate through the streets. Happy smiling people filed past us. The orchestras were happy, the food sellers were happy, even the police seemed happy.

Lucy put her arms around my waist and buried her face in my chest. She whispered, 'Eamon, I'm so happy, I love you so much.'

20

After Carnival Lucy seemed to belong to Portobello. She walked around the neighborhood as if she had been there all her life - although she didn't have the accent. I caught glimpses of her buying vegetables at the market, talking to shop owners and people she knew as she walked down the street. With a happy smile and flowing, curly blonde hair, she was radiant.

For a while, we were oblivious to the impending deadline of her visa expiration in December and we carried on as if we were destined to live our lives together down the 'Bella forever.

But, a niggling thought entered my psyche, and I couldn't ignore it for long. It was the memory of the bittersweet nights, the rustle of sheets, hot lips and quivering kisses of Amanda. I heard her whispers in my ear, and saw her long eyelashes flutter millimeters from mine in the dark, enveloped night. I smelled her passionate musk, and felt her bosom brush my chest. I stared at the shelves in the supermarket as my hallucinations took me to this other place, a shadowed scented room until the lady next to me said, 'You alright luv? You look as though you've come over all queer.'

I sat at a table in the Duke of Wellington with an untouched pint of bitter ale in front of me and contemplated the payphone in the corner. Why did Gwyneth give me Amanda's number? I knew the answer, it wasn't her fault. She was just being her normal, meddling self. She didn't know what the outcome would be. Gwyneth just liked the idea of being a catalyst - an agent of change. She just made things happen.

I gulped some beer and shoved my 5p in the slot. 'Amanda? It's Eamon.'

'What a surprise to hear from you.'

'Gwyneth gave me your number.'

'She mentioned that to me, but that was weeks ago.'

'I got caught up in Carnival fever... but... do you want to have a drink?'

'Alright, why not? I do think about you now and then, and hope that you're alright.'

'I'm fine, just fine. Shall we meet at the Water Rat, for old time's sake?'

'Funnily enough I don't live far from there now. We could meet some evening if you like.'

I finished my beer in a daze. I walked the short distance back to the basement and entered the cold, empty room. Lucy was at work, but I felt as though I had chased her away from me, and I was now abandoned, on my own.

Don't be ridiculous, I told myself, you're just going to have a pleasant drink with an old friend, Amanda, the girl who drove you to distraction, the first cut, the one who broke your heart, that terrible, and for so long obscure object of your most ardent desire.

'Stop it Eamon!' I shouted out loud. I rushed out into the street and back to the pub. A few pints later I felt decidedly merry and pleased with myself. Oh yes, I'm going to have a drink with Amanda, the girl, Amanda!

Lucy had already returned home from work, and as I stumbled into the flat she cheerily said, 'Hi, did you have a nice day?'

She threw her arms around my neck and kissed me all over my face. 'You've been drinking, so early in the evening!'

'I met a mate down at the Duke, you don't mind do you?'

'No of course not. Would you like me to cook dinner, or shall we go out tonight?'

'You make dinner darling, I spent all my money at the pub in any case.'

I hadn't actually spent all my money, but the next evening I was going to meet Amanda and would need some cash.

As per usual, I propped up the bar as she chopped and boiled mountains of vegetables. But, all evening I thought of nothing, other than my rendezvous the next day.

As Lucy left for work in the morning I called after her, 'Lucy, I'm not sure when I'll be home tonight. I have to meet my old friend Bill for a drink.'

'Oh, okay, is he the guy that girl gave you the number for?'

'Yes, that's him.'

It was autumn and the clocks had just been moved back so the sunset was an hour earlier. Leaves were tumbling from the plane trees as the 31 bus made its way from Notting Hill Gate, through Earl's Court to

Limerston Street, and it's final destination opposite the Magpie and Stump at World's End. I nervously crossed the street and walked towards the entrance of the Water Rat. I glanced in the window, and there, resplendent, was Amanda, sitting at the same table, in the same seat where I had spied her in that age gone by, cheating on me with.

The memory jolted me like an electric shock. But my eyes rested on Amanda, her scarlet lips, vibrant henna-red hair, and the bitterness drained from me. My heart was pounding as I slipped unnoticed into the chair beside her and closed my arms around her shoulders. My lips met hers and our tongues entwined.

Until, she pressed the palm of her ever more insistent hand against my chest forcing the two of us apart. Amanda's molten, grey-green eyes pierced mine, and she whispered, her voice palpating, 'Eamon, what are you doing? You must stop, now.'

'I'm sorry, I didn't expect my reaction to seeing you. I just thought that it would be nice to have a drink, but I was overcome when I saw you. You look ... you look, like I haven't seen you for so long.'

'Alright Eamon, calm down. Why don't you go and buy us a drink? I'll have a Britvic Orange and vodka, okay?'

As we sipped our drinks, she spoke animatedly, her arms wafting gracefully up and down with her hands turning descriptively like a Balinese dancer. Her eyes shone, and her red lips sparkled. When we first met she looked younger than me, but now, she was a sophisticated woman, and I felt like a scruffy boy in comparison.

'Gwyneth mentioned to me that you were in Munich?'

'I worked at the Country Cousins for some time after you and I split up. Then, I got offered a job as stage crew for Nina Hagen, so I quit. She had a European tour, and we traveled all over the place. We ended up in Munich where I got a job in a theatre. That only lasted a couple of months, so I came home to London.'

She threw her head back and laughed, 'Oh, it was such fun working in Germany, they are so straight laced. So what about you Eamon, what are you up to now?'

'I have market stalls at Portobello, Swiss Cottage and Camden Lock. Yes, it's a lucrative game I must say,' I said nodding my head insistently.

'You're engaged aren't you?'

'Engaged, no not at all, where did you get that impression?'

'Gwyneth told me that you were in a serious relationship and going to be married, she said, "They're bound to get married, I can see it in Eamon's eyes."'

I laughed nervously, 'No, no, I'm actually quite alone at the moment. I did have a thing with a girl, but that ended a while back.'

'Oh, how sad, what happened?'

'Happened? Oh nothing, I just didn't want to be tied down. I want to keep my independence so I can grow in my art. I just told her it was over.'

'Are you doing much art nowadays Eamon?'

'Ah yes, well, uh em, there is my poetry. You know Amanda, it was you that brought out the poet in me.'

She burst out laughing uncontrollably and shaking her head from side to side, 'My round,' she said, smoothed her tight pencil skirt down, composed herself and gracefully stood up to go to the bar.

My art, oh I'm a poet... pillock, get it together, or you're going to blow this, I thought.

'So, Amanda, how about you, are you seeing anyone special at the moment?'

'No, I'm not. I've been in a couple of relationships since we split up, but they didn't last.'

'Were you hurt?'

'Yes, a little, well a lot actually, but I'm over it now. I'm not looking for anyone Eamon.'

Oh good, she's single, how wonderful. 'Well Amanda, perhaps now after all that's happened we can be friends again?'

'Yes Eamon, friends, why not?'

We chatted and drank until eventually the barman rang the closing bell.

... ting ting.... ting ting

'Finish your drinks please ladies and gentlemen.'

We stood outside the pub, and Amanda said, 'Good night Eamon, see you again soon I hope.'

'I haven't asked where you're living now, close by you said?'

'I have a council flat in Battersea. It's not far, just over the bridge.'

'I'll walk you home.'

'No Eamon, no. I'll be fine really.'

'Don't be silly,' I said and linked my arm in hers. We walked down Beaufort Street to Cheyne Walk and continued along Chelsea Embankment to Albert Bridge.

Thousands of lights illuminated the bridge and it sparkled in the moonlit sky with the gleaming river slowly flowing upstream as the tide was coming in. 'Eamon, this is far enough, I want to go on alone from here but thank you.'

I ignored her command and we continued to walk across the bridge. As we reached the middle Amanda stopped and turned to look at me. She was about to speak, but I put my arm around the small of her back, drew her quickly towards me and kissed her. She resisted, but soon melted, and her sweet lips pressed against mine. As quickly as she melted she froze, and once again pushed her palm into my chest to force me away. I tightened my arm around her, but she pushed and squirmed away from me.

'Eamon, you must stop doing that, you must.'

'Amanda, you know you like it. You still want me.'

'I'm only flesh and blood, but this isn't a good idea for either of us. Turn around and go home now, before you upset me.'

'Do you want me to go forever?'

'No, we can still be friends, I'll call you. What's your number?'

Her question threw me. This time I already had her number so I could call her. I certainly didn't want her to ring the basement and for Lucy to answer the phone. 'Er, 370 3700,' I blurted out.'

'Isn't that your old number at Royston Gardens?'

'Oh, yes I suppose so. Er, I have your number already. I'll call you tomorrow.'

'Alright Eamon, call me sometime. It's been nice seeing you. I always cared about you. Please look after yourself.'

I approached her motioning as if to give her a goodnight kiss. She kissed my cheek, but lingered a fraction too long, or so I thought, for it to be without desire.'

'I still need you Amanda. Maybe we could try, just one night.'

'Not tonight Eamon.'

'But some night?'

'No, I ... I don't think so. I'm going now. Don't spoil everything, goodbye.'

She turned on her high heels and with her hands in the pockets of her trench coat, her head bowed to the wind, she disappeared across the Albert Bridge and into the darkness of Battersea.

I slowly turned around and walked home through Chelsea and Kensington. The full moon lit up the autumn sky, and white clouds crossed swiftly from west to ease obscuring the moon as they went.

I felt exalted. Amanda had kissed me. It was not just I that had kissed her, she had kissed me. She said she might spend a night with me sometime... at least, I think that's what she said. I ran down Kensington Park Road but slowed as I turned the corner into Blenheim Crescent and crept down the steps of the basement. Lucy was already sound asleep as I slid into bed. I spent the night engulfed by vivid dreams of red hair, ruby lips and the tinkling sounds of moist kisses.

I woke up late, and Lucy had already left for work. I was glad she wasn't there to see my guilty eyes. In the afternoon, I called Amanda, but no answer.

Lucy came home from work, and we resumed our normal routine. She asked me, 'Where did you go last night with Bill?'

'We went to the Water Rat on King's Road. When the pub shut I walked all the way home. It was a beautiful moon bright night.'

She smiled and turned away to wash some dishes in the sink. Over her shoulder, she said, 'Bart called last night. He got our number from Gene.'

'Bart, we haven't seen him for so long. What did he say?'

'Oh nothing, he'll call again.'

'Did you get his number?'

'Yes, I have it somewhere.'

I sensed a change in Lucy that she could tell that I was up to something. I gave it no more thought, and I forgot about Bart as well. All I could think about was Amanda.

I called Amanda every day at different times but never got an answer, until finally a week later, 'Eamon, how are you? I would have called you but you didn't give me your number.'

'Yeah, well, I've been so busy at the markets you know. Business is booming, and I only thought to call you just now.'

'Too busy to write any new poetry?'

'I wrote one poem ... for you.'

'You did? Go on, recite it for me.'

"Er, well I haven't *actually finished* it, but it starts with, er, the eyes of Amanda, I think ...'

'Oh well I must dash, do call again.'

'Wait a minute, let's meet for a drink or dinner even.'

'I'm going to be busy from now until the end of October. I've got a job.'

'What doing?'

'I'm working on The Clash tour. They'll be playing some dates around the country in early October, and then doing a week at the Lyceum in London towards the end of the month.'

'Wow, that sounds great. Can I come on the tour with you?'

'Very funny Eamon. Of course, you could go to the Lyceum gigs. I could get you tickets if you like?'

'You bet, I'd love to see The Clash. How many tickets can you get?'

'Well you only need one right?'

'Er, oh of course, there's only me. Just one would be fine.'

'I can probably get you a ticket for a few of the gigs if you're that keen.'

'Sure, I can see you at the shows I hope?'

'Yes, we can meet up there. Give me your number and I'll call and let you know about the tickets.'

I searched my mind for an idea, but it was blank, 'Er. er, oh, 907 4709.'

'Okay, Eamon, I'll call you in the next few days, byeee,' click.

The next three days were torture. I didn't want to leave the basement for fear of missing the call or even worse, Lucy might answer the phone. I imagined their conversation, 'Hello ... you want to speak to Eamon?.... Who am I? I'm his live in lover, who the hell are you?... Oh, he said he ditched me to write poetry?...'

Lucy and I were just sitting down to eat diner when the phone rang. I jumped across the floor and grabbed the handset. 'Hi, er ... that's good news, thanks so much. Wow, I am looking forward to it... okay... sure... yes, I know where to go. See you then ... yes me too... no ... no ... no, just little old me ... see you ...' click.

'Who was that?' demanded Lucy

'On the phone?'

Her eyes turned to daggers. I blurted out, 'Oh, that was Bill, yes Bill, amazing really. He's working on The Clash tour. He's got me tickets for the shows.'

Lucy's ambience changed, and she smiled, 'Fantastic, we're going to see The Clash!'

'Actually, he only got tickets for me.'

'But you keep saying tickets - plural?'

'You see, they are playing for a whole week, and he got one ticket each night.... for... me.'

We ate our dinner in silence and Lucy didn't mention the shows again.

The next day was Portobello market day and I carried my stuff down to the flyover. I was relieved that I no longer had to sit by the phone in case Amanda called. I bought a portion of chips with a pickled onion and mused, maybe I'm not cut out for this type of double life. How do people handle having two lovers? It must drive them insane. As the dull, grey morning wore on, slowly, people strolled past the stall, and my thoughts turned once again to the scent and sensual feeling of Amanda.

Perhaps it was the way I glared at the market goers that day, but an unusually large number of people picked up a piece of junk that I was trying to flog, gazed at it and said 'I think I'll just leave it,' and walked away.

Later in the afternoon I was at home, dreaming about Amanda, while sorting through my bric-a-brac when Lucy arrived home from work.

'He fired me.'

'What? Who fired you?

'The owner of the shop. He demanded to know if I had a work visa for the UK.'

'What did you tell him?'

'I said sure, I was all legal and allowed to work.'

'He didn't actually ask to see your visa, did he?'

'He was pretty heavy. He said he didn't want to get into any trouble and that there were plenty of French, Portuguese and other Europeans looking for work who were legal and wouldn't cause him any fuss. I don't think he believed me. Anyway, he said that next week I had to show him my work visa or I was fired.'

'Well never mind. It wasn't the best job in the world. You can look for another one.'

'What if I get asked to show my visa to any new employers?'

'You won't get asked. He must have been paid a visit by the immigration department or something. Most people don't care about visas.'

'How do you know? You're not an illegal alien. You don't know what it's like. I feel desperate, lost. I'm just a bloody foreigner.'

She sobbed uncontrollably and slumped her head into her chest. 'Even my tourist visa expires soon.'

'I guess we can ask for another renewal.'

'Maybe… It'll be a tremendous hassle and what if they refuse? I think I should go home.'

'What about us?'

'I don't know. What can we do? It's all so short term Eamon. I can't just work in clothes shops forever, I have to do something with my life. Even if they do extend my visa it'll still only be a tourist visa.'

'We'll find a way to get your visa extended'

'Maybe, but what then?'

'We'll figure that out later, don't worry,' I said trying to be reassuring.

'I like it in London Eamon, but it just doesn't seem to be feasible for me to stay here. You say you love me but I don't know if you really do or not.'

'Lucy, of course I love you.'

'Eamon ... I don't think I can ...'

'Oh don't tell me, you can't take responsibility for this any more.' I stormed out slamming the door behind me.

'Eamon, EAMON come back!'

I ran up the stairs to the street. Our next door neighbours were engaged in one of their regular arguments. The husband, a Scotsman, was standing on the pavement yelling up to his wife who was leaning out of the first floor window.

'Don't ye fuckin' tell me wha te du ye stupid bitch!'

His wife, a cockney, yelled back, 'You're no kind of bleedin' husband you lazy drunken pig! Get down the shops and buy me some soddin' cigarettes you tosser!'

'You t'ink I'm gonna buy ye some bloody fags? Go piss off. I'm gein doon te fuckin' pub!' Off he strode brushing past me on his way to the Duke of Wellington.

I walked without stopping my eyes half closed following the pavement. After about two hours I found myself sitting in the dark on the bench underneath a statue of the painter Whistler, beside Battersea Bridge on the Chelsea Embankment. I watched as a barge made its way down the river, lights blinking and engine churning under the Albert Bridge and then Chelsea Bridge. The tide was high, and the muddy waters sparkled in the autumn light.

Lucy was right. She couldn't stay in London and had to go home. But could I go to America? I would have the same visa problems as Lucy. I walked back up Beaufort Street to the King's Road and stopped in at the Roebuck for a swift pint. I continued up Royston Gardens and Gloucester Road and Kensington High Street.

When I reached home Lucy was cooking dinner and she glared at me, 'You're so mean. You know I love you. I just don't know what the future holds for us. I'm scared, can't you tell?' Her blue eyes sharpened to fierce points then quickly diffused to deep pools of quavering love and emotion.

'Lucy, what do you think we should do?'

'I love you, but I don't know. I want to be with you.'

We ate dinner in silence staring at our beans and rice.

I lay awake in bed all night. I turned on my left side and had visions of Amanda, onto my right side, and there was Lucy. I lay on my back, and asked myself, who you are kidding Eamon? You're not going to end up with either one of these girls.

The next day we carried on as if nothing had happened, ignoring our problem. Lucy told her boss that her work permit was being posted to her, and he gave her until the end of the month to show it to him.

21

I read in the New Musical Express that The Clash were playing in Glasgow, Manchester, Liverpool and Saint Austell over the next two weeks. I would just have to wait for the tour to reach London before I could see Amanda. Unable to face Lucy, every evening I drank alone. When the pubs shut, I stumbled home to find her sleeping and by the time I woke up in the morning, hung-over, she had already left for work. Until at last, the day of the first concert arrived.

I was to collect a ticket that Amanda said would be left for me at the Lyceum box office before the show. It was Sunday so I put up my stall at Camden Lock market, but Lucy didn't join me that day. When I returned home in the mid afternoon Lucy was out. Just before it was time to go to the concert I called Amanda's number hoping to arrange to meet her after the gig, but as usual no answer. I put the handset back in its cradle and immediately the phone rang. 'Amanda?' I said expecting a serendipitous return call.

'What?' barked an American voice. Man, you're fucked up. What the fuck does Lucy see in you man? I mean, you are a prize tool.'

'Bart, is that you?'

'Yeah, who did you think it was?'

'I was expecting someone else, not you calling to tell me I'm a dick.'

'I didn't call to speak to you.'

'Well who did you call to speak to?'

'Lucy of course.'

'Lucy?'

'Yeah, Lucy. Can you put her on please?'

'Lucy is not here Bart. You're freaking me out. Do you think I need this aggravation? What is up with you?'

'You're going to lose that girl.'

'Oh yeah?'

'If you don't treat her right my friend you'll come home one day, and find her gone.'

'Yeah, are you going to be the one to change her mind?'

'Maybe, if you don't wake up! Tell her I called,' click.

I slumped down into a chair shaking with rage. Lucy ran down the steps and in the door. 'Aren't you going out again tonight Eamon? I didn't expect to see you here.'

'Yes I'm on my way out the door. Bart called you.'

'Oh good thanks for telling me.'

'Why did Bart call you?'

'Maybe because he's my friend, my only real friend in London.'

'Have you been seeing him?'

'What do you mean seeing him?'

'I mean *seeing* him, just like it sounds. He wasn't exactly friendly to me on the phone.'

'What difference would it make to you anyway? I haven't *seen* you for weeks.'

'I've got to go now. We can talk when I get back.'

'You promised you wouldn't let me down and that you would always love me.'

'I do love you Lucy.'

'Oh really? Do you love me as much as you love Bill?'

'Don't be ridiculous, look, I have to go.'

'Okay, you just run away again. I should have known. I love you Eamon, but I feel like such an idiot. You're just waiting for me to get thrown out of the country aren't you?'

'No, I'm not but I can't talk now, see you later.' I ran out the door and up to Notting Hill Gate tube station.

Lucy with that oversized boy, I was incredulous. I thought Bart was my friend, but now I despised him. My conscience said I should turn around and go back home, but I kept going forward unable to stop myself. Could I look Bart in the eye and tell him to leave Lucy alone after I had convinced Amanda to spend the night with me?

I took a Central Line to Tottenham Court Road then the Northern Line one stop to Leicester Square. I brushed past the crowds of theatre goers, walked down Garrick and Henrietta Streets, past Covent Garden to Wellington Street and the Lyceum.

I was early, but there were already dozens of people milling around outside the theatre. A crowd huddled up against the box office windows. I joined in and asked a guy in front of me, 'Are you collecting tickets or trying to buy one?'

'We're seeing if there are any returns, the show's a sell out.'

The bloke ahead of him quipped, 'The Clash, they'd never sell out!'

I forced my way to a window and shouted at the woman on the other side, 'You should have a ticket there for me. One of the stage crew organised it for me.'

'What's your name luv?'

'Eamon Curran.'

'Here it is, be careful in there, it's going to be a bit of a crush tonight,' she said passing the ticket to me. I pushed my way back out to the street and looked at the square, white ticket.

Lyceum - Strand WC2

Straight Music Presents

THE CLASH

Sunday 18 October

STANDING

Eventually, the doors to the theatre were opened, and I filed in with the crowd. The entire ground floor of the elaborate Victorian theatre had been stripped of seats and people poured in the entrances like flowing water.

Soon a massive throng had gathered pushing and straining to get as close to the stage as possible. It looked far too crowded for me, and I stood at the back. The house lights cast us all in a stark white light, and I had some time to have a look at the crowd. A few years earlier the audience at a Clash concert would have been mostly punks, but this night a large cross section of London youth seemed to be there.

I watched everyone milling around. They soon merged together in my mind, and I could hardly tell one person from another. Over the years, the hippies had changed. Many of them had cut their hair and now wore different clothes. The punks had grown their hair, and wore the same patchwork of styles as the hippies. Some of the white guys had matted their hair into dreadlocks to look like West Indians. Some black guys had bleached their hair white. In 1977 the youth cultures became polarized, now, they had merged together to form some new hybrid counter class.

I noticed an old hippie who was a familiar sight at music events. I was sure I remembered seeing him at every gig that I had ever been to. He looked different now, wearing a flowing hippie shirt, but his hair was short and he had pointy shoes on. Even he had morphed into a new wave mutant. I wondered would this merging lead to a new and as yet unthought-of flowering of culture? Perhaps in the future everyone would be bald.

On the stage Amanda emerged from the curtains behind the drum kit. She walked with Catlike, deliberate, stylized movements. Her hair was brushed upwards and even from a distance her dramatic eye makeup was striking. Wearing red footless tights and a long military style shirt she grabbed a mic stand and I thought she was going to perform. Instead, she plugged in a microphone. She was not the main act, but she was clearly part of the mood creation - a performer.

Somehow I had to find my way to the stage so I could talk to her. I moved forward inexorably squeezing in between like an amoeba growing in a desired direction. One by one I moved the packed bodies aside and inched closer to the front and Amanda.

Finally I was on the railing at the foot of the stage, the ultimate and final front row, in the centre. Amanda reappeared carrying a roll of cable and passed in front of me. I pressed myself against the rail and called, 'Hey Amanda!'

She bowed down towards me and smiled. 'Eamon!'

Her eyes twinkled with excitement, 'Come to the stage door afterwards and ask for me, okay?'

'Sure see you then.'

She blew me a kiss and my heart skipped a beat. I blew a kiss back, and she disappeared again. Moments later the house lights went down and the stage lights sparked on. A blue light flashed and a siren sounded

... Bwamp - Bwamp - Bwamp - Bwamp ....

Spot lights illuminated Joe Strummer and Mick Jones standing right in front of me. Joe grabbed the microphone and called out,

'It's up to you not to heed the call up ...'

The audience surged forward and jumped upwards, my chest was crushed against the rail. I hung onto it as if to save myself from being flung overboard. I could hardly hear the band over the shouting and screaming. The mass of people bounced up and down carrying me along with them. Up we went as high as we could jump and down with such a force my knees crumpled beneath me, but again, I was carried up, up, higher then down.

Joe belted out the lyrics his spit splashing our faces. Breathless and crushed I was faint as the words echoed in my head.

'There is a Rose that I want to live for ...
There is a dance, and I should be with her
... It's fifty five minutes past eleven ...'

With the crowd I crashed to the ground again, and I fell to the floor my head buried in a wall of legs, smashed against the rail, spinning into oblivion. My only thought was of Lucy, and that I should be with her. I had an overwhelming desire to hold her, to be in her presence. I stuck my arms above my head, grabbed the railing and pulled my self off the floor as Joe Strummer wailed like a banshee.

When the song finished the crowd backed off a few inches. I caught my breath and decided to get out of there. I had to go home to Lucy. What had I been thinking? But the band began to play again.

I had heard these songs many times on the radio or on vinyl, but I was struck that they didn't just address petty concerns, but the burning issues that faced people each day, and they demanded that we ask ourselves, who are we? They urged the listener to take sides, to act, to be part of a revolution.

Song after song played at a furious pace, with such force and energy driving us to ever more wild jumping. I had no way out, and realised that I would have to wait until the show was over before I could escape. I was in an unstoppable tide being carried away from the one who loved me, the only one I truly loved. I turned and squirmed yet I couldn't move, save up and down with the surge of the phalanx. Hands thrust upwards, bodies pushed forward, ever forward. I had a vision of myself floating above the stage looking down on a writhing sea of arms and bobbing heads.

The crowd was excited, not just by the spectacle, or music but the feeling of unity with the band. The audience were drawn to the Lyceum that autumn evening not to see a concert, but to be part of a collective expression. The circle had closed, the punks and hippies were now one amorphous body.

Finally the band played a lightening fast

'White riot - I wanna riot
White riot - a riot of my own ...'

Without warning, as tumultuously as it began the show was over, and The Clash walked off stage.

Like a discarded rag doll I was left hanging on the rail with my back to the stage as the now silent crowd herded out of the theatre. My eyes were clouded, my limbs stretched, my ears ringing. I was dehydrated, and my knees were unable to support me. Someone called my name as if from far away the sound barely reached my consciousness, but I turned towards it. Amanda was kneeling on the stage craning towards me.

'Eamon, Eamon! Are you alright? Come this way,' she said pointing, 'I'll let you in up here.'

I edged to the side of the stage and she opened a barrier ushering me up to the back stage area. She took me to a small room, and I crashed down in a chair.

'Eamon, you look as if you crawled out of a trench. I don't think you should have come right up the front like that.'

'No kidding, I couldn't get away once I was there.'

'Did you enjoy the show?'

'I don't know if enjoy is the right word,' I said, regaining my breath. 'It was the most intense experience I have ever had, that's for sure.'

'There is a party later, you can come along if you're up to it.'

'No, no thanks Amanda. I have to get home to Lucy.'

'Lucy? Is that your girlfriend?'

'Yes, we live together, I love her, and I shouldn't be here.'

'You're right, you should go home to her. I knew you were lying in the pub. "Oh, I just told her it was over ... for my art." You are silly Eamon.'

'Amanda, I never stopped loving you.'

'Perhaps you do love me, I don't know, but that doesn't mean that we were meant for each other.'

'I know that now Amanda. I've made such a fool of myself. As you said, I need to grow up.'

'You need someone to take care of you Eamon. You're not terribly good at looking after yourself.'

'You're right, but who will look after you?'

'Don't worry about me, not too much anyway. I'll be alright.'

I paused, and then said, 'Can you forgive me?'

'Forgive you for what?'

'For being so selfish, for hurting you.'

'Yes, I forgive you Eamon.'

'Oh good ... I have to go home. I hope it's not too late.'

She put her arms around me, kissed me on the cheek and showed me to the stage door. Exhausted as I was, I found my way back to Leicester Square and took the tube home.

22

The basement was dark, and I assumed that Lucy was asleep, but I couldn't see her shape in the bed. I felt the blankets and switched on the light. My heart sank, oh no. Don't panic she probably just went out with Bart.

I turned off the light and sat in the empty, dark room waiting for her. The hours passed until the dawn light slowly found its way down the outside staircase one step at a time. Timidly, the light crept up to the window, peeked inside and fell, exhausted on the breakfast table. There it lay, looking up at me, the grey, motionless, lifeless light, challenging me to some glimmer of hope. My head bowed I sat still, and my eyes struggled to take in the light. My world was now colourless, like the primordial sludge before the dawn of creation - nothing, limbo.

Eventually one thought came into my mind then disappeared like someone who had opened the wrong door then quickly closed it again. My numbness turned to a dull ache. Then flashes of sharp pain struck me as a memory emerged out of the sludge and confronted me. Another memory came then another, each one more painful than the last. I clenched my stomach in a vain bid to stop the feeling of nausea and entangled twisted intestines. The pain eventually subsided just enough for me to see into the future instead of the past. But there too I saw only pain, consequences.

Oh my, who have I been all these years? I realised now, at long last, that everything I had ever been told about myself by my mother, father, Amanda, Lucy, teachers, was true. 'Eamon could do better.'

I knew now, too late, how much I had hurt everyone who had ever loved me. The more they loved me, the greater was the pain that I inflicted on them. I had torn my love down. I had grabbed the love that people gave me and tumbled it to the ground.

Albert's words rang in my ears, 'It's all about identity, finding out who you really are, not who people say you are.'

I remembered Amanda looking at the twisted Francis Bacon figures in the Tate, '... it's because that's what we're really like, on the inside.'

So who was I? Was I a trapped soul? I closed my eyes to shut out the torture of existence. I tried to stop it, but again, and again the thought welled up in me, strong insistent at first, then slowly fading until it became just a vibration with no apparent meaning. It faded further and became just a thought, pure thought, then nothing at all, just the memory of a thought, until finally it was just a potential thought, beyond thought but possible, perhaps...

Who am I?

Who?

I

i

I touched my cheek, and it was wet. I cracked open my eyes and saw my hands were damp and felt that my whole face was covered in flowing tears. I grasped the hard table and squeezed it with my fingers as if trying to make it bleed. Then I realised that I too was hard, as hard as felled seasoned wood, impervious to all, unyielding. An image of Lucy came to me. She was soft with no hard edges. Then I felt my own vulnerability, and perhaps that was why I had made myself become hard, deluding myself that my shell would protect me.

Who was I? Am I different now? I remembered Olaf assuring me, 'You are nobody, so you can become anybody. You are a free man and you can do whatever you desire.'

No, that isn't true. No, look at the terrible mess I had made. I remembered Mum teaching me, 'You should always clean as you go. By the time the meal is cooked the kitchen should be all cleared up and spotless.'

I couldn't just leave my skin behind and be reborn, at least not until I had put everything to right. I had to clean up the mess. I felt a determination growing inside of me, I listened, listened, and sure enough I heard it.

Softly, it splashed, like an oar touching the water, as gently as a young man strokes his lover's hair, like milk pouring slowly from a jug, soft rain falling on green meadows. Then the sound softened still more as if happy it had been noticed at long last, and was now just a gentle summer breeze lightly stirring the leaves of a hazel tree. I wanted a brand new start, but the sound told me to go back, back, and tend the garden I had planted.

I stood up and washed my face at the sink. The light coming in the window was stronger now. I pressed my face to the glass and peered up to see a blue sky with puffy white clouds dancing by. Who do I love? I asked myself. I love them all, that's the truth. My family, friends, the science teacher at Chelsea School, sergeant 'Fatgut', the immigration official on the boat, the police at carnival, the Mangroves, The Clash, all of them - except the skinheads perhaps. Yes, I love Amanda. How could I stop myself? Love, it seemed to me, was not something that was temporary, but permanent. Once the candle is lit it never goes out. How could it and why should it? But I knew now, that the one I wanted, the one I loved more than all, more than I loved myself, was Lucy.

It was early, so I made breakfast. Lucy started work at 10am, so at 10:30 I walked to the Hindu Bazaar to see her. 'Lucy is not coming to work today. She called in sick, you didn't know?' said her boss. I walked home again and called Bart, but there was no answer.

The phone rang, and I jumped, afraid to pick it up this time. Gingerly I lifted the receiver, 'Hello?'

My sister Katie said, 'Eamon, come over quickly, Mum's not well.'

'Where's Dad?'

'I don't know he went out somewhere. Come right away, she's terribly ill.'

I ran out of the house and hailed a taxi on Ladbroke Grove. When I arrived at the shop, Mum was upstairs in bed almost unable to move. Katie said, 'I called the Doctor, he said he had no idea what could be wrong with her, but he called an ambulance to take her to Charing Cross Hospital.'

I held Mum's hand. It felt icy cold with the faintest pulse. We waited nervously until loud cockney voices echoed in the shop downstairs, 'Alright, where is she then? We ain't got all day come on take us to the sick old dear.'

I ran downstairs and explained that Mum was upstairs and led the ambulance men to the foot of the stairs. 'Cor blimey, 'ow do you imagine we are going to drag a stretcher up that narrow stairway? I ask you, bleedin' ridiculous.'

I glared at the two men, 'Have some respect there is a sick woman upstairs.'

The ambulance men eventually brought a wheel chair to the bottom of the stairs and then the two of them carried Mum down and dropped her in it as if she were a sack of potatoes. She looked as white as a sheet and was nearly unconscious. As they closed the double doors on the back of the ambulance, Mum woke up and said, 'Don't let them take me to Charing Cross. No one ever comes out of there alive.'

The doors slammed, and the ambulance whirred away. Leaving my youngest sister to look after the shop, Katie and I hailed a taxi and followed behind. The ambulance pulled up outside the hospital, and she was whisked away to intensive care. A nurse told us that we could wait but that it was clear that Mum was going to be in hospital for at least one night.

Much later Dad arrived and found Katie and me sitting forlorn in the intensive care waiting area. After another hour of waiting Dad spoke to a doctor in the corridor. 'They are running some tests in the morning, and tonight they are just trying to stabilise her and make her comfortable. They say she is in no immediate danger. You go home Eamon. I'll take Katie back to the shop a bit later on.'

I walked out of the hospital onto Fulham Palace Road, opposite the old shop where Albert used to live. I walked home through the cold twilight and called Bart, but no answer. I made dinner and went to bed early for the first time in months.

In the morning the phone rang. 'Hello, it's Dad. I've just spoken at length to a senior doctor. I am sorry Eamon I have bad news. Your mother has a heart condition. She had an angina attack and her heart is frail. She is recovering well at the moment. We are just going to have to wait and see what the long term implications are.'

'Can I visit her?'

'Yes you can. She will probably be in hospital for a few days.'

I walked the length of Shepherd's Bush Road to Hammersmith Broadway and around the corner to the hospital. I found my way up to the ward, and bumped into Dad walking out with my sisters. 'Good timing Eamon, we just left her side so now you can stay with her for a while. We're going down to the canteen to have a cup of tea and something to eat. We'll see you a bit later.'

Mum smiled at me through half open eyes as I entered her room. She was propped up in the big hospital bed with a tube in her nose and another stuck in her wrist. A small machine with green lines on a screen showing her vital signs sat on a table next to her.

'How are you feeling?'

'Not so bad Eamon, I'm full of drugs. But I'm worried about the poor girls.'

'Don't worry about any of us Mum you just get better. We can look after ourselves.'

'I don't know that I'm going to get much better Eamon. I might be in this awful place for a long time.'

'Don't be silly you're going to be alright, sure you are.'

'Eamon you've always been such a worry to your father and me.'

'I'm sorry I've been a disappointment to you both.'

'Well Eamon you know I'll always love you no matter what you do. But you've got to stop letting people down. You've always been the strong one, more independent than your brothers and sisters. But you only use your strength to help yourself. You don't seem to think of others but only what you want.'

'You're right, I am so selfish.'

'How about your girlfriend, Lucy, how are you getting on with her?'

'I love her, and we're getting along okay I think. She has to go back to America soon though, and I don't know what I'll do.'

'Have you thought about getting married?'

'I'm not ready. I can't commit to anything for the rest of my life.'

'It's always about what you want. What does Lucy want? Does she want to go home, to leave you?'

'I don't think so, I mean, she loves me too. Perhaps she would be better off at home. I have no future, there's nothing I can do.'

'Eamon, you can't just give up. It's time you decided to stick with something. You have to apply yourself, work at something. That's the only way you'll make a success of anything, including your relationship with Lucy. You can't just drift along for ever.'

'I guess I always want to run away from difficulties. When I was little we moved so often, and I went to so many schools that it felt natural to leave everything behind. I would put something down, and go find the next toy to play with.'

'That's the way it is for children. You're not a child any more Eamon.'

'Please forgive me Mum.'

'Of course, I forgive you, my precious little boy.'

On the way out of the hospital I stopped at a payphone and called Bart's number again, but no answer. Not answering the phone? I'm not having this. I took the Piccadilly Line from Hammersmith to South Kensington and walked to Flood Street. The Coopers Arms was down the road from Bart's apartment with a corner window that gave a view of the entrance to his building. I bought a pint, sat in the window and waited.

For two hours I sat and watched for any sign of Bart or Lucy. I was doodling on a beer mat when a white van drove down the street. As it passed I caught a glimpse of a scarf and curly blonde hair, but the van stopped obscuring my view. I ran out outside as the van continued on its way. Yes, Lucy was walking away from Bart's apartment, alone. She glanced up and saw me standing on the corner, but bowed her head and continued going. I caught up to her as she reached the corner of King's Road. 'Lucy, Lucy, I'm sorry.'

'No you're not,' she snapped at me and kept walking.

'Lucy, please we have to talk. Let's have a coffee.'

'What's there to talk about?'

'Us, we have to talk about us.'

'Is there an us?' She stopped and glared at me.

'Antiquarius is right here, let's have a coffee.'

We sat at a table in the small cafe on the ground floor of the arcade and stared into our cups of milky instant coffee. 'I got quite a shock when I got home on Sunday night, and you weren't there.'

'Really? I didn't think that you were intending to go home on Sunday night. How was the concert?'

'It nearly killed me, but I had a revelation.'

'What was the revelation?'

'What a fool I've been. I don't know Lucy, I think I went crazy because I didn't know what to do about your visa situation. I was running away I guess.'

'Well I guess it doesn't matter anymore.'

'Of course it matters. We have to stay together somehow.'

'I'm going home Eamon, I truly am this time.'

'Where is Bart?'

'He's in Switzerland with his folks.'

I was so surprised to hear that Bart was not around that I spilled my coffee, 'When did he go to Switzerland?'

'On Monday morning. I'm house sitting for him and his parents while they're away.'

'You mean, you haven't been...'

'No, I haven't been seeing him. Who do you think I am, some two-timing floozy? I'm not like you.'

'Oh Lucy, I'm more sorry about my lack in faith in you than I am about anything else.'

'What else do you have to be sorry for?'

'Not what you think.'

'Oh, not for cheating on me with Gwyneth?'

My heart soared, once again I had been let off the hook. 'I swear to you that there has been nothing going on between me and Gwyneth. I just went a bit crazy that's all. I neglected, shunned you, tried to drive you away from me, and I succeeded.'

Her shoulders slumped, and she looked out the window at the busses and taxis streaming down the King's Road. 'Why should I believe you?' she whispered, her breath condensing on the windowpane.

'I'm sorry Lucy, and I love you. Please come home.'

'I have to house sit for two weeks.'

'Can I house sit with you?'

'No, but maybe we can go out at night or something.'

'That's a nice idea, we've never actually dated have we? We've always lived together. I never had to go anywhere to pick you up.'

She smiled and sipped her coffee. A wave of relief came over me. The ice was broken, and I could see in her eyes that she didn't hate me, but still loved me.

For the next two weeks, we carried on like dating school kids. We took walks and held hands. We sat on the bench under Whistler's statue on Chelsea embankment licking Dayville's ice cream. Some nights, Lucy came home with me, but she was gone by the time I woke up in the morning.

Mum was released from hospital after a few days, but she had to stay in bed at home. When I wasn't with Lucy, or working at the markets, I helped out at the shop.

Lucy had a few days off pretending to be sick, but then returned to work, waiting for the dreaded day that she was to front up to her boss with her work permit. She wrote to her parents asking for money for an airline ticket home. The day that Bart and his parents were due to return, I asked her, 'Will you move back in with me now?'

'I guess so. I've got nowhere else to go.'

'Are you afraid that I'll persuade you not to go home after all?'

'Yes I am afraid of that. But, in any case I have to pack up all my stuff and get ready to go. I'll be home before Christmas.'

'I don't want you to leave me.'

'If I go to America, at least for a while, I'll be able to get another visa and come back.'

'I can visit you in California in the meantime.'

'But I don't want you to.'

'I know.'

'I think we should separate for a while, maybe only a little while. If you love me, you won't forget about me. If you do forget about me, it'll mean we weren't meant for each other.'

'What if you fall for someone else while you're there? What about you're poet?' I asked disconsolate.

She packed her small back pack left a note on the kitchen table for Bart, we closed his front door, dropped the keys in the letterbox and caught the bus back home to Notting Hill.

23

On Saturday, rather than admit that she did not, after all, have a work visa, Lucy told her boss that she had another job and quit. My heart sank as she recounted her tale of woe, her failure, which I had caused. 'What did he say?' I asked.

'He just looked at me as if I were an idiot. He knew I was lying, and he just turned and walked away from me.'

I looked back at my life, and I realized that I had been like driftwood, at the mercy of the waves. When I was young I was taken around by my parents, told what to do, which school to go to.

I met Amanda, not through design but by chance. I had chased Lucy across Europe, afraid to be apart from her because I didn't want to be alone. I was abandoned by my parents - left in a great big apartment it was true - nevertheless, I was never in control of myself or my circumstances. I merely reacted to events as they unfolded around me. Now, I felt a determination to take some control of my life, to be a driver rather than the passenger I had been all this time.

I had never felt that I fitted into English society, but I asked myself, so what? Why do I have to fit in? I'm not a child any more, I can do what I like; become who I want to become. I don't have to fit in with anybody. This is my country now, not just theirs - someone else's. I was a member of this society whether anybody wanted me to be part of it or not. As the Dub Vendor said, I was here to stay in England. I was one of the people - only one - but I was one of the people who would determine the direction, the future. I sensed that I had a role, a part to play.

I was in fact free, but with freedom came responsibility. If I could shape my future, then I had to be accountable for it. Whether I liked it or not I had to take my place in society. I had to engage with it, put my arms around it.

I felt as if I had been on a journey and now I was back. No, London was not perfect, some paradise, but it was my place, I was part of it and it was part of me, and I wanted to be a part of its future.

Lucy was more sensible than me. She wanted us to split up because I was behaving like a child and preventing her from developing. In any case, she was right that she had to find her place in the world and start her life. But, I was now more determined than ever that we would walk through life together.

Even though our romance had lasted for two years, I had still not won the heart of the fair lady. I had failed to complete our union. It wasn't just that I was unable to commit to her. She didn't want to throw her lot in with me, and I couldn't blame her.

Yet, I thought, I can't bend to the norms of society and be forced into actions I don't want to take. I want to do it my way, and make it our way, mine and Lucy's way.

I didn't want to be defeated, like my old science teacher - they, the authorities, the un-seen forces, the government was not going to decide whether Lucy and I could stay together.

Lucy was right that marriage was not the solution. I didn't believe that a public act would change what was in Lucy's or my heart. It seemed that so many people wedded hoping that marriage alone, would bind them to one another, but so often it proved to be an illusion, like dust slipping through their fingers. No, I had to win her fully, only then could we make a true union. But we had to get around her visa problem somehow. We were trapped.

I thought that Albert, the punks, skinheads and West Indians felt that they were backed into a corner, they could see no escape. The only escape they could see was to fight, destroy, burn down the house so that there were no walls, no barriers any more. The trouble of course, was that in the process, apart from hurting others, they ended up destroying themselves.

The trick was not to get backed into a corner in the first place. That was why I had to be in some control. I had to create some room for manoeuver.

I felt as if I were on the fine point of a star that could explode into oblivion, disappear 'puff bag of shit', at any moment. This feeling gave me an urgent desire to say thank you. I wanted to make a public expression of gratitude. After all, I felt no grudge against the world.

On the contrary, I loved life, where else was I going to go? I wanted to embrace the world, squeeze it for all it was worth. But, I felt I had to give something back, make some kind of contribution.

Had I gone too far down the wrong path as my father had warned me? Perhaps, but I thought that I owed it to the society I was in, to the people I knew, to the city itself, to cut a new path. I still had to figure out exactly how to do it, and I set to work.

A few days later I asked, 'Lucy, do you think we should celebrate Thanksgiving? I mean, we won't be together for Christmas.'

'Yes, sure, that would be lovely. Who will we invite?'

'Everyone! Everyone we know that is.'

'I can cook the meal all right - turkey, pumpkin pies and all the rest. You'd better let me know how many people to expect. It's less than three weeks away.'

Thanksgiving is the last Thursday in November, which in this year was 26 November just eight days before Lucy's visa was due to expire. Over the next few days, I called all our friends and invited them. Very few of them had ever heard of Thanksgiving. They were intrigued, and everyone said yes.

'Lucy, I've called everyone, so I can give you a number to cater for.'

'Great, how many?'

'Twenty-four people, including us'

'You're kidding, twenty-four? That many people won't fit in this room! We only have that ancient stove. We don't have a dining table, no chairs. I thought there would be six people or something.'

'Hmm, I was surprised, but everyone said yes including Olaf who's coming over from Copenhagen.'

Lucy had a point. We didn't have enough of anything for a dinner party of that size, especially cash. What should I do? Call it off or ask everyone to meet at the Prince of Wales and have a pint? I though it over for a day or two and developed a plan.

'Lucy… I have a plan.'

'Oh God, I hope it doesn't involve hitchhiking.'

'We can cook two turkeys in my mum's kitchen, and I can borrow cutlery and plates from her. I'll hire tables and chairs from a catering company. You can cook the vegetables here and hey presto!'

'Okay, I guess.'

'What do you have at a Thanksgiving dinner anyway Lucy?'

'Well, you have to have a roast turkey with stuffing, sweet potatoes, corn bread, pumpkin pie and Jell-o salad.'

'Jell-o salad, what on earth is that?'

'You make Jell-o and put tinned fruit in it.'

'So you have that as a dessert?'

'No, you have it as part of your dinner.'

'Doesn't it melt?'

'No, you take it out of the fridge at the last minute.'

'Humm, what are the origins of Thanksgiving anyway?'

'The Pilgrim Fathers founded a settlement at New Plymouth. They nearly starved to death during the first winter. But the Indians helped them to plant native crops like corn, potatoes and pumpkin. After bringing in their first harvest, they had a big meal to celebrate.'

'Did they invite the Indians?'

'No, they had all died of smallpox.'

Lucy went to the market and began gathering the ingredients for our feast. 'In America they sell pumpkin in cans to make pies with. But they don't sell it that way here,' she complained. 'I'll have to buy fresh pumpkins at the market, and cook them and mash them up myself. I've never done it that way before!'

To cater for twenty-four people we needed to make lots of pies. As it was autumn, pumpkins were in season, and Lucy bought two huge ones from Portobello. 'Pumpkin pie is best when it's cold, so I'll make them in batches.'

She carefully cut the pumpkin into slices and boiled them. Our little stove had two gas burners, but they were so close together that Lucy could only boil one pot at a time. She carefully scooped all the pumpkin flesh away from the outer skin and strained it to get rid of the excess water. Then she mashed it and made pumpkin custard by mixing it with eggs, milk, brown sugar, cinnamon, ginger and nutmeg.

She made all the pastry by hand, mixing butter and flour with a fork and rolling it out with a rolling pin. We bought disposable aluminium pie pans and lined them with pastry and filled them, batch by batch, with the pumpkin custard. We could bake two at a time in our tiny oven, and the tantalizing aroma of sugar and spices filled the house.

I tasted the first one out of the oven. 'Mmmm, that is delicious. We should make a whole pie for everyone, mmmm.'

'Don't be silly. No one's going to eat more than one slice.'

'Are you kidding? I'll eat a whole pie, so will Gene and Vincent will eat two. This is the most scrumptious stuff I have ever tasted.'

We agreed to make thirteen pies, or roughly half a pie per person. In the end, we simply used up all the pumpkin and made a total of twenty four pies. It took us a week to cook them all. As we had no room to keep them in our fridge, we gave them to some of the guests for safe keeping. Mum took several, and so did Lachlan and Gene. I was afraid that everyone would gobble them up, and we would end up with none for the feast. I warned Gene, 'Don't you dare touch these pies or Lucy will be furious!'

Lucy went to Tesco on Portobello and bought two enormous turkeys. 'We have to make stuffing with the giblets, so take them out.' She chopped up white bread into small bits and put trays of it in the oven to roast until it was dry but not brown. While the bread was roasting, she put the giblets on to simmer to make a stock. Then she chopped a mound of celery and onion and sautéed it. She poured the stock onto the dry bread with the onions and celery, added salt, sage and thyme, and mixed it all together.

Gene drove over in the MG to take me to my folks place with the turkeys for my mother to cook. 'Hi Mum, here they are, two turkeys and lots of stuffing.'

'This must be a grand party you're having.'

'Yes, twenty four-people. Are you feeling well enough now? Do you mind cooking the turkeys for us?'

'I'm much better now, and of course I don't mind. It's going to be a wonderful meal. You're lucky to know so many people.'

Gene and I nearly stripped my mother's kitchen bare. We loaded the MG with cutlery, plates, serving bowls, gravy dishes, pepper grinders and drove back to Blenheim Crescent. The darkness of late autumn set in quickly and as we drove it started to rain. The little windshield wipers of the MG squeaked up and down, and I could hear the swish of the tyres as we growled along Goldhawk Road and up through Shepherds Bush.

'Thanks for helping me, Gene.'

'It's my pleasure Eamon. What are you and Lucy going to do about her visa? Doesn't it expire soon?'

'Lucy is going home, for a while anyway, a few months or so.'

'You two seem so much in love.'

'Yes… but she'll be better off without me.'

'Do you really want to split up with her?'

'No I don't. In a way that's what this dinner is about. I'm not sure how, but I'm trying to work things out.'

'Maybe you should get a job mate. I mean a real job.'

'Thanks, Gene, a job - it sounds so sordid.'

'A man has to work. Things happen when you work for a company. You meet people, and opportunities come up.'

The next day was Thanksgiving. As it was a Thursday I didn't have to work. When the catering supply company arrived in the morning, I helped them unload three large, round tables with fold-up legs and twenty-four plastic chairs.

To make room for the tables I up-ended the mattress and base of the bed and moved them into the passageway. I moved our breakfast table upstairs to the main hall of the house, shoved all my market goods into the passageway, put everything else in the cupboard and moved the bar against the wall. I unfolded the three tables and arranged chairs around each one.

'Well Lucy, they fit.'

'Only just, there's no room for anything else in here now,' she said, stacking my mother's serving bowls on the bar. The only other things left in the room were the fridge and stove. With the walls covered in posters, photographs and postcards, and round tables, the place looked like a speakeasy.

Lucy set about making corn bread. She mixed eggs, corn meal, flour, baking powder and milk, poured the batter into cake tins and put them in the oven. 'How long does the corn bread bake for?'

'About twenty minutes.'

Next she carefully chopped the sweet potatoes into thick slices and steamed them in a pot until they were nearly cooked. She then put them in a baking dish, poured in some milk, added cinnamon and a little brown sugar and baked them for half an hour.

The Jell-o salad was easy. Together we made bowls of jelly with tinned fruit salad mixed in and put them in the fridge. 'Can I help you chop up the vegetables Lucy?'

'No, you'll make a mess of them.'

I sat at one end of the table, and she placed a chopping board opposite me. I watched as she carefully chopped carrots, Brussels sprouts, cauliflower and broccoli. I looked at her face and hands as she took each vegetable and examined it with a delicate smile. She placed each one down and took our antique kitchen knife, bought as part of a lot in an auction, curled her finger tips in slightly and made a graceful incision. After each slice, she regarded her handiwork before preparing to make the next. Lucy carried herself with such grace and poise that it was like watching an elegant Japanese woman perform a tea ceremony. That is the way she does everything, I mused, with love and dedication. Her handwriting was graceful and artistic. The way she walked, spoke, smiled, her whole being was so serene and beautiful.

The sun cast a soft grey-blue slanted light illuminating both Lucy and the vegetables like a Vermeer painting. She was such a contrast to me. Opposites attract, I supposed. I could have watched her all day. How could I exist apart from her? How could I let her leave me?

Children ran past our windows, their legs rushing by, twisting and turning as they punched each other and laughed, 'Give me that back!'

'You gotta catch me first, don't ya!'

The light gradually changed in a seamless vignette to dark grey. As the last feeble glimmer of the winter sun faded, rain splashed in the street and cascaded down our steps. The frozen moment thawed. I shook my self, and stood up from the table while Lucy continued chopping.

We were less than a month from the shortest day of the year and the cold, dark night set in. I heard a clip clop on the steps and a rat-tat-tat on the window. It was Bernie, the Yorkshire Cowboy, my colleague from Haymarket Publishing. 'Pumpkin pies,' he cried holding up two pies that he had been keeping in his fridge for us. He arrived early, so we could go and fetch the cooked turkeys.

Bernie had a new car. It was a 1955 Zephyr Zodiac, and he was very proud of it. 'It's called Trigger.'

He had stuck a cardboard cut-out of Prince Charles and Diana to the back passenger window, with a cut-out hand attached to it, weighted at the bottom. As we drove along, the movement of the car made the hand wave. The car had semaphore indicators that popped out and flashed on either side, plush leather seats and a large, pearled steering wheel. He drove around the block so he could show it off to me, like a big kid with a new toy. 'Oh look, those people like my Charles and Diana.'

The people in the car beside us were laughing and pointing at the royal couple waving at them. 'Ho ho ho, this car is fun,' he laughed.

He straightened up and drove over to the shop attracting attention all the way.

'Mum, thanks so much. The turkeys smell delicious.'

'They're beautifully cooked. Just keep them covered, and they'll stay warm. Have a lovely time.'

As we drove back to the basement Bernie put the Four Tops on the car stereo, and we sang *Baby I Need Your Lovin'* as we drove back home.

We waved our hands out the windows in time to the music. People waved back at us and Charles and Diana in the rear seat. When the song had finished, Bernie calmed down a bit and as we sat at the traffic lights at Notting Hill Gate he said to me, 'Have you thought about getting a job?'

'Not you too Bernie, have you been talking to Gene?'

'No, but you should probably get a job. There are openings at my company you know.'

Bernie was working for a publishing company in Clerkenwell, just north of Fleet Street.

'Are you enjoying your job, Bernie?'

'You know me. I'm here for a good time - and are we going to have a good time tonight!'

We brought the turkeys in and set them out on the bar. 'Bernie, I thought I would make a punch to jolly everyone along. Can you nip down to the supermarket and buy a bag of ice?'

'Right you are,' he said, and off he went.

I rummaged around and found the punchbowl that mum had lent us for the evening. I poured in two cartons of orange juice, a bottle of soda water and a few dashes of Angostura bitters. Then I poured in a bottle of vodka. The fridge was full of beer and wine bottles, and I had borrowed a tub from Lachlan to put more bottles in. When Bernie came back, we poured some ice in the punch and the rest in the tub.

It was still early, and most guests were not due to arrive for another hour, but rat-tat-tat on the window. Vincent and Gene had arrived with their girlfriends followed by Bart. I ladled out drinks, and we all clinked our glasses and threw the punch in our hatches.

I put on some music and Gene, Bart, Vincent, and Bernie began dancing in the bay window, twisting, turning and clicking their fingers like the Four Tops.

…du, du-du-du-du...

They were all so different to the guys I'd known a year earlier. Bernie was a man on a mission. He had a full moustache and beaming eyes. Oh yes, he was 'gonna have a good time'.

Bart looked so mature now, no longer the lanky bicycle boy from Pow-alto. He had grown into an urbane American-in-London that people took for a record producer or a film director.

Vincent was not the studious lawyer he had been planning to be, but seemed liberated, self assured and in control.

Gene didn't look like a nerd any more. He now wore contact lenses instead of glasses, a fluffy white shirt with one too many buttons open, an expensive watch on his wrist, and long black hair which he swished around. He danced with a wild maniacal smile and glazed eyes as if he had been freed from all his earthly inhibitions. He was like a magnificent pagan beast.

Another tap-tap rattled the window, signaling the arrival of a guest, first one and then another. Soon the room was filled with people. I gave everyone a glass of punch as they arrived. I kept making batches until all the vodka was used up. By the time all the punch was gone everyone's voices had grown louder with shouts and whoops.

Olaf arrived, and I opened the door to greet him. 'So, my young adventurer, who did you decide to be in the end?' he asked me.

'I decided to be me, Eamon. I tried, but I couldn't become anyone else. I found out that actually, I am not free. I'm bound up in this bundle of flesh and bones called Eamon. Try as I might I have been unable to escape myself.'

'Are you just flesh and bones, or is the whole more than the sum of the parts?'

'I don't know yet, Olaf. Maybe history will remember me in some small way. I may make some kind of difference in this crazy mixed up world.'

'Ah ha, you mean that perhaps you are not just a hill of beans?'

'Oh, you are as much of a movie buff as I am?'

'Of course, we are all part of this living, manifest world. But have you found your real self, your transcendent being?'

'No, I have not. But, maybe I don't need to find my real self. Either I am real, or I am merely a delusion. Does it matter if I am aware of the ultimate truth or not? I either am or I am not. What I think or know about it may make no difference.'

'Ignorance is not bliss, it is just ignorance. You my friend are not ignorant. You are aware, and, the one who is most aware carries the greatest burden of responsibility.'

'I'm beginning to take life more seriously now Olaf. I'm going to try, make an effort, and see how far I can get.'

'Ah, good Eamon, enjoy the journey.'

Lachlan came downstairs and I counted the animated heads bobbing around the room. Twenty-four, we were all there. Most of the guests were sitting around the tables with little space to stand up. Lucy was taking the last pot of vegetables off the stove as she chatted to Bart. I caught her attention, and she said the feast could commence.

Bernie and I carved the turkeys. While everyone was seated, it wasn't possible to move from one side of the room to the other, so Lucy passed around plates, and serving dishes filled with steaming vegetables, corn bread, and sweet potatoes. Everyone was served and waiting for a sign to dig in when I remembered the final ingredient. I yelled across the room, 'Lucy, the Jell-o salad.'

Our guests looked puzzled, as we passed around the bowls of green goo and told them to help them selves. Finally, when everyone had a plate of food in front of them and a full glass, I rose to my feet to speak.

'Friends, I wonder if we will ever all be in the same room together again? Before tonight many of you were strangers, but now all of our friends have at least met one another. You are our most excellent extended family - Lucy, and I love you all.'

The room erupted in a great cheer. 'To absent friends and family. Let us give thanks to God and providence.'

'Hear, hear! Give thanks!'

'Let the feast commence!'

When we had finished our turkey dinner with all the trimmings, Lucy passed around the pumpkin pies. The room fell silent, save for chomping and munching sounds, as we gobbled up all four and twenty pies.

24

By the time I woke up the next morning, it was too late to put up my stall at Portobello market. Lucy and I spent the rest of the day cleaning the room. The catering company came by in the afternoon, and I helped load the tables and chairs on their truck.

Lucy was pleased that our home was back to the way it was before the feast. She smiled at me with a distant forlorn look, sat down and her shoulders drooped.

'Lucy, I love you.'

'I know, I love you too.'

'You can't leave. If we go anywhere, we have to go together.'

'Alright Eamon, where will we go, what will we do?'

'I'll come to America with you.'

'I guess you could,' she said with her eyes fixed to the floor. 'You won't be able to work there or anything - at least not legally.'

'I'm just grasping at straws I suppose.'

'Before I met you, I wanted to go home. I had no idea what I was going to do when I got there, but now I don't know. I want to be with you, somewhere. It's just that I've grown to like it here in London. I feel comfortable here. I love Portobello and the people - our friends. Don't you like it here?'

'I don't know. I think I've always rejected England. I never actually wanted to fit in. I've always wanted to go home.'

Lucy stood up and said, 'Come on, I want to go for a walk.'

We walked, talking all the way through Kensington to the Thames.

'I have an idea, why don't we go to India!'

'You want to hitch hike all the way to *India* now?'

'We don't have to hitch; we can take the bus - the Magic Bus. I don't know what route it takes nowadays. It can't go through Iran because of the revolution, and there's a war on in Afghanistan. Honestly, there is a company called Magic Bus that goes to India.'

'What would we do in India?'

'Travel around, live on the beach, it'll be great, you'll see. Then we can see how we feel. When we get fed up with India, maybe we could go to Australia.'

'Eamon, we don't have much money.'

'That's a good reason to go to India, it is extremely cheap. I'll borrow some money off my Dad as well.'

So we had a new plan. Lucy would see if she could get her visa extended for a few weeks until we could vacate the basement and arrange bus tickets. Lucy sighed, turned around, and we began to walk back up to Notting Hill.

I felt a pang in my heart at as I passed all my old haunts. How did I feel towards England and London? Somehow I did feel different now I was here with Lucy. I felt more at home than I ever had before even though I was living with a foreigner. Maybe it takes a stranger's eye to see the beauty in what becomes mundane, even ugly, to someone who sees it every day. Could it be that I had found my home at last? We continued on in silence and spent the weekend working out the details of our plan.

***

First thing Monday morning, I called Bernie at his work, and he put me through to his boss, the publisher. I made an appointment for an interview the following week. 'Lucy, I have to go get a haircut and borrow a suit from my brother, see you later,' and I rushed out the door.

The following Monday, I went to my job interview. The company had offices in several buildings dotted around Clerkenwell, on the fringe of the City of London. The building Bernie worked in was on Clerkenwell Road, and I stopped by to say hello to him before the interview. The open plan office on the fifth floor had a magnificent view of the large dome of St Paul's Cathedral, juxtaposed by the Old Bailey Central Criminal Courts, with the statue of Themis, Lady Justice, atop it.

My interview was in a different building around the corner on Farringdon Road, next door to *The Guardian* newspaper. I was ushered into a small office, where a short man with frizzy brown hair jumped out of his chair nervously. 'How 'r ya, Eamon, sit dian,' he said in a broad Belfast accent.

He asked me numerous questions about my previous job with Haymarket Publishing. I blabbered out answers that seemed to fit with what he wanted me to say. All through the interview he looked agitated and intense. At one point, he hit the table in front of him with his index finger, his arm out stretched, 'Nia, we don't need any slackers here. No, this is a place for dedicated people, hard workers. We only want serious people, hungry people who are ambitious. How are ambitious are yee, Eamon?'

'Er, oh yes, you bet ambitious. Me? I'm determined to make a mark in this world. Er, no back slacking or whatever, no no no. Ah ha! No way on earth by goodness!' I psycho-babbled.

He became sullen and crouched in his chair pulling at his eyebrow with his finger and thumb. He pensively skimmed through my brief résumé, eyes darting around the pages. I wondered how much he knew about Chelsea School.

'Alright Eamon, call my secretary tomorrow. She'll let you know when you can start.'

He jumped up and strode out of the room, leaving me to stare at his vacant, swivel chair, spinning around. I stared at the chair transfixed. No, I thought. That chair is too small. I want a bigger one.

With so much to do the rest of the week flew past. On Friday morning, the alarm clock sounded

…beep beep beep…

'Lucy, today's the day.'

We quickly dressed and caught the 31 bus to World's End. From our seats at the front of the top deck we watched the street scene displayed before us as the bus swayed and rumbled slowly along its route. The 31 bus meanders all the way from Camden Lock through Swiss Cottage, Kilburn, Notting Hill and down to World's End cutting through the city like a tributary of the Thames. The weather had turned milder, and it was sunny but with a pallid wintry look. A few remaining leaves clung to the trees then, set free at last, they floated, copper-green, gently past the windows of the bus.

The people on the street seemed relaxed and happy as we looked down on black London cabs, Bobbies on the beat, newspaper sellers, queues of people waiting at bus stops, West Africans wearing Grand Boubou robes, Indian women in saris. People of all shapes, sizes, ages, and races were out on the streets walking, talking, and wandering in and out of shops.

As the bus inched down Earl's Court Road memories of every bus ride, of every step I had taken and of all the people I had met in London crowded my mind. I still felt like a walking encyclopedia knowing just enough about most subjects to be annoying, but I was determined to put my knowledge to some good use.

The conductor moved along the top deck calling 'Fares please.' We kissed passionately as he approached us, and he turned around to make his way back down the length of the bus leaving us in peace. It was a pleasant way to avoid paying the bus fare.

One by one passengers pulled the cord, and the bell went ting. When the departing passengers had jumped off the open back landing of the bus the conductor rang the bell twice, ting ting, to signal the driver to get moving again. Eventually we reached the end of the line at Limerston Street.

We strolled up the King's Road past Seditionaries which had been renamed, World's End. Across the road, the caff where Albert and I used to drink tepid tea and listen to Lou Reed was still there, unchanged. I remembered the day that we noticed that Too Fast to Live, Too young to Die had morphed into SEX, and the day Amanda made me try on a pair of bondage trousers. We walked past the Chelsea Pot where Lucy and I had our first meal together and the Roebuck where I hallucinated with Tim.

Soon we arrived at Chelsea Town Hall. Bart's apartment on Flood Street where Lucy and I first met was just one block away. We waited on the steps of the town hall at the entrance to the Chelsea Register office. I reassured Lucy, 'They said they would meet us at a quarter to ten.'

'How will we know what they'll look like?'

'The agency just said it would be one man and one woman.'

A voice spoke to me from the bottom of the steps, 'Eamon?'

'Yes, you must be from the agency.'

'Indeed, I am Karin, and this is Richard.'

We all shook hands and I ushered them in the door. I approached the desk and said to the receptionist, 'We are the ten o'clock.'

Her face illuminated, 'Oh, right you are, lovely, please do come this way. Isn't it a beautiful day? You both look so lovely, oh my, yes indeed.'

She brought us into an ornate waiting room and asked us to take a seat, 'The Registrar will be with you presently.'

We sat nervously waiting while Karin made polite conversation.

'How long have you known each other?'

'Almost two years,' I said

'How nice, do you not know anyone in London?'

'No one we can ask.'

'I see, how romantic this all is. Normally we just do TV commercials and the odd flan-o-gram.'

Two middle aged gentlemen immaculately dressed in black suits with waistcoats and impossibly shiny shoes entered the chamber followed by a lady in a frumpy black dress. The older man smiled and asked, 'Which of you are the bride and groom?'

Lucy and I presented ourselves. 'Lovely, now will you all follow me, please' he said.

The lady opened a double-sided door into a large room with ornate high vaulted ceilings and enormous windows facing out onto the street. Several dozen chairs were arranged in rows on the rich red carpet. At the top of the room up two steps, stood a large wooden desk and a lectern, arranged like an altar in a church. The registrar asked us to be seated. He stood in front of the desk flanked by his two assistants.

'We are gathered here today for the marriage of Eamon Curran, and Lucy Morris.' Lucy looked at me, and I held her hand. Eventually the Registrar asked me if I had a ring. 'Oh yes, here it is.'

I took a ring for Lucy out of my pocket. It was an Australian opal from Lightening Ridge mounted in sliver. I bought the opal from an Australian girl at Swiss Cottage market and had it set by a jeweler. The Registrar spoke to me, and I said, 'I do.'

Lucy said, 'I do.'

'Under the authority granted to me by the laws and customs of the United Kingdom I hereby declare that you now legally married as husband and wife.'

We embraced and kissed, our tears mingled on our cheeks. Lucy looked beautiful in her colourful clothes, all bought at Portobello Market. We signed the register followed by our witnesses and were handed our certificate.

As we departed, Karin and Richard shook our hands and kissed Lucy. We stood on the steps, and I took the envelope with the money for the witnesses out of my pocket and handed it to Karin.

'No, no,' she said. 'We can't possibly charge you for this. It was lovely, and we wish you both great happiness.' I insisted and tried to give the money to Richard, but he wouldn't take it. We thanked them, and they skipped down the steps and left us there alone.

Lucy and I looked out at the King's Road. I remembered the first day I walked past the Chelsea Town Hall and thought of the rich old men in double breasted suits, soldiers with stiffened moustaches, fashionable women in pink boots and white plastic mini skirts, elegant men wearing flounced white lace shirts, girls with see-through blouses and mini skirts, furry freaks, followed by more girls wearing even shorter mini skirts.

'What will become of us now, Eamon?'

'We're together, that's all that matters.'

'I guess life doesn't just turn out like a stupid cake. Ta da! Here it is all baked.'

'No I suppose it's more like a stew. You just keep adding things, herbs, spices, fish and tomatoes - eat some, then add some more ingredients.'

I didn't know how things would turn out. I just knew that she was my girl, and I loved her. I didn't just love the way she was on that sunny autumn day standing on the steps of Chelsea Town hall looking out at the carnival of life swirling past us. When my eyes were closed I still loved her. When I was asleep alone, I loved her. I didn't just love the way she talked or what she talked about. I didn't just love her sensibilities or the way she moved or smelt. I didn't love her because of what she loved, or did, or stood for. I just loved her, and there we were, holding hands and staring into each other's eyes on the King's Road.

****

Sean De Siun spent his early years in Australia before moving to London in the early 1970s.

His written works include non fiction redactions, documentaries, screenplays and short stories. He currently lives with his wife in Sydney Australia.

Also by the author and available
from Fileata Fiction

Artists
Man of the River
Avatara
Desire
Canice and the Book
Katie
Chatter

Copy Sales
Kings Road is available on **amazon.com**
Purchase direct from **artcamino.com/fiction**

www.ingramcontent.com/pod-product-compliance
Lightning Source LLC
Chambersburg PA
CBHW052029020726
47501CB00004B/1312
9780980604948